GAME OF PAWNS

Gino Ranno Takes Control

LOUIS ROMANO

Also by Louis Romano

Detective Vic Gonnella Series

INTERCESSION

YOU THINK I'M DEAD

Gino Ranno Series

FISH FARM

BESA

GAME OF PAWNS

Poetry Series

ANXIETY'S NEST

ANXIETY'S CURE

Acknowledgments

Very Special Thanks to the Following:

To Jack Berisha who again was a huge help in me understanding the Albanian language, proverbs and traditions

To my new friend and great actor Ari Barkan who guided me through Brighton Beach, Brooklyn and things Russian

International Grand Chess Master Nigel Davies was generous with his time, loaned me his knowledge, and gave his advice on the game and its terminology

Danny Rivera, my dear friend, helped me with police stuff and was available night and day for my 911 calls

To Damian Albergo Esq. who introduced me to Dr. Sandip Kapur, Chief of Transplant Surgery, New York Presbyterian Hospital Weill Cornell Medical Center. He and his staff do amazing things every day

To Jim Guardino who really gave me some great ideas

To the one and only Frank Cali

To my great pre-readers, all seven of them

To my editors, Pamela Fuchsel, Dana Paul, Matt Engel, Anita Sancinella, and the great staff at Vecchia Publishing

To Centurion Associates Marketing & Publicity

...and to the few gangsters that I met along the way.

This book is dedicated to my ancestors and extended family from Lecara Friddi, Sicily, and Balvano, Pacentro, and Armento, Italy,

to those who have come to the United States,

and to those who will come after me.

CHAPTER 1

Despite what many people may think, not every Sicilian is in the Mafia.

However, they all have a telephone number should the need arise. It's a birthright that emanates from centuries of oppression and control on the embattled island of Sicily and from the tough toil and bigotry that Sicilian immigrants found in America.

There is a certain attraction, a pull if you will, that the mob life has had on Sicilian-Americans and Italian-Americans in general. The notion that Americans of Italian extraction are embarrassed and insulted by their association with their underworld brothers is total nonsense. If anything, being associated with the mob is a dynamic that is both mythical and empowering. There is a sense of pride in the accomplishments of great Italians on both sides of the law. The Renaissance, all the great artists and architects, Enrico Fermi, Marconi, DiMaggio, and on and on. Great people all of them…but nobody ever feared them.

Most people would rather watch old, black-and-white film clips of Lucky Luciano getting locked up by burly Irish cops than view Michelangelo's statue of David. It's far more interesting, it seems, to follow the short, swarthy Sicilian dressed in a top coat and fedora slightly pulled down over his dark, shifty eyes than to look at a stunning masterpiece in white marble.

1

The mob life flourishes in America. It really couldn't make it big in mostly socialist Italy. Capitalism fosters success and greed, and the mob life is all about the money and power.

In Gino Ranno's case, it was never about the money, and he couldn't care less about power. In his case, the mob life is in Gino's blood and has lain dormant until now, when he considers himself nearly an old man.

In his early sixties, Gino had become the right-hand man of Carmine Miceli, Junior, and a new underworld life for him was about to begin...

CHAPTER 2

Marty Craig has an idyllic life. Some would say a perfect life, one that is full of success, happiness, and glory.

At fifty-one, he is the perfect male specimen. 6'1" with zero percent body fat obtained from his ritual of daily exercise at four- thirty every morning with his personal trainer without fail and his balanced and weighed diet prepared by his live-in executive chef.

His large, black olive-like eyes, perennial tan, and combed back, jet-black, full head of hair made him the envy of his friends and the target of every magnificent-looking woman from eighteen to sixty who crossed his path. As if that weren't enough, his nine-million- dollar, nine-bedroom, eleven-bath-room, sixteen-thousand-square-foot estate on Sterling Lane in Sands Point, Long Island, along with his gorgeous, Scandina-vian blonde wife Erika put him in a stratosphere that few men could hardly even dream about.

His New York City-based hedge fund was sold for just under a half-billion dollars a week after his fiftieth birthday. All he had to do now was watch his money grow and make sure his two kids were not overly affected by his wealth. His daughter Gianna was a junior at the Wharton School, top in her class, and his son Lloyd was a junior at a private prep school, Roxbury Latin, in Boston, Marty's Alma Mater.

But fate dealt Marty Craig some shitty cards.

Lloyd, the apple of his eye, was a sickly child. Squadrons of the best doctors were unable to diagnose his problems properly until he was three years old.

Dr. Pretesh Gupta, a young nephrologist at Columbia Presbyterian Hospital, did a full workup on young Lloyd. It fell upon Gupta to be the bearer of bad news. The conversation took place at Dr. Gupta's stark, unassuming office at the world-renowned children's hospital. The doctor sat across from the concerned couple. The meeting with Dr. Gupta was forever burned into Marty Craig's brilliant mind.

"Mr. and Mrs. Craig, your son has a rare genetic disorder. Usually, it is an inherited disease, so we are unsure why he contracted this without family history. I would say that, if you were thinking about having more children, it would be wise if you meet with a geneticist for a full evaluation. Either one or both of you have passed this disease to your son. He has Alport Syndrome. Alport generally affects the glomeruli, which are tiny capillaries in the kidneys that filter waste products from the blood. We term this *hematuria.* This is why his urine has been so dark. It's from his blood. He will almost certainly develop severe hearing problems and possible eye abnormality as he gets older. Not in all cases, mind you, but some Alport patients develop anterior lenticonus, which is deformity in the shape of the eye lenses. As he grows, he will exhibit additional symptoms of kidney disease," Dr. Gupta explained.

"What kind of symptoms?" Erika Craig inquired. Her voice was quivering. Marty was stone silent.

"Well, by his teens, he will experience proteins in his urine and is at risk for high blood pressure. Patients with Alport Syndrome experience progressive kidney damage."

"Is there a cure, Doctor?" Erica asked.

"There is currently no specific treatment for this disorder. Hopefully in the future, gene therapy may cure this disease. However, he can live a normal life until the disease progresses. Generally, dialysis and or a kidney transplant are indicated. Kidney transplants are quite successful in Alport patients, typically, in the patient's late forties or early fifties. Some rare cases progress much quicker," Dr. Gupta explained. His manner was clinical. There could be no sugar coating Alport Syndrome.

Marty Craig finally spoke.

"What about our daughter? She is a few years older than Lloyd, but she is very healthy. Never sick a day in her life."

"Then the recessive or dominant gene did not affect her. Anyway, Alport is generally not as problematic with women."

"Can we give him one of our kidneys now, Dr. Gupta?" Ericka said. The tears were rolling down her cheeks. Marty reached out and took her hand in his in a futile attempt to comfort his wife.

"His kidneys are not at the point of failure at the moment, so surgery is not indicated. He will likely need both of his kidneys replaced if he experiences renal failure in the future. The risks are too great for him to function with just one kidney knowing this disease. For a successful transplant, he would likely need the organs from one donor. We are putting the cart way before the horse at this juncture. We will monitor him closely on a monthly basis."

As he grew, Lloyd did experience all of the symptoms that Dr. Gupta predicted. Following the doctor's advice, Erika watched Lloyd's diet and fluid intake, and his blood pressure was monitored and logged on a daily basis for signs of deterioration. His hearing was the biggest issue. He was slowly losing that sense. In crowded, loud places, he would wear earplugs or avoid these situations entirely so as to protect his ears. The normal life that Dr. Gupta had predicted was not so normal after all.

Lloyd insisted on going away to prep school. His dad graduated from Boston Latin before going to Yale University, and he was determined to leave a legacy at both schools. Marty and Ericka reluctantly agreed and were frequent visitors at BL. The Craigs purchased a three-bedroom condo in tiny Cambridge just to be able to spend weekends near their precious son. A nephrologist at Boston Medical Center was the boy's local doctor and conferred with Dr. Gupta whenever changes in Lloyd's condition warranted. No expense was spared. No chances were taken.

Lloyd excelled academically and had as great a social life as any all-boy preppy could imagine. Things were as good as could be expected under the challenging circumstances.

Then almost suddenly, severe bleeding and back pain stopped Lloyd cold in his tracks early in his junior year at Boston Latin. A visit to Presbyterian and Dr. Gupta confirmed the Craigs biggest fear.

Lloyd's glomerular filtration rate, the rate of filtered fluid through the kidney, was way out of the normal range. He was experiencing the beginnings of renal failure.

Thirteen years of Lloyd and his family visiting and being monitored by Dr. Gupta softened the doctor's clinical bedside manner toward the Craig family. The years of service grew into a great friendship. Enormous contributions to the renamed New York Presbyterian/Morgan Stanley Children's Hospital Foundation by Marty and Ericka Craig naturally enhanced the relationship.

Dr. Gupta pulled Marty Craig aside for a one-on-one meeting. Gupta brought Marty into the executive board meeting room without Ericka on the twelfth floor of the hospital complex so they would not be disturbed. The mahogany-paneled walls and heavily framed photographs of doctors and hospital administrators dating back to Dr.s Sarah and Julie McNutt, sisters who founded the hospital in the late 1880s, seemed to be silent witnesses to the conversation. The time had come for a frank discussion.

"Marty, the time is near that Lloyd will need to start dialysis. This brings certain issues that you need to be aware of. First off, dialysis is an imperfect treatment to substitute kidney function. In no way does it correct the compromised endocrine kidney functions," Dr. Gupta said.

"Pretesh, this is way ahead of schedule," Marty said.

"His disease is in its advanced stages. Like any genetic disorder, there is no rhyme or reason. The reality is here upon us."

"What are the next steps?" Marty asked.

"He needs to come home for the rest of this year. We need him close by to monitor him and administer the dialysis temporarily and get him on a transplant list as soon as possible, today as a matter of fact."

"How much dialysis?"

"Three days a week, four hours a day until we can find suitable kidneys for Lloyd. But I am not going to kid you, Marty. The wait list is long."

"Long? How long?" Marty asked. His dark eyes grew darker.

"In New York City right now, the kidney-transplant wait list is between six and seven years. There is no…"

"Fuck that, Pretesh. I know you have an idea of how many millions of dollars we have pumped into this place. That doesn't account for anything? This is my son, God damn it!"

"Look, Marty, I am sure certain things can be done, but this sudden turn of events came out of the blue. There are protocols and procedures that we cannot ethically bypass. I can't snap my fingers and throw a new kidney into your boy," Gupta said.

"Are you kidding me or what? What the hell is money for if I can't save my own son or at least lessen his torment? By the time we get these organs, he can be deaf and blind if not dead!"

"As a friend, I can only tell you what I would do if I were you. I've grown very fond of Lloyd. He is like a son to me, too."

"Go for it."

"I will deny it if you say anything about this conversation. I can lose my license to practice medicine. I can likely go to jail."

"I swear on my life."

"There are ways of getting organs outside of the normal system. I can put you in touch with someone who knows someone. Don't ask any questions. I will give you the proper specifications, blood type, tissue type, and a lot of other medical stuff that you don't need to know about. These people will know what to do and get the organs relatively quickly. I will care for Lloyd right here post-operatively."

"He can't have the surgery here?"

"No, but I will be there for him…all the way. After surgery, we will get him in here for the proper immunosuppressant meds. If all goes well, he will be back at Boston Latin next year. I will fix the paperwork."

Marty Craig inhaled deeply. He knew where this was heading. He exhaled slowly.

"Money is no object, Pretesh. Please save my son."

CHAPTER 3

Her real name is Barbara Black. The pregnant sixteen-year old from Canton, Ohio ran away from home a year ago to have her baby. Barbara's beautiful baby boy was sold to his barren yet enthusiastic adoptive parents in the Riverdale section of the Bronx. The parents were found on an online site that paired young, unwed mothers to their children's grateful adoptive parents. What a wonderful world we live in.

Barbara's idea was to take the money, all thirty thousand dollars, less the ten-percent fee to the web site-a discounted sum for an American, white child-and start a new life some-where. Her plan did not include the necessary details for it to work, and it didn't factor in Ari Mamantov.

Ari Mamantov is a twenty-two-year-old member of the Petrov *Bratva* out of Brighton Beach, Brooklyn. His job, his only job, for the Russian mob is to recruit young, good-looking girls for a stable of sex slaves operating out of a well-appointed brothel on Bath Avenue a few blocks from Coney Island. Like any pimp, Ari was expert at getting the girls to fall for him while getting them addicted to heroin within as short a time as possible. In the sex trade, Ari was known as one of the best "Romeos" in the business.

Barbara Black became known to her clients as Stacie. In no time, Stacie was a big earner. Not for herself but for Ari's bosses.

The 5'11", wavy-blond-haired, muscular, tee-shirt-wearing, tattooed bad boy, Ari was the perfect snare who attracted Stacie and many other hapless young women who wound up servicing as many as fifteen men per day. The girls had to perform a menu of sexual performances to meet any and all desires. The kinkier the act, the more it cost. Supply and demand like with anything else in life… just follow the money.

Poor little Barbara Black from Canton, Ohio, was blessed or, in her case, cursed with amazing good looks. 5'4", killer body, saucer-sized steel blue eyes, straight, almost platinum-blonde hair that went down to the middle of her back or just past her full breasts depending on how she styled it. The last thing her parents did for her was to make her smile orthodontically perfect. When she smiled, it finished the entire package. Johns paid eight hundred dollars per visit to Stacie for an hour of her valuable time. Stacie saw a lot less than that. Food, room and board, and her daily heroin fix left her a tad more than seventy-five dollars a day.

The *Bratva* paid for Stacie's bi-monthly doctor visits. On her first visit to the medical facility owned by the Petrov *Bratva* on nearby Cropsey Avenue not far from the Bath Avenue apartment building that doubled as her apartment and workplace, a total medical examination and blood work-up was completed. The *Bratva* needed Stacie healthy and clean. The Petrovs did not take kindly to sick days. Time was money. Big money.

After a while, Barbara was getting disenchanted with Ari's promises of marriage, a nice, big house on Long Island, and a baby to replace the one she had sold. The work was not at all appealing to Barbara. She was doing it for Ari and her future. The thought of being with so many men was beginning to disgust the homesick teenager. She realized after a short time that Canton was not such a bad place after all.

Argument after argument ensued with her "boyfriend", Ari, who was coming around less and less frequently. Barbara loaned Ari the money she received from her baby early on in their relationship. He used her money to buy a bagel shop in Brighton Beach. Ari swore he would pay Barbara back, and the two of them would be able to have a nice, comfortable life together. There was just one small problem. There was never a bagel shop. When she insisted on seeing the place, Ari made numerous excuses until he finally told her the shop burned up in a fire. A total loss because his partner forgot to pay for the fire insurance.

Barbara was now a hooker and a drug addict without money and with a boyfriend who turned out to be a real scumbag loser. She had had enough. Then Barbara made a mistake that made Ari very angry.

Barbara went to the police.

Between tricks one day, Barbara walked over to the "Six O", the NYPD precinct that covers Brighton Beach. Her idea was to file a report against Ari to reclaim her money and make her way back home to Ohio. A detective took her name and some information before he told her she was just another hooker. The detective told her there was nothing that could be done about her money.

Little did she know, the cop she spoke with was on the Petrov *Bratva* payroll.

Ari showed up at her apartment later that day.

"Baby, how could you do such a thing to me? How could you go to the cops? You know I love you. Just a little while longer, and this life will be behind us," Ari said. Even now, she found him, his good looks, and his Russian accent to be irresistible.

"Ari, you lied to me. I'm tired of doing these disgusting men. Don't you even care about my feelings?"

"Of course I do, baby. I just need to get back on my feet. Then we can move out of here and be together. We can go looking for a house very soon," Ari said calmly.

"You took my money, Ari. It was all I had. I need that money to get back home to see my parents. I just need to see them. I'll come back in a few days," Barbara said. Her lie was not at all convincing to Ari the pimp.

"Okay, I will get all the money for you by tomorrow. I swear to God. Look, I have a friend coming up in a few minutes. He paid a thousand to be with you. I will give you the total amount. As a matter of fact, here it is," Ari said.

He fanned out ten new, crispy, one-hundred-dollar bills and handed them to his "lady".

"See? I mean what I say. Just one more trick, and it's over. Now let me help you get straight," Ari said.

Ari took the works and a packet of heroin that was Barbara's fix from the right pocket of his jeans.

CHAPTER 4

The intercom to Stacie's apartment made a gravely, grindy, buzz sound. She got a sinking feeling in her stomach followed by quivering butterflies. This was nothing new to her. Every time a john rang, she had the same sickening experience.

Ari had left her with explicit instructions after her 20 ml fix. In two hours, after she came down from her high, her last trick in her short career in prostitution would be over. His name was Freddy. She was to do whatever he asked. Freddy was a high roller.

As she was trained, Barbara waited at her apartment door, which was just to the right of the elevator on the fifth floor of the building. The smells of different foods always permeated the light gray, tiled hallways. Today, it was cabbage and maybe beef stew, favorites in the mostly Russian building. Barbara, or, really, Stacie, stood holding the brown, heavy, metal door open with her rounded hip. She was wearing a favorite ensemble of many if not all of her clients. Skin-tight blue jeans, flame-red high heels, and a hot-pink halter-top, which exposed four inches of her rock-hard abdominals. Her body did not show a hint of having given childbirth. The halter had no buttons. Stacie tied the bottom of the blouse in a slipknot allowing her ample breasts to expose a big gash of cleavage. The tips of her flowing, blonde hair were like a moving curtain that begged to be moved away for a better view.

Freddy was ferociously built. All muscles and no neck on a 5'5" body. His muscles seemingly had muscles. A three-day stubble made his low forehead and shaved head look something like a Neanderthal freak. Freddy forced a smile and walked right by Stacie without a word. The teen rolled her eyes, allowing herself a silent editorial on Freddy's looks. She noticed a Puss-n-Boots- Cat-in-the-Hat tattoo on her john's hand but was not aware of the significance. Freddy was a member of the Petrov *Bratva*. There were many other body markings of different shapes and meanings, which Freddy had etched into his leathery skin while in prison in the former Soviet Republic. He served five of his twenty-five years for stealing a scooter that belonged to a policeman. Freddy was as dumb as he looked.

"Freddy? Really? Freddy? You look more like a Boris or a Viktor. Okay, I'll call you Freddy. Unless you like "baby" better?" Stacie said.

Freddy, or whatever his name really was, ignored her remarks.

"Ari said you will do whatever I want." Freddy's accent was heavy, almost a parody of a Russian accent.

"Well, unless it's really kinky, I usually am good enough to get my job done.

"I want to fuck you in your ass....dry."

"Ohhhh, hold on, cowboy. I don't know about that," Stacie said. The teen took a few steps backward into the apartment's living room, trying to figure out an exit strategy.

"I paid Ari two thousand. He said I could do whatever I wanted to you. That is what I want." Freddy moved toward Stacie, his broadness and hairless, huge arms made an escape to the front door impossible for Stacie.

"Look, Freddy, I'm not saying I don't want to be with you, baby, but that sounds like that will be a little painful for a small girl like me. Let me call Ari, and he will pay you back. I have a thousand in the bedroom. Let me get it for you," Stacie said. Her soft voice began to quiver. She knew she was in trouble.

"No fucking refund. No calling Ari. *Tupa shmara.*"

Freddy grabbed Stacie around her waist with his left arm like she was a ragdoll. He carried her toward the bedroom. Stacie's throat closed and her mouth went dry from fear. She thought of screaming for help, for the police, and then remembered the detective at the Six 0 telling her she was just another hooker.

Freddy threw the young girl hard onto the quilted and multi- pillowed, king-sized, four-poster bed. Stacie hit her chin on one of the posts, almost rendering her unconscious. That would have been a blessing. She reached for the telephone. Freddy attempted a laugh, which sounded more like a lion's growl, as he pulled the phone from Stacie's tiny hand, smacking her hard on the side of the head with the receiver.

"Please don't, baby, I'll do what you want," Stacie said.

"Of course you will, bitch."

Freddy flipped Stacie onto her stomach with a simple flick of his wrist. His brute strength from obviously spending more time lifting things than any human being needed allowed Freddy to shred the poor girl's jeans at the seams. Freddy was now on the bed, on his knees, tearing at Stacie's thong, ripping it as if it were a cellophane seal on a pack of cigarettes.

"No, no, please! I'm going to throw up!" Stacie screamed. She felt her sphincter muscle tighten and bile rise into her throat.

"Shut your fucking mouth, bitch, or I will snap your skank neck for you."

Freddy held the teen down at her neck with his left hand. The panicked girl could hardly breathe from the power of her assailant. With his right hand, Freddy opened his pant buckle and pulled out his beefy cock.

Tugging on it a few times until it hardened, Freddy used his penis like a probe to find his victims anus. Stacie was whimpering and gasping for breath at the same time.

Freddy loosened up his grasp of the girl's neck only for a second. He lifted his hand from her and smashed his fist onto the back of her head, parting her blond hair with the blunt force. Stacie nearly blacked out again.

Anus found, Freddy jammed his cock into the teen's small hole, ripping the walls of the organ with the violent penetration. Stacie attempted a scream but passed out from the pain.

When Stacie regained consciousness, her entire body seemed to ache. Her rectum was numb. Instinctively, she felt for her vagina. It was dry. Then she touched her anus. Her hand came back a bloody mess.

Stacie went into the bathroom, looking into the rest of the apartment for her rapist. He was gone.

Stacie trembled and cried while she found a washcloth. She ran some warm water over the cloth and gently applied it to the brutalized area. She then felt the pain ripple up her spine.

Stacie glanced into the medicine cabinet mirror.

The normally bright whites of her eyes were totally bloodshot. Her hair was matted with blood and sweat. Her chin was scraped and almost bleeding. Her neck had big, black and blue marks that reminded her of the huge hickies she used to get from and give to her first boyfriend, Conrad. Conrad was the one who impregnated her and put her into this mess of a life.

"That fucking prick! That...rat...motherfucker! Stacie shrieked, surveying the damage to her neck and face. The first invective was for Conrad, the second for Freddy.

"Ari, he hurt me! Please, honey, get here as soon as possible. I need help." Barbara sent this text to Ari after having tried to call him ten times in the last half hour. The calls all went into Ari's voice mail.

A few minutes later, Ari was in the apartment, holding onto the sobbing Barbara Black of Canton, Ohio, all the while checking the time on his Tag Heuer watch.

CHAPTER 5

The Meatpacking District of Manhattan no longer has the two hundred and fifty slaughter houses and meatpacking plants that made the area virtually uninhabitable save for a few rough-and-tumble tenement houses. Today, fancy boutiques, luxury hotels, overpriced apartments, packed nightclubs, and pricy restaurants make the neighborhood from Gansevoort Street to West 14th Street and from the Hudson River to Hudson Street one of the most glamorous areas of New York City.

The district also serves as the dividing line between the Albanian Mob and the Italian Mafia. Neutral ground, both factions have their hands in illegal activities there. They share in the profits of the once Italian-Mafia-controlled neighborhood.

What better place to have a sit-down than at *Macelleria*, on Gansevoort Street? In Italian, m*acelleria* means butcher shop, harkening back to a long-gone era in the neighborhood. *Macelleria* is owned by a legitimate Albanian restaurateur with an Italian name. The interior of the place boasts an antique, mahogany bar that looms over a small dining room with butcher-block tables. Normally not the best place to have a quiet talk about illegal activities, but, on this day, the restaurant was closed until noon. The three guests were well known to the owner, Sergio.

"Two enemies rest their heads on the same pillow," Ilir Marku, the head of the New York Albanian mob, said to Carmine Miceli, Jr., and Gino Ranno of the Italian mob. The three men sat at a large table that could easily have accommo-dated six people.

Bodyguards for both sides stood at the ready outside, pretending to be looking in the boutique windows or at the passing hipsters.

"Ilir, I thought that word, "enemy" would have been buried a long time ago. We don't view you like that," Gino said, a bit surprised at Ilir's choice of an old Albanian proverb.

Carmine, Jr., gave Ilir a puzzled look. He had taken over the infamous Miceli family upon the death of his father. Carmine, Jr., was learning not to lose his cool or be insulted easily. Gino Ranno was Carmine, Jr's. advisor and mentor. Gino had done a good job teaching the once-petulant child.

"I apologize. I see everyone as an enemy since I buried my son. Today would have been his twenty-eighth birthday. You have proven your friendship since that terrible time. Please forgive me," Ilir said.

"Rest in peace. It was a terrible tragedy," Carmine, Jr., said.

"What is bothering you, Ilir? You seem, well…you seem angry," Carmine, Jr., said.

"These Russians are animals. It is bad enough that we must share the streets with them. What they are doing, I cannot tolerate," Ilir said.

Suddenly, the door to the restaurant was opened by one of the Albanian bodyguards. A familiar figure walked in, shading his eyes to adjust from the bright sunlight to the darkened dining room. It was Hamdi Nezaj, advisor to Ilir Marku.

Gino and Carmine, Jr., immediately stood. Carmine, Jr., out of respect, Gino, out of friendship.

Hamdi walked over to that table and, as it should be, shook Ilir's hand and kissed him on both cheeks. He then turned his attention to Gino, smiling broadly.

"My dear friend, I haven't seen you in so long it seems," Hamdi said. He embraced Gino and kissed him in the Albanian fashion.

"How are you, my old friend? How is your family?" Gino asked.

"We are all fine, thank God, and you and your family?"

"Some good, some not so good. We can discuss things later," Gino said.

"Hello, Hamdi. You are looking well and very fit," Carmine, Jr., said.

Hamdi took Carmine's extended hand in both of his, bowing his head ever so slightly in a sign of respect.

"Thank you, Mr. Miceli. I hope you and your family are well."

"Sit, everyone, let us continue our conversation," Ilir said. Ilir made a gesture to Sergio, who immediately sent a waiter to gather the coffee orders and to offer a few dishes of bread, feta cheese, and olives. A bottle of homemade *raki* and Marie Brizard anisette were already on the table.

"You had mentioned the Russians, Ilir. What is the problem? Can we help in any way?" Carmine, Jr., asked.

"I see only bad things in the future for both of our affairs, my friends. These people have no limit to their cruelty and greed. My dear friend, your father, Carmine, would never have permitted them to grow their tentacles as we have allowed. Perhaps, our feud clouded our judgment, and they acted quickly when our backs were turned," Ilir said.

"What are you referring to, Ilir? Are they encroaching on our territories, our business interests?" Carmine, Jr., asked.

"If I may. With all respect, I would like to speak for Mr. Marku on this matter," Hamdi said.

"By all means," Gino said.

"We have interests very similar to your own. Your family has been in business for many, many years. As things became difficult for you with the Justice Department, the RICO laws, and your own associates who made themselves very visible, our people made inroads, and we both sipped from the same cup. Mostly, we have made small issues not come between us. The larger issues are now behind us," Hamdi said.

"Another of my famous Albanian proverbs for us to consider, 'Wise men make big problems into small problems and make small problems disappear altogether.' These problems with the Russians are very large," Ilir said.

"There is no secret that the Russians in Brighton Beach have a disdain for us. They think we are ignorant mountain people and show us no respect at all. But...no problem, our shoulders are big. We have lived with this yoke around our necks since we arrived here," Hamdi said.

"Tell me, my friend. What are they up to?" Gino inquired.

"Unspeakable things that the Shqiptar, the Albanians, would never contemplate. We would never sell young people into bondage for sex. I don't believe your people would either," Hamdi said.

"Absolutely not," Carmine, Jr., confirmed.

"Prostitution has its place in this world. Kidnapping children, little girls, young boys for money is beyond our understanding. Our culture, our *Kanun*, does not allow this behavior. Even among criminals. They must be stopped," Hamdi said.

"May I interject, *kumar*?" Ilir said as if he needed permission. Hamdi put his right hand to his heart, lowering his eyes in deference to his friend and leader.

"This ugly business is only part of what these, what we call *Gjin të egër*, the "wild people," are doing. We will explain more. What they are doing will put us in the same pot with them. The heat from these activities will fall on us and you and your people. We, none of us, need more scrutiny," Ilir said. His face was twisted in disgust.

"Bad enough they are selling children into sex slavery. They are selling human organs as well. Medical murder, I'm not even sure what to call it. They chop people up and sell the parts like they are a car," Hamdi said.

"Organ piracy. They sell the organs of people they kill for money. I know of this in places like Iran or India or Russia. I wasn't aware that it was here in New York," Gino said.

"Their people are trained in Russia, Iran, and other places around the world. And, yes, it is here in our city. They have set up a surgical center that is more like a slaughterhouse. I don't know the proper word in English to describe that kind of thing," Hamdi said.

"Abomination, atrocity, disgrace. Take your pick," Carmine, Jr., said.

"We must shut them down and send a message that this cannot be allowed to continue. Let them bring this mess back to Russia," Hamdi declared.

"Have you discussed this with them on a high level?" Gino said.

"We have tried several times. They will not sit with us. They believe we are beneath them," Hamdi said.

"It seems that we need to first have a discussion. One of the families in Brooklyn had some dealings with the Russians. The gasoline and diesel tax business was shared for some time. I'm sure you remember this. Hundreds of millions were made on both sides. Tax money was collected but never paid to the state and federal government. Then the suits, the politicians in Albany and Washington got wise, and the rats scattered. With your permission, I will reach out to them for a sit-down," Carmine said.

"I agree with you. However, I do not think we should be at the meeting. The feeling they have toward us, and, now, we toward them, will be like playing with dynamite. It is better that you feel them out," Ilir said.

"Agreed. But we will speak for you as well as our people," Carmine, Jr., said.

"And if they refuse?" Hamdi asked.

"Let's cross that bridge when we come to it," Gino replied.

Hamdi looked at his old friend Gino with a serious frown. He spoke slowly.

"I'm afraid the toll will be very costly,"

CHAPTER 6

The moment Ari and Barbara walked out of the five-story, pre-World War II-built, tan, brick apartment building, a car appeared as if on cue to take them to the doctor's office. Ari had called ahead to make the emergency appointment. Barbara felt comfortable that she would be seeing the doctor who had once given her a physical. On a second visit, the doctor prescribed an allergy medication. He also gave her a large supply of body creams and lubricant samples which Barbara could use in her work.

Dr. Mickele Abramoff had a gentle manner and was not at all judgmental. Barbara told him what she was doing for a living when they first met. He seemed to understand the difficulties in her life and made her feel comfortable. In some ways, Dr. Abramoff reminded Barbara of her own father.

The two-story, two-hundred-feet-wide, grey, metal-and-brick building had only a few windows, which were black. No lights or movement inside of the building could be seen from the street. The only sign in front of the property facing Cropsey Avenue read, "Klinger Pavilion". Two rotating security cameras panned the front of the building and entranceway. Access was gained with a sophisticated voice-and-fingerprint-recognition device that accepted Ari Mamantov instantly.

Ari and Barbara took the elevator to the second floor. The couple was met by a female nurse who wore surgical greens and carried a medical folder with "Black, Barbara" printed in bold letters along its side. The nurse asked Ari to wait in a small reception area. She escorted Barbara to a nine-by-nine foot medical waiting room. The room was typical of many medical examination rooms with a scale, an examining table, a short stool, and a large wall chart of the internal human anatomy.

There were medications and syringes on a white, Corian counter, which had an inlaid sink with a soap dispenser above it. The nurse asked Barbara to undress, handing her a blue, patterned hospital gown to wear.

Dr. Abramoff entered the room a few minutes later after a gentle, polite knock on the door.

"My dear Barbara, what happened to you?" Abramoff said.

"A crazy man almost killed me."

"How unfortunate. Let me take a look. Oh my, these lacerations on your neck look quite serious. Are you in any pain?" Abramoff asked.

"Not as much as the back of my head and my butt. He forced himself on me, Doctor. I was bleeding a lot, but that seems to have stopped. He punched me in my head here, and I feel a bump," Barbara said. She began to tear up.

"I want to start you with an IV and some antibiotics. The risk of infection is great in an attack like this. Lie down on the examination table. Nurse, please start the IV. I'm going to also give you an injection to calm you down a bit, Barbara. You are traumatized," Abramoff said.

"Thank you so much, Doctor," Barbara sighed.

The nurse dutifully found a vein in Barbara's left hand and started the IV drip. The doctor injected her with ten milligrams of Valium. Within a few minutes, Barbara was floating like she had just taken a fix of heroin. She welcomed the high.

Another man in green scrubs appeared and introduced himself as a doctor.

"Miss Black, I am going to help you take a nice rest. Just relax for a few minutes. We have your records here, and we are familiar with your medical history and drug use. We will be taking you to another room in just few short minutes."

Barbara couldn't care less. She was floating on a cloud from the Valium and the sedative that was in the IV. There were no antibiotics administered. There was no need.

Barbara didn't try to move. And, if she had, she would have discovered she could not move an inch.

Ten minutes later, two male nurses joined the female nurse in wheeling Barbara to a room down the hall from where she was lying. The florescent lights and acoustic tiles seemed to be racing by above her. She was now so drugged that she started to smile from the experience.

The two men and the nurse wheeled Barbara into a room with a sign above the door that read OP ONE. The operating room was full of machines, laptop computers, and various instruments to prepare for the teen's surgery.

The nurses moved Barbara from the gurney that transported her to an articulating surgical table. There were four people standing around the table all dressed in blue, surgical gowns, blue masks, and beige gloves that rose halfway up their forearms. The table had many stainless-steel clamps, scissors, probes, and scalpels, neatly arranged on top of heavy, blue sheets.

Dr. Abramoff entered the operating room in sterile blues with surgical mask, a tight-fitting surgeon's hat, and gloves. His glasses had surgical loops to assist him in magnifying the detailed work that was soon to occur.

The last thing Barbara saw on this earth was the word, "Maquet". Maquet is the manufacturer's name written across the sides of a four-armed lighting unit attached from the ceiling, which also served as a docking station for two video monitors. To the side of the table, a machine with slushed ice and a stainless-steel deep tray made a slight hissing noise. The slush pump pulsates up and down to regulate the vessel's temperature.

Soon after, Barbara Black's organs were surgically removed and placed in the tray for their recipients.

CHAPTER 7

"I want to know what love is...I want you to show me..." The music of Foreigner played in the background of the operating room. The anesthesiologist, a Russian-trained woman with bad teeth and even worse body odor, administered two milligrams of the drug Versid. She quickly attached the appropriate tubes to keep Barbara breathing and signaled Dr. Abramoff to begin the shark bite incision into Barbara Black's abdomen.

There was no thought about a small cut or a bikini line cut in this case. There would be no vanity for the unwitting donor to be concerned about.

Barbara's blood type and antigen match were perfect for the waiting organ recipient. These issues were predetermined by the tests taken on the unsuspecting teen during her first visit to Abramoff's office.

Barbara's left kidney would be harvested for an exceedingly special patient, who would receive the organ within the next hour. They don't get much fresher than that. The teen's right kidney also had a new home planned for a now-daily dialysis recipient in New Jersey the next morning. Barbara's two corneas, pancreas, and spleen, and even her soft, supple, young skin would also be used within the next forty-eight hours. That is pushing the time frame for successful transplants. Anything over that time frame would render the chilled body parts useless.

Barbara's leg bone marrow, her ligaments, and even some muscles would be used for waiting patients.

Total take for these pirated parts would exceed seven hundred and fifty thousand dollars in gross profits to the Petrov *Bratva*. After expenses, including the nurses, surgical staff, and Dr. Abramoff and his assistant, it would be in the area of a half-million dollars in cold cash. Barbara would have had to spread her legs thousands of times over many years to earn that much profit for the Russian mafia.

Within twenty minutes, Dr. Abramoff uttered his first words.

"Okay, I'm ready to remove the first kidney. We are fortunate this kidney doesn't have multiple arteries. That is such a pain in the ass," Abramoff said.

The doctor's assistant, who slightly resembled Igor in the original Frankenstein movie, mumbled an agreement.

"Retractor please. So where are we off to this weekend, Sonja?" Abramoff inquired. It was his way of flirting with the long-legged nurse who met Barbara and Ari Mamantov at the door to the house of death.

"My boyfriend and I are going to Miami for a few days. We love the clubs and the action down there," Sonja replied.

"All the way to Miami with that young boy. He has no idea how to please you, my dear. You need an older man…a patron to take his time with you and make you gush with excitement," Abramoff said.

"He knows exactly what to do, believe me. We dance at the Clevelander on South Beach. Dancing is almost as good as sex there. You have to see it to believe it, Doctor," Sonja said.

"Rotate the table away from me please," Abramoff ordered his assistant to move the operating table slightly to get a better angle at the kidney.

"So explain how dancing is like sex. I guess my generation views dancing a bit differently," Abramoff said.

"As the hip-hop music pulsates I bend down with my butt against my boyfriend's crotch like this, and we move as one to the beat," Sonja explained. She demonstrated her movement so that her tight butt pressed against the sterile, blue surgical pants. Her ample and impressive breasts strained against her tight-fitting, V-neck, surgical top.

"Sounds like a pretty fun thing to do. You must admit, though, you are probably the talk of the club with that great body," Abramoff said. The doctor looked up for a few seconds over his spectacles to get the full benefits of his nurse's demonstration.

"Okay, I'm ready to remove the organ. All that's left is to clamp off the urethral tube and artery," Abramoff said. The surgeon used a long, two-pronged surgical device that both cut the kidney away from artery and tube and clamped it at the same time. He was as calm as a barber buzz cutting the hair on the back of his customer's neck.

"And what do you wear during this *voyeurs* picnic, Sonja? Certainly not these blues," Abramoff said. He now stepped away from the table to get the full visual of the nurse.

"Well, spiked heels for sure, a mini up to about here, and a skin- tight blouse just to about here," Sonja answered. She pointed to an area on her thigh just below her crotchs and to one just below her breasts.

The Igor impersonator growled aloud.

"Let's leave your boyfriend home this trip. I can be your escort," Abramoff said. The sweat on his surgical cap was becoming a problem.

"Maybe next time, Doctor. I want you to imagine me with someone else this weekend," Sonja said. She knew that Abramoff would pay dearly for the pleasure of her company. Not in cash money but in plastic. All she wanted was his Platinum Amex card for a jaunt around the shops and boutiques on millionaire's row in Great Neck, Long Island. Abramoff was hers just for the asking.

Abramoff put his attention back to the work. He could barely concentrate.

"Okay, here is the first kidney. Please rotate the table back, and prepare for the second abdominal slit," Abramoff said.

He removed the organ through the original incision. The kidney came from Barbara's body in a tight, mesh bag that Abramoff molded around the organ. He turned slightly to his left and placed the kidney in the stainless-steel tray, which was surrounded by ice. The Igor impersonator made the second cut into the donor's lower abdomen.

As if on cue, the sound of the musical group America came on the disc player and seemed to fill the room.

You can do magic
You can have anything that you desire
Magic, and you know
You're the one who can put out the fire

You know darn well
When you cast your spell, you will get your way
When you hypnotize with your eyes

A heart of stone can turn to clay
Doo, doo, doo...

"Okay Sonja, I am captivated by you. How about three weeks from this Friday? Tell your man that you have a medical convention to attend. Where are we staying?" Abramoff said. He was not focused on the kidney, which looked more like a bloody, seared roast beef then a kidney when the mesh bag was cut away.

"Only place I will stay is the *Fontainebleau.* Everyplace else is a dump in comparison," Sonja said. For the first time her big, blue eyes looked right into Abramoff's. The surgeon's cock tingled with excitement.

"I will get us the penthouse," he said.

The song ironically ended at that moment.

You're the one who can put out the fire
You're the one who can put out the fire
You're the one who can put out the fire...

Sonja laughed for the sake of the others in the room, but she knew she had made the score of the year. He was hers, and Sonja could just imagine what her wardrobe and shoe closet would look like by the end of the year.

The Russian-trained, female anesthesiologist kept Barbara unconscious and ventilated through the process of removing all of her organs. The moment her corneas, the last of her parts to be removed, were taken, Barbara would be left to take her last breaths, never knowing that her beautiful, young body was ravished for the profits of an organized crime family in Little Odessa, Brooklyn.

LOUIS ROMANO

Within the hour, Barbara Black would be dead, Freddy, the rapist who beat her, would be removing her body to a grinder in Sheepshead Bay, and Dr. Abramoff would be on the phone with American Express to make travel plans to Miami Beach.

As easy as that.

CHAPTER 8

One of the best structural criminal groups in this country and for the world for that matter is the Russian mafia. And take a guess where they poached it from?

In 1931, Salvatore Maranzano separated the five Italian mob families in New York City. Using a brilliant organizational mind, Maranzano established the *Cosa Nostra* code of conduct and structure. He borrowed heavily from the Roman Legion chain of command to delineate the *capo*, or head, from the *soldate*, the soldiers. Lieutenants, captains, and underbosses, were the managers who ran each family. There was however, a major flaw in Maranzano's character. Maranzano's greed was larger than his ego.

Maranzano appointed himself *capo di tutti capi*, the boss of all bosses, taking a tribute or a tax to himself from each family. In effect, every family worked for him. In short order, within six months of Maranzano setting up his organization, Salvatore Lucania, a.k.a. Lucky Luciano of Lercara Friddi, Sicily, had Maranzano assassinated. Luciano set up the famous "commission", allowing the families to have set territories and act independently of each other. Eighty-five years later, that organization is still in existence, albeit not as strong as they once were.

The Russian mafia or *voy v zakone*, thief-in-law, or more literally translated as "thieves who follow the law," have virtually followed a carbon copy of the Sicilian-American mafia, which, like the Sicilians, are not a singular criminal organization. Each family stands on its own. The law they follow is their own code.

In the Russian mafia, the *pakhan* is the boss. He is assisted by a brigadier and an underboss, who, like the Italian mafia, has *boeviks,* or soldiers, who pay tribute to the p*akhan*. The *boeviks* are also *kryshas*, the literal meaning is "roofs", and they are the violent enforcers of the family.

The *pakhan* employs two spies who watch over the action of the brigadiers to ensure loyalty from everyone in the family.

Similar to the Sicilian mafia *consigliere*, the *pakhan* also appoints a *sovietnik,* or a councilor.

The family also has torpedoes, or contract killers, like the mafia's button men. Among their ranks there are *obchchaks,* or "bookmakers," and *byk*i, literally meaning "bull", as bodyguards. Any man of honor, or a "made" man, is called *vor*. The lowest rank, like the Sicilian mafia associates, are called *shestyorka.*

Their honor code differs from the Sicilian mafia in several distinct ways. One of the major differences is, when a man joins the *Bratva*, he must renounce his own mother and father. He refers to his mother as *suka*, a bitch, and his father as *friar*, or worthless piece of shit.

Renouncing their own family in favor of their treacherous life is an abomination to their counterparts in crime.

The Albanian mob and the Italian mafia now would draw a line in the white sands of Brighton Beach.

CHAPTER 9

Vadim Orloff looked more like an animal than a man. Orloff's steel-blue eyes, long, stringy, brown hair, and low forehead were framed with a strong, square jaw and pockmarked complexion. His smile, more like a snarl, displayed gray and nicotine stained teeth. A wide diasthema in the middle of his two front, capped teeth made him resemble Cro-Magnon man.

Orloff is a krysha, a "roof" or protector of the Petrov *Bratva*. His only job was to make certain that he fulfilled any job that his brigadier ordered. Broken bones, murder, maiming, and arson are his specialties and he is the very best the *Bratva* had.

Ilir Marku wanted to send a strong message to the Petrov *Bratva*. The Albanians were no longer going to sit idly by and watch as their earnings were decimated at the hands of the greedy Russians. Ilir patiently awaited the right time for the message to be sent.

Orloff made the mistake of leaving the Coney Island Peninsula in Brooklyn, making the forty-minute ride to Arthur Avenue in the Bronx. His mission was to fulfill an order from his boss, Timur Maksimov. One of the Marku Albanians reneged on a serious gambling debt. Forty thousand dollars was enough for Maksimov to have Orloff strike fear into the deadbeat gambler.

The truth is, Ilir Marku had his man purposely lose in a card game and defy the Russians, refusing to pay on a marker. The trap had been set.

At ten o'clock on a lazy, sunny, Sunday morning, Orloff and his driver, a low level *shestyorka,* or Petrov soldier, found a parking spot on Arthur Avenue near East 187th Street. The two Russians walked a block until they spotted a storefront with a small, Albanian, double-eagle insignia on the front door. The windows of the store were tinted black for six feet and green for the top half. Orloff could not see inside the place.

A well-used set of brass knuckles was in Orloff's jacket pocket, and a Serbian-made, Zastava, M-88, 9mm pistol wrapped inside a copy of *Novoye Russkoze Slova*, an American, Russian-language newspaper, was in Orloff's right hand-his tools of his trade that morning. His right hand had a tattoo of what looked to be a skeleton head, a symbol that he was a *voy v zakone*, a thief-in-law.

"You wait here. If you hear anything, you come in blasting. Kill all those filthy bastards," Orloff told the soldier in Georgian Russian. The soldier had an automatic pistol under his poorly fitting, wrinkled sports coat.

The *krysha* walked into the members only club and sat down at a table near the entranceway.

The six men in the club looked at him quickly and looked away, ignoring his presence. One of the six stood and approached Orloff.

"Sir, forgive me, this is a private club."

"I know," Orloff said.

"Well, I will ask you to leave, please. We do not serve the public."

"I will leave when I am ready. I am waiting for an old friend who I know comes in this place," Orloff said in a thick Russian accent.

"And who is that friend?"

"Jack Daci. Do you know him?"

"I know of no Daci who comes in here."

Two of the men lit cigarettes under a no-smoking sign, listening carefully to the conversation. They never looked at Orloff.

"I will wait for him. Or maybe you can tell me where I can find him. We go back a long way, Jack and me," Orloff said.

"Leave me your telephone number, and I will ask a few members if they know this man."

"Get me coffee," Orloff demanded.

"Sir, I said to you, we only serve members."

"Fuck you, pig Albanian. Get me coffee."

The two men with their cigarettes dangling between their lips quickly pushed away from their table, and a third, unseen by Orloff, came from behind a colorful, beaded curtain that led to the bathroom. The two men at the table brandished pistols, and a sawed-off Beretta shotgun was in the hands of the man who came from behind the beads.

"Don't move, you motherfucker. Put the newspaper on the table. Do as I say, and you will live," the shotgun guy said.

One of the men with the pistol put the gun to Orloff's temple. The man who was talking with Orloff quickly locked the front door.

Outgunned, Orloff placed the newspaper on the table. The second pistol guy quickly removed the paper. He tucked Orloff's Glock into his waistband.

One of the other Albanian men in the club, a large, heavy-set guy, quickly walked to the rear of the club. He exited the rear door and walked up the small alley that led back to the street. Orloff's Russian associate was trying to see inside the club, placing his hand on the window, trying to shade his eyes to see through the tinted window. The last thing he saw was a shadow of the baseball bat that crushed his skull. The door of the club suddenly opened, and two of the other men inside the club along with the big man pulled the lifeless body of the Petrov solider inside the club.

The trap was sprung.

Joey Nanariello started his gravy at five o'clock every Sunday morning so it would be ready for his loyal customers by noon. By twelve-thirty, there was an hour wait for a table. People came in from New Jersey, Westchester, and as far away as Connecticut to enjoy the best Sunday gravy on the planet.

His Neapolitan family passed down Joey's secret through many generations. He had made a good living for many years on his family recipes.

Into a one-hundred-quart, heavy, double-stainless-steel stockpot that had a depth of nineteen inches and a circumference of twenty-two inches, Joey placed the ingredients as if they were part of a sacred ritual, a people's mass if you will.

First the olive oil. Not that extra virgin, first-pressed, cold -pressed hipster stuff. Just plain, old olive oil. The least expensive that he could buy across the street at Teitel Brothers' grocery store. Joey's great grandparents bought all of their provisions at the Jewish-owned store. The Nanariellos had a "trust" account at Teitel for decades. They had bought their oils, tomatoes, olives, garlic, seasonings, and cheese at this store since 1905. Old man Teitel would put the amount owed in his composition notebook, and Joey's people would settle up every Friday evening with cash. No checkbook, credit cards, debit cards, ATM machines-nothing like that was ever even dreamed about.

As the thick cloves of smashed garlic browned in the quarter inch of oil, Joey added the canned San Marzano tomatoes, fresh parsley, fresh basil, and Trapani sea salt. Black pepper was the last ingredient added before the gravy simmered for the better part of an hour. The Nanariellos called it gravy and would defend themselves against anyone who called it sauce.

Next came the large chunks of pork in one-pound pieces that were first browned in an iron skillet before being delicately placed into the simmering tomatoes. The same process was followed with sweet and hot sausages. Sixty or seventy healthy links were added two or three at a time. Joey's fingers could feel the heat from the gravy as he placed the sausage gingerly into the it. He burned himself once when his Nona was showing him the art of the gravy back when he was fifteen. That was all it took. Joey was never burned again in fifty years of gravy making.

Then the *piece de resistance*...the famous, Nanariello family meatballs were taken from the heavy frying pans and placed into the huge pot. More than one hundred meatballs were made with no one outside the family ever seeing the ingredients that were put into the chopped beef, pork, and veal meat. That was the best-kept secret in the world history of Italian food.

The gravy then simmered for hours. Five hours on a low flame with Joey stirring the gravy every ten minutes or so. After every hour, he would "make *mocca*" by dipping a piece of hard-crusted, Italian bread into the sauce. Joey would raise the soaked bread to his mouth, blow away the steam, and wait a few seconds for the heat to subside before eating it. This was as a progressive taste test. Maybe more salt? Pepper? Something may not be enough. The bread could never have any seeds. God forbid if one seed would fall into the gravy.

Joey's restaurant was next door to the Albanian social club where Vadim Orloff was about to experience some summary Bronx justice.

Calls were made, and, within the hour, mysterious-looking men-all dark and swarthy, some short, some tall, all with a look about them that said, "don't fuck with me"-entered the Albanian club one by one. A few had that Albanian-high-forehead and broad-cheekbone look; a few had that combed-back-hair look of Italian gangsters. The Italians were easy to spot. They were dressed better in their front-pleated pants and Italian loafers, and it was clear who was whom.

Mickey Roach, the Miceli family enforcer, arrived last with two of his Sicilian henchmen.

Mickey tapped lightly on the social club door. He had an unfiltered cigarette dangling from his mouth, which he flicked into the gutter when the door to the club opened. On the floor of the club was the dead Russian with the bashed-in skull. Orloff was hog-tied just a few feet from his comrade.

"Where do you get the balls to come into my neighborhood looking for trouble?" Mickey demanded. He stood over Orloff, who strained his neck to see who was addressing him.

"My business is not with you," Orloff replied.

"Sure it is, my friend, sure it is. Everything that happens here is our business. This is our home. Just like that piece of beach is your home in Brooklyn. How would you like if we came in there looking for one of you people?"

"You are Italian. We have no beef with Italians. It's these Albanian swine that I come for," Orloff said. The Russian was trying very hard to get onto his side, to continue the conversation.

"These good people are our friends. You come for our friends is like you come for us. I can't have that you have the crust to come here," Mickey said. He lit another cigarette, spitting a tiny piece of tobacco onto the floor.

"I get the message, my friend. I will go back and explain your loyalty to these dogs."

"Who sent you here?" Mickey asked.

"I came on my own."

"I will only ask you again, Ruskie. Who sent you here?

"Your mother. That's who sent me here," Orloff said. His face was now touching the ceramic tile floor.

"Nah, my mother died in Sicily many years ago. I can see that you need some convincing."

Mickey Roach stepped away from Orloff and motioned to the men standing around him, two Sicilians and two, tall, husky Albanians.

"Bring him downstairs. We need to take him next door for a little hospitality. We haven't even offered him anything to eat. Now what kind of hosts are we anyway?" Mickey said.

The four men lifted Orloff up by his tied limbs, carrying him like a rag doll down into the dark cellar. The old, wooden steps strained from the weight making creaking and cracking sounds all the way into the dank basement.

The huge Albanian who mashed the skull of the roof's soldier, opened a bolted door that separated Nanariello's restaurant from the social club. They carried the Russian up a flight of black stairs that led to Joey's kitchen. Joey was startled by the intrusion as he just finished stirring the bubbling gravy.

"Joey, that smells like my mother's kitchen. It brings tears to my eyes," Mickey said.

"Mickey, I don't want no trouble," Joey said.

"Don't worry, Joey. Out of respect for you, I will give this mutt one more chance to answer my simple question."

The four men placed Orloff on the greasy, black and white tile floor near the busy stove. Mickey bent down on one knee to ask the question again.

"One last try, Ruskie. Who sent you to my neighborhood?" Mickey asked Orloff.

"Fuck you and your dead mother, guinea," Orloff said.

Mickey calmly raised to his feet, brushing off the knee of his right pant leg.

"Joey, go put a sign on your front door: "Closed due to illness". Don't worry, you won't come out second. My guy will stop by tomorrow with the right amount for you in an envelope," Mickey said.

"You will all die. My people will slaughter you like the pig fuckers that you are," Orloff yelled. He was squirming on the floor.

"You know something, my friend? In this country, they have a children's game. They play it around Halloween. It's called bobbing for apples. But, in this neighborhood, we call it bobbing for meatballs. Let's see how many of my good friend's meatballs you can pick up," Mickey said.

Mickey motioned with a flick of his wrist to dunk the Russian into the boiling, bubbling, famous, Nanariello gravy.

The two Albanians and two Sicilians lifted Orloff over the huge stockpot, placing him head first into the hot gravy.

Orloff let out a scream that sounded like the squeal of a beast as his head was submerged. After ten long seconds, the men lifted him from the gravy. Orloff's face had become a red, blistered mess. He tried to gasp for air. Orloff's eyes were sealed closed by the hot oil that formed on the top of the gravy.

"C'mon, my friend. You're supposed to come out with a meatball. Don't you understand our game?" Mickey nodded his head to the side, signaling another dunk. Orloff tried to yell out again but the lack of air prevented the noise.

Again, he came out without a Nanariello meatball.

"Again," Mickey ordered.

After five dunks, Orloff's lifeless body was unceremoniously dropped onto the kitchen floor.

He never got a meatball.

CHAPTER 10

Valbona Marku was not in a good place in her life. A little over a year ago, she had everything to live for. Valbona had a handsome, attentive husband, and her precious baby boy was about to be born in just a few short weeks. But a situation between her husband and another man changed their futures forever.

Her husband, Lekë, came from the Marku clan with his father, Ilir, being the head of the Albanian mob in New York City.

And as with all mob troubles, things got ugly. So ugly, in fact, that an all-out war was going on between the Albanian mob and the Italian mafia. Not a storefront was safe in the Bronx.

But that was then, and this is now. Today, she sits with a man, a friend and confidant, who had totally fallen in love with her. There was a bond between Valbona and Adem, but not in the way in which Adem had hoped.

Adem fell deeply in love with Valbona, and, in his mind, began courting her in the Albanian fashion with all respect and understanding of her horrible ordeal. Valbona had deep feelings for Adem although she did not want what Adem had in his mind.

Adem and Valbona took a ride to their mutual friend Skander's restaurant, the Sparkill Steak House in Sparkill, New

York. During the forty-five minute drive to suburban Rockland County from the Marku Estate in Westchester, Adem felt that something was not right with Valbona. He chalked up Valbona's distance to the roller- coaster moods that he had already experienced with her over the last year.

Skender saw to it that the two were given a quiet table away from the other patrons this night.

"Are you okay, Valbona? You seemed distracted on the ride here," Adem said.

"I'm fine. Just a bit tired," Valbona said. She took a sip of *Tignanello* wine that their friend Skender sent to the table with his compliments.

"You don't look tired at all. As a matter of fact, you look gorgeous tonight."

"Thank you, but I don't feel anywhere near gorgeous at the moment. As a matter of fact, I want to discuss something with you, Adem," Valbona said. She took a larger sip of her red wine to fortify what she was about to say.

"By all means."

"You have been my rock, Adem. I can never repay you for what you have done for me since…"

Valbona gazed out into the woods from the bay window next to their table. Her eyes filled with tears.

"There is no reason to thank me, Valbona. Two things I know for sure: I love you with every fiber of my being, and I want to marry you and start a life together," Adem said.

That's what I want to discuss Adem. I love you, too, but I'm afraid we can no longer see each other."

"Excuse me?"

"I don't want to sound ungrateful for all you have done for me. You pulled me from the brink. I never told you this, but I thought of ending my life several times since last year. I never, ever want to lose our friendship, but anything else is out of the question.

"You are not ready now, I understand that. I will be as patient as I need to be," Adem said.

"There will never be another husband or children for me. Never."

"The wounds of what happened are still fresh, honey. In time, your..."

"Adem, stop. You are not listening to me. I will never change my mind. My feelings toward you will never change. My spirit is damaged, damaged beyond repair. I don't want to have that kind of relationship with you or any man now or ever," Valbona said. She took a long draw of her wine, draining the glass.

"We can slow things down," Adem said.

"You are the most wonderful man. There is no reason for you to stick around and be part of my drama."

"The old timers have a saying: 'one fool tosses a stone into the lake, and one hundred wise men cannot retrieve it.'"

"I never understood what that really means," Valbona said.

The waiter refilled Valbona's glass, and the couple went silent until he was out of their space. Valbona reached for the long-stemmed, crystal glass. Adem gently put his hand on the glass to stop her from drinking more.

"What it means in simple terms is that you can make an uncorrectable error with your life. The way you see things now may not be how you feel in time," Adem explained.

"Adem, go on with your life. Your career means so much to you. Your talent will bring great things to you and to the entire world. 'With patience, you will drink an entire ocean sip by sip.' Another old timer's proverb."

"You are my life," Adem said.

"No. Singing must be your life, not me. You decided not to join your father in his business affairs and for good reason. God gave you a gift. Your destiny is right in front of you. Don't be that fool with the stone."

"Do you feel this way because of my relationship with Lekë? That he was my half-brother? I never even knew him."

"I feel this way because my soul is empty. I don't love you that way. I will never love that way again."

CHAPTER 11

Carmine Miceli, Jr., had moved into his father's townhouse on East Seventy-Ninth Street in Manhattan after the mob scion passed away. His mother moved down to Boca Raton, Florida, to be with her sister to wait her turn to die.

The morning after the killing of Orloff, which Carmine, Jr., sanctioned after meeting with Ilir Marku, the doorbell to the townhouse buzzed incessantly along with a few loud raps on the front door. Carmine, Jr.'s wife jumped from bed and shook her husband awake.

"Carmine, what the hell is that? Someone is pounding at the door. Oh, my God. It's five-thirty in the morning."

Carmine, Jr., reached over to his nightstand and quickly entered the code to a small safe that was tucked away in the furniture. The trap door of the safe popped open. A loaded Heckler and Koch nine-millimeter pistol was in his hand within ten seconds.

"Go into the kids' room, and stay there," Carmine, Jr., said to his panicked wife.

In his underwear, Carmine moved slowly down the two flights of cherry-wood and marble staircases. The gun's safety was flicked off. The pounding at the door continued. The pounding in Carmine, Jr.'s chest was now beating into his ears.

Carmine looked out the beveled glass window, standing defensively behind the wall near the door. He could see several NYPD police cruisers and four or five black, unmarked cars, which blocked the street. Seven men in suits along with several uniformed police officers stood in front of the townhouse entrance.

"Yeah, who is it?" Carmine yelled. He stood aside the unopened door.

"Carmine Miceli? FBI. We have warrants for your arrest and to search the premises. Please open the door."

Carmine rubbed his eyes and ran his hand over his head to even out his bed hair. He put the HK behind his back and opened the door.

"Mr. Miceli, please step away from the door," an agent said.

"I'm armed," Carmine, Jr., said.

Another agent reached out and removed the pistol from Carmine's hand.

"This is a warrant for your arrest. These men have an order to search your home. I will give you a few minutes to get dressed."

"My wife is upstairs with my children. Can I ask you not to send them into hysterics?"

"Not our first day at the rodeo Mr. Miceli. Tend to your family, and come downstairs within five minutes."

The agents began swarming into the home's first level, walking in different directions as if on cue.

"Can I ask what this is all about?"

"The paperwork is specific. Extortion, racketeering. You can call your attorney when we get to our office downtown," the agent explained. There was no sympathy in his voice. He was all business.

The United States government had arrested Carmine Miceli, Jr.

Carmine, Jr., walked calmly back up the stairs, where his wife was waiting at the top of the staircase.

He gently took his wife's hands in his and looked into her tearing eyes. Carmine, Jr., kissed her on the lips and calmly let her know that everything was going to be fine.

"I have a bit of a problem. Don't get nervous. It's part of the life. Call Gino. Tell him it's the feds. He'll know what to do. Put the gravy on. I'll be back before one for dinner."

CHAPTER 12

Lloyd Craig sat in a chair by the window of Room 1909 at Columbia Presbyterian Hospital. His kidney transplant was performed at a private surgical center in Cedarhurst, Long Island, under the watchful eyes of his nephrologist Dr. Pretesh Gupta. Gupta had promised to be there for Craig every step of the way, and he was true to his word.

Lloyd, admitted to Presbyterian for a few more tests, was feeling glum as he watched the few barges motor down the dark, green waters of the Hudson River. The New Jersey skyline offered little except for the boring apartment buildings that lined the once- majestic Palisades.

Marty Craig tapped on the door to alert his son that he had visitors. Lloyd's mom and dad were all smiles when they saw their son out of bed and sitting comfortably. Lloyd did not look happy to see them.

"Hey, buddy, how ya doin?" Marty asked.

Ericka moved quickly to hug her son as he sat, kissing him all over his frowning face.

"Hi, guys," Lloyd said.

"What's up?" Marty said.

"I was just thinking that I may not go back to BL."

"Why, honey? You love that school," Ericka said.

"I'm just thinking I should stay close to home for now. Maybe enroll in a school nearby and commute."

"What's bothering you, son?" Marty asked.

"My friends will be moving to the next level, and I'll be left behind because of this," Lloyd said, pointing to his back.

"I'm sure we can work something out. Independent study, something that will keep you sticky to your classmates," Marty said.

"Honey, you seem sad. What's really bothering you?" Ericka asked. She pulled up a second chair and sat close to her son.

"I wish I never heard the word "Alport". Look what it's done to me," Lloyd said.

"You were dealt some crappy cards. The doc said you would be fine with this new kidney and live a long and full life," Marty said.

Dr. Gupta walked in, carrying Lloyd's records in a metal box folder. His broad smile was an indication that the doctor was pleased with the results of the transplant.

"Everything is great. Just a few more tests today, and you will likely be released tomorrow sometime. How are you feeling, Lloyd?" Gupta asked. He could sense there was a somber mood among the three Craigs.

"Doctor, whose kidney do I have? I would like to thank him," Lloyd said.

"That's very thoughtful Lloyd, but the donor is deceased. By the way, it was a female who gave the kidney," Gupta said.

"Okay. I would like to thank her family then. After all, her kidney has given me a new chance and saved me from a lot of distress and dialysis. I owe it to them," Lloyd said. Lloyd had tears in his eyes.

Gupta glanced quickly at Marty and returned his attention to his patient.

"That isn't possible. The donor's family wants to keep their kindness anonymous. Many families feel that way," Gupta said.

Lloyd returned his gaze to the Hudson.

"Feeling blue is very typical of organ recipients. You have been through a lot over the past few days, but let me assure you, you have tolerated the rejection medication perfectly. Your body is performing as if the kidney were yours. All of your tests indicate that the operation was a total success. After a few months of rest, you can go back to normal activity," Gupta assured him.

"Dad, you can find out who these people are. At least I can send them a letter thanking them," Lloyd said.

"Lloyd, this would be a violation of the agreement with the donor. Your father does great things for our donors, and he will certainly continue his work in this arena," Gupta said.

Lloyd did not look away from the view of the river.

"Let's get those tests taken so we can go back to Sands Point and celebrate. Then I will contact the Dean at BL and see what we can do to get you back to Boston as soon as possible," Marty said.

Gupta motioned with his head for Marty to leave the room with him.

"I will see you in the morning and sign the release form. You may be home in time for lunch," Gupta said to the back of Lloyd's head.

In the hallway, Gupta reassured Marty. Ericka sat next to Lloyd, holding his hand, just being there for him.

"His behavior is normal. Almost classically predictable. Remember, he is still in adolescence, which has its own litany of issues without being a transplant recipient. In a few days, he will be back to normal. You may want to consider a psychologist to get him through some rough spots," Gupta said.

"And what about the dad? What do you suggest for me?" Marty said.

"What do you mean?"

"I'm having sleepless nights. Bad dreams. I guess I'm conflicted about how and why I did what I did to get the kidney."

"Well, my friend, you know why. You wanted to save your son from years of a crummy life. And who knows if he would have survived? You did what most people in your position would do, I suppose," Gupta said.

"Would you have? Would you have saved a child at the expense of another's life?" Marty asked.

"Look, Marty, you need to come to terms with this. Lloyd and Ericka will never know what happened. This is a tough world, and you made a tough decision. Put it behind you."

"You didn't answer my question, Pretesh."

"It's a silly question if you want me to be totally honest. Not being in that position, my answer would only be theoretical, only conjecture. I cannot answer."

"Some young woman is dead because of my decision. She had a mother and father somewhere. Maybe they were great parents, maybe not, but she may have been loved. I took her life because I have money. That's fucked up in a way, isn't it?" Marty asked. He was searching Gupta's face for an answer. He needed to hear it was okay to do what he did.

"You can view it another way. She would have been dead anyway, and her organs would have gone to someone else. These people in the black market are very serious people. They have no conscience. In time, your guilt will subside. I don't expect that you will be able to talk to anyone about this. Technically, you would be complicit to murder. Just let it go, my dear friend. You have other work to get done. You have helped thousands of people. Throw yourself into that," Gupta said.

"What do you think a priest would say?" Marty asked.

"For the right price, you will find a priest who will say anything you want to hear,"

CHAPTER 13

A few days after Valbona closed the door on having a romantic future with Adem, she asked to see her father-in-law, Ilir Marku, privately.

Valbona felt that she owed Ilir an explanation about her decision on Adem. She was also seeking his blessing on another life- changing situation.

The Marku estate in Scarsdale, New York, was now a virtual fortress. The Petrov *Bratva* was now aware that they had lost two of their men. Orloff and his soldier sidekick never returned from their visit up to the Bronx. Although no bodies were yet discovered and likely never would be, it was clear that some form of retaliation would soon befall the Marku family.

Thirty heavily armed Albanians, all soldiers in Ilir's association, worked in three shifts to protect Ilir and the compound. While the Italians would not generally attack a man's home or family, the Russian mafia had no such barriers. They attacked the Marku estate once before. They would certainly come stronger this time. Ilir expected the Russians would come at him or his family with bad intent. His wife was now safely in Tirana, Albania, with her sisters. Ilir would send for her if and when the danger had passed.

Ilir would never come down from his room without being fully dressed in a buttoned, dark suit, white shirt, and silk tie. This particular morning was no exception. Valbona waited in Ilir's study. A massive oil painting of the Albanian hero, Skanderbeg, loomed over the diminutive Valbona as she sat patiently, waiting for Ilir to arrive.

Ilir walked into the dark, mahogany-paneled room with his arms outstretched and a forced smile on his face. Seeing Valbona was a constant reminder of his son, Lekë. The sadness of losing his boy would never leave him. Although Valbona still lived at the estate, the two rarely saw each other. Ilir was not home very much and Valbona kept to herself. She was practically in a perpetual state of mourning while at home.

Qika e Babës, it is so good to see you," Ilir said. He embraced Valbona and kissed her on both cheeks.

"Babë, thank you for seeing me today. I have been wanting to discuss a few things for some time," Valbona said.

"I am always here for you, *nuse,* until the day I close my eyes."

"Babë, I wanted you to know that I have told Adem that he should go on with his life. My grief and sorrow are too overwhelming, and I do not wish to marry again. He has too much to offer, and there is no future for him with me."

"And how did he respond?" Ilir asked.

"In time, he will understand that this is best for both of us. His wounds will heal. Mine never will," Valbona said. She cast her eyes toward the floor.

"Now I understand why Adem suddenly went back to Tirana. The timing is right for him to return to Albania as the situation here is getting a bit dangerous for all of us. You, too, must be guarded closely. My men will see to that."

"Babë, I hope you understand my feelings," Valbona said.

"You owe me no explanation. You must continue your life in your own way."

"I am so grateful for the way you have treated me. I have no words to express myself."

"The day you married Lekë was the day you became a Marku. Our tradition demands that."

"That leads me to my request, dear Babë. Our tradition also respects a woman's desire to take the oath of *Burrnesha*. I have decided this is the future for me."

Ilir was visibly stunned by Valbona's words. He sat in silence for the better part of a minute.

"*Qika e* Babës, do you know what you are saying? Are you aware what this involves? This may not be the life that you really want to live," Ilir said.

"I have thought long and hard about my life. I know what to expect."

"Becoming a sworn virgin is a custom that is rarely used in our culture. Yes, it may have been seen from time to time especially in the mountains of Tropoja. But here? I don't believe *Burrnesha* has ever found its way into our new lives in this country."

"My heart and soul tells me that my pledge to have the rights of a man, to be a *virgjinehse*, is my destiny."

"In this country, women have many equal rights to men. I know many of our women here are doctors, lawyers, professors, or any profession they want. These women have the respect of our men. To reach back into our tradition, over five hundred years ago for such a thing is something that I find difficult to imagine."

Babë, it is not my right?" Valbona asked.

"According to the *Kanun*, yes. According to this society it will be looked upon as…."

"I really don't care how I will be looked upon. For those who will think I'm a lesbian they will be in for a fight. I simply want to continue my life with all of the privileges and rights of a man."

"Dear nuse, we are not back in the mountains. I have worked hard to make sure that the women in our family have every opportunity for education and advancement. Why go back in time?" Ilir asked.

"So you expect me to be an a-la-carte Albanian? I can pick from a menu of things that suit me and eliminate certain aspects of our culture if the mood fits? No. I choose to be a total traditional woman with ALL of the rights a woman has including this choice. I will be Burrnesha, and you must approve of it so I can live my life as I see fit."

"I need to think this through, nuse. This is not something that is quickly decided."

"The decision is already made. With or without you, Babë, with all respect, I will begin dressing as a man dresses, my hair will be cut as a man. I will expect to sit with men and discuss what men discuss and to smoke just like a man. I will work just as a man. If I must paint houses, do construction work, whatever it takes to be accepted as a man, I will do all those things. When *gjakmarrja* is needed, I will take the revenge just like a man does," Valbona said. Her hands were now trembling as she spoke.

"What are you really looking to accomplish, Valbona?" Ilir asked. Ilir was more perplexed than angry.

"Babë, please, I say this with all respect to you. Your son and grandson are dead. Taken from us by this life you have chosen. Your other son, Adem, has no interest in this life, but I do. I want to learn from you and keep the family going. You are like the river that I am named after. So many of our people rely on you for their livings. When you are gone, will these men around you now act as you have? Most of them are selfish with no idea how to help others. I will see to it that your legacy continues."

"So marry Adem, and have babies. That is a better answer to your life."

"Impossible. I will do what is necessary without lying to myself and to Adem. My mind is made up," Valbona said.

"I will think this over, I will take counsel with a few of my closest advisors. We will talk again. I feel like the old proverb we use: '*Hyp se t'vrava zhdryp se t'vrava,*'" Ilir said.

"Climb up, or I'll shoot you, climb down, or I'll shoot you," Valbona said.

"As the Americans would say, 'between a rock and a hard place.'"

"Ilir, the next time you see me, I will be as a man. I will answer to the name 'Val.'"

CHAPTER 14

Gino picked up Jim Rem at his apartment on Sutton Place and East Fifty-Sixth Street. They would drive down to Twenty-Six Federal Plaza together to find out what the charges were and post bail for Carmine, Jr. Rem was Carmine Miceli Sr.'s, lawyer for the last ten years of the Don's life. Carmine, Jr., kept him on retainer for just the kind of headache the feds now dropped on him.

"I'm sure it's a media circus right about now," Rem said.

"Oh, for sure. These bloodsuckers are all lined up for Junior's perp walk," Gino agreed.

"All orchestrated by the real mob, the federal government. These guys are worse than any wiseguys I ever represented. The news will be all over television, entertaining the viewers while they have their breakfast this morning. Ya gotta love the technology."

"I wonder what they have on him."

"Christ knows. Now I have a ton of paperwork to sort through. Great way to start a Sunday. I was supposed to take my wife and kid to the Bronx Zoo. She's having a fit. As if I have any choice. Have the feds been nosing around?" Rem asked.

"Not a peep."

"They are like the savages in the jungle. When you don't hear the drums, they pull a surprise attack. The world is a veritable jungle, Gino."

"I'm concerned about a few areas of the business. We've had a couple of problems with the Laborers' Union, but I thought they were all resolved. And, of course, that damned waterfront commission. Can't think of anything else off the top of my head."

"No sense racking your brain. We will have an answer in about five minutes unless they decide to really break balls and have us cool our heels until midafternoon. It's all a game, my friend. I've seen it all," Rem said.

"At least Junior hasn't made that *bella figura* like Gotti. His father taught him to keep a low profile. No fancy suits, no guys kissing him on the streets, none of that goomba stuff to piss of the feds and the judges," Gino said.

"That's half the battle. When you wave the red flag in front of a bull, the bull attacks. Carmine, Sr., taught him well."

Gino found a parking spot on Lafayette Street. The early, Sunday morning ride was a quick one.

On the fifth floor of the towering federal building, Carmine, Jr., waited in a holding cell for a federal judge to arrive. The judge would hear the prosecutor's case then make a determination if bail would be set. Jim Rem was working his magic with the assistant prosecutors.

"I need to wade through this paperwork to review all of the charges unless you want to give me a heads up, which would be the right thing to do," Rem said.

"It's really simple, Jim. Carmine Miceli, Jr has two RICO predicates. That's enough to put him away until he goes gray and then bald," Don Wilson said. Wilson was the golden boy, an up-and-coming assistant prosecutor with a Columbia Law degree and five years of federal prosecutorial experiences. He was earmarked to take over for his boss, Eamon Fitzpatrick III.

"Mr. Miceli, to my knowledge, never ordered anyone to commit any crime that falls under the RICO statute. This is plain and simple another demonstration of the federal government prosecuting a business man because his name ends in a vowel. Enough already," Rem said.

"You will have plenty of time to discover what evidence we have on your client," Wilson said.

"And you will force him to cop to lesser crimes that will put him away for a while. Off the record, is that really justice?"

"Off the record, you must admit that your client is the head of the Miceli crime family. Let's start with that."

"Carmine Miceli, Jr., is a business man with an impeccable record. He's never been arrested in his life," Rem said.

"Until today," Wilson pointed out.

"Look, we are two lawyers just talking. The Catholic Church is among the biggest racketeers in this country. How come you guys never brought a suit against Archbishop Bernard Law in Boston? They buried dozens of sex abuse claims. That guy should be in a federal prison somewhere instead of sipping espresso in the Vatican," Rem argued.

"We brought a case against the church in Cleveland a few years ago. A jury cleared them of criminal racketeering. Bad analogy, Jim."

"Okay, maybe so, but my guy is as clean as can be. Only problem is he doesn't have a billion followers and God isn't in his corner."

"Be that as it may, we have some credible evidence against your client," Wilson said.

"I'm telling you, Don, he is not what you think."

"There is a guy who says otherwise. He rubbed out an officer of the Painters' Union. He claims the orders came directly from your client," Wilson said.

"That's crazy. What did you guys offer him? There is nothing that will stick."

"I guess that's why we have judges and juries," Wilson said.

"What about bail? Is Fitzpatrick gonna play hardball on this?" Rem asked.

"Of course, he is. A simple slap on the wrist is not what RICO is all about. Miceli and his family have a pattern of behavior that's put him here. It's our intention to break the back of the mob. Miceli runs a mob family. This is not just a fishing exhibition, Jim."

"He runs several legitimate businesses. We will prove that."

"And we will seek an injunction to seize his assets."

"And set a high bail and choke the life out of him," Rem said.

"If I were you, I would get my fee up front,"

"I'm so confident in my guy's innocence that I will wait. He's a stand up guy," Rem said.

Carmine, Jr., was wrong about being home for Sunday sauce. The Honorable Carl De Angelis, the federal magistrate, did not appear until after four in the afternoon, at which time he set bail for the defendant at ten million dollars. Carmine wouldn't be home until late afternoon on Monday at the very least.

Those federal guys really know how to play the game.

CHAPTER 15

Two days after the hit man Vadim Orloff and his sidekick went missing, there was a meeting of the Petrov *Bratva* at Tatiana's Restaurant in Brighton Beach.

It was seven in the morning when the members showed up one at a time. They were each greeted at the door by a Petrov *Biki*, a bodyguard who looked like a cross between Karl Malen and Jaba the Hut, and another heavy, KGB-throwback dressed in a rumpled, black suit without a tie. He, too, didn't have a neck.

Once inside the nightclub, which closed three hours earlier, the men went to a long, linen-covered table, adorned with several bottles of *Serebryaniy Zamok* Vodka and a two-feet high, silver, samovar tea server.

Boris Petrov, the *Pakhan* of the *Bratva* arrived last. Mikhail Andratova, his *Brigadier*, Vladimer Kuklowski, Petrov's *Sovietnik*, or counselor, and two "spies," Vlasislav Milhailov and Oleg Zhvkovsky, both *Vors*. A *Vor* is akin to a "made man" of the Sicilian mafia.

Boris Petrov took over the leadership of the Brighton Beach mob three years ago from Grigor Grigorovich, who was referred to as the *Czar*. Grigorovich ruled with a brutal iron fist and died suddenly while having dinner one evening with Boris Petrov and Mikhail Andratova. The official cause of the *Czar's* death was myocardial infarction. The real cause was cyanide poisoning, administered by Boris Petrov.

With his men seated at a long table at Tatiana's, Petrov offered a toast with a tumbler of Vodka, neat.

"*Dla Shahsiya*," Petrov said. "*For happiness.*"

Each man held his glass high, repeating the toast.

Petrov paused, looked into the eyes of each of his associates, and then began the meeting.

"We have a serious problem. It is evident that two of our men were taken out by the Albanians up in the Bronx," Petrov said. His deep, blue-green eyes showed his intense anger. Petrov was a large, intimidating man, clean-shaven with enormous hands and full head of wavy, gray hair. He was dressed in a tailored, dark-blue business suit with a red tie.

"I'm wondering if there were any Italians involved with this. After all, isn't it still their neighborhood?" Androtova asked. The second in command, Androtova had the look of a ferret. He was short and lean with a long nose and nicotine-stained fingers. The *Brigadier* was a respected mobster who hailed from Kiev. He served five years in prison in his country for his role in a truck-hijacking ring. His father and grandfather were noted mobsters in the former Soviet Republic.

"Very doubtful. We have a good relationship with the Italians since we earned together on the gasoline deal. They were happy with our success," Kuklowski said.

"The Bronx crew is a different family. They are renegades who sleep with those filthy, smelly Albanians," Androtova said.

"We have no way of knowing for sure unless we find out the old-fashioned way," Kuklowski said.

"Either way, we cannot stand for this. If it means breaking our friendships with the Italians, we must show that we are stronger than them and their Albanian dogs combined," Petrov said.

"The Italians have a way of stabbing their friends in the back. We may have to send a message that we no longer fear them," Androtova said.

"*Nye day bohg*. God forbid the Italians are part of this killing," Petrov said.

"And, if we find that those Bronx Guineas are with the Albanians in this thing, then what?" Androtova asked.

"Let us cross that bridge after we are sure. Like the old saying, 'Draw not your bow until your arrow is fixed,'" Kuklowski said.

"Vladimir, if we have two enemies, we must teach them both a lesson they will not soon forget," Petrov said.

"With all respect, none of this is good for business," Kuklowski pointed out.

"They both understand the meaning of revenge. They have not tasted our *mest*, good, old-fashioned, Russian revenge. If we show weakness or fear we will lose all respect. We may as well hide our heads in the sands of Brighton Beach like cowards," Androtova said. He refilled his tumbler with Vodka.

"What are you saying?" Petrov said.

"Verify if the Italians had a hand in killing our men, and react without delay," Androtova replied.

"Why not just assume it was only those Balkan pigs and hit them hard now?" Petrov asked.

"I suggest we have patience. If Italians were in this, then we hit them with a two-pronged attack on their streets," Androtova suggested.

Petrov cleared his throat, a signal that he was in control of the *Bratva,* and about to decide on which action would be taken.

"Val, go to your contacts with the Brooklyn Italians. Tell them we know their people in the Bronx acted against us. See how they react. In the meantime, get a couple of the Bronx Albanians. Find out what we need to know. Use the methods that you stated. If we know that the Italians are truly our enemy, we strike them both without mercy." Petrov went silent and stared at his own meaty hands, which were folded on the table in front of him. Petrov slowly raised his glass. "*Vashee zda rovye.*" He toasted to everyone's health.

"Let us discuss other business. This problem will soon be solved," Androtova said.

CHAPTER 16

Lloyd Craig woke from a nightmare, crying hysterically. The horrible dream happened only two days after the family was back home, safely ensconced in their palatial estate.

Marty Craig and his wife, Ericka, were going at it pretty good when they heard Lloyd sobbing. Ericka quickly jumped off of her husband and threw on her robe. Craig had to wait a bit longer to allow this throbbing manhood to go limp. Ericka got to Lloyd's room first.

"Lloyd, what is it, honey? Are you in pain?" Ericka asked.

The teen's crying turned into sobs. Marty came into the room, wearing only his underwear.

"Son, what's wrong? Are you okay?"

Lloyd snapped out of his dream and started to regain his composure. The boy's hair and body were sopping wet from perspiration. Ericka sat on the bed next to her son. Marty stood behind her.

"Oh, my god. Oh, my god! She was killed. They fucking killed her!" Lloyd screamed.

"Who, honey? Who? You just had a bad dream is all," Ericka reassured him.

"My new kidney. This stupid new kidney. It was taken from a young woman," Lloyd insisted.

"Okay, settle down, son. Sure it was. Dr. Gupta said the kidney was from a female, remember? Nightmares can happen after surgery. It's because of the anesthesia. Remember Doc Gupta said to expect some changes. This is one of them," Marty said.

"She was in my dream. She told me they killed her for her kidney. They took other stuff from her too. My God…she had no eyes. Gone! They took her eyes."

Marty was dumfounded. He could not find words to comfort his son at that moment.

"Lloyd, that is what happens with nightmares. They don't make any sense. The mind works in very mysterious ways, honey," Ericka said.

"She was very pretty. Long, blond hair and very polite. She told me she had a baby. I'm telling you, she was real. Her whole body was butchered. I can't…I just can't."

"Son, she is not real. It's all a dream. There is nothing to get all nuts about. Let's all go down to the kitchen and make some hot tea or warm milk or something. Then get back to sleep," Marty said.

"Dad, warm milk, really? That's only done in the movies. Warm milk tastes like shit," Lloyd said.

"Well, at least your sense of humor is coming back. Let's just sit and chat for a few minutes until you feel like falling back to sleep," Ericka said.

"Why can't I know? I want to know who gave me their kidney," Lloyd said.

"Lloyd, there are certain rules that can't be broken. This is one time we can't use our influence to get something done. The rights of the donor and the family are very sacred," Marty said.

"I've heard where people were given up for adoption, and years later, were able to find who their parents were. It's the same thing. I just need to know," Lloyd said.

"Look, just put that out of your mind. You need to concentrate on recovering and going forward with your life. It's a chance to enjoy yourself and live a long, long life," Marty said.

"Okay. I'll do my best. I'm sorry that I woke you both. It was just that the dream was so real. It was as if she were sitting right here talking with me. Weird."

"Okay, sweetie. Let me get you a towel. You're all sweaty. Then back to sleep. Tomorrow, you have physical therapy. Dr. Patel insists that we keep you moving and that you get mild exercise," Ericka said.

"You'll be fine, kiddo. Trust me. In a few months, you will be better than ever. After all, you're a Craig!" Marty laughed at his comment.

Ericka brought a bath towel and tried to blot Lloyd's perspiration. The teen took the towel from his mother.

"C'mon, mom. I'm not a baby."

"You will always be my baby, and you know it," Ericka said.

"G'night, son. See you in the A.M.," Marty said.

"Relax, and get some sleep, honey. A good breakfast in the morning, and you will feel like climbing Mount Everest," Ericka said.

"G'night, Mom. G'night, Dad. Thanks for being there for me."

"Honey, I know you're all grown up and stuff, but, when you were little, I would always sing your favorite song. Can you indulge your dopey mom?" Ericka asked.

"Sure, Mom. Anything you want."

Come with me, and you'll be
in a world of pure imagination
Take a look, and you'll see
Into your imagination.
We'll begin with a spin,
Traveling in the world of my creation.
What we'll see will defy
Explanation.
If you want to view paradise,
Simply look around to view it
Anything you want, do it.
Want to change the world, there's nothing to it.
There is no life I know
To compare to pure imagination.
Living there, you'll be free
If you truly wish to be.
If you want to view paradise,
Simply look around, and view it
Anything you want to, do it
Want to change the world, there's nothing to it.
There is no life I know
To compare with pure imagination.

Living there, you'll be free
If you truly wish to be.

"That was great, Mom. I have a confession to make," Lloyd said.

"A confession?"Ericka said. Her eyes were moist from the words of the song.

"Every once in a while when I was alone in my dorm at BL, I would pop in the *Willie Wonka and the Chocolate Factory* DVD and watch the scene when Mr. Wonka sang that song to Charlie. I would sing along," Lloyd said.

Ericka hugged her son tightly, fighting back her tears.

Ericka and Marty walked toward the door of their son's bedroom. Marty thought for a moment about his wife riding him like a cowgirl and realized the mood had passed. Ericka snapped the light switch off as the couple left their sons room.

"Oh, Mom, Dad…one more thing," Lloyd said.

Ericka switched the lights back on. Both she and her husband put their heads through the doorway of the bedroom.

"She said she lived in Brooklyn. Weird, right?"

CHAPTER 17

Two days after Valbona declared her intentions to become a sworn virgin, she went to Ilir Marku's office in the Bronx. Going to the place that her husband had worked was difficult enough. It brought back too many memories of another life. Showing up for the first time as a man made her knees shake.

Her long, black hair was now cut into a man's style. Short and slicked back with gel, only her large, beautiful, green-blue eyes gave away who she was. She wore one of her husband, Lekë's, blue, pin-striped suits, which she altered herself. She wore a pair of men's, brown, Italian loafers that she bought for her size at Ferragamo. One of Lekë's shirts still smelled of his cologne. Valbona reformed the shirt to fit her body. She also wore a pair of her late husband's favorite gold cuff links. The Albanian double eagle insignia adorned the links. His gold Rolex watch was on her left wrist. The combination of the watch and cuff links looked rich.

Two of Ilir's bodyguards stopped the unknown man at the front door of Ilir's office building.

"Excuse me. Sorry, no unannounced visitors," one of the guards said. The other one put his hand inside of his suit jacket, fingering his firearm.

"I'm Val Marku. I want to see Mr. Marku. Please tell him that I'm here," Valbona said.

"Val Marku? We know of no such person," the guard said. The second bodyguard removed the 9mm from its holster. He brought the pistol behind his leg, ready to use it if needed.

"Dude, get used to it. Just fucking go inside and tell him I'm here. I'll wait right on the street until he sends for me," Valbona said.

The bodyguard looked closely at the man standing before him. The face was familiar. For a second, he thought the man looked like Ilir's daughter-in-law. He looked at the man's chest as his associate frisked the visitor. No gun.

"Open your jacket," the first bodyguard demanded.

"Why?" Valbona said.

"Just do it."

Valbona opened the jacket and put both hands on her hips. The bodyguard could see there were small mounds where her tits were. They were mashed against her chest by a tight undershirt.

"Jesus Christ! Are you Valbona Marku?"

"I'm Val Marku. Now please, tell my Babë that I am here and I would like to see him."

The lead bodyguard told his associate to keep her where she was then turned and walked into the building. The second man returned the nine to its holster.

"Mr. Marku, there is a man outside who wants to see you. Well, it may not be a man. Forgive me, I think it's your daughter-in-law dressed like a man."

"Bring her in," Ilir Marku said. Ilir put his right hand onto is forehead and ran it through his hair. He wasn't sure what to expect.

Valbona walked into Ilir's office with both bodyguards on either side of her.

Ilir was visibly shocked at what he saw. The boss of the Marku crime family had an instantaneous flashback. In his mind's eye, he saw a nine-month-pregnant Valbona and his son, Lekë, standing in front of him not very long ago in the same spot where this new person was standing.

"Please leave us. Bring us some coffee, please," Ilir said to the bodyguards.

"I must say, Valbona. This is shocking to me. You are very headstrong *nuse*. I thought we would have more time to discuss this. I'm not prepared in my mind for such a transformation."

"I'm Val now. Val Marku. Every man in our world must treat me just like one of them. That is our tradition. That is what the *Kanun* allows. I claim my right to be a man from this day forward," Valbona said.

"I am not questioning your right. I would have liked more time to inform the community and my people."

"So there is no better way than to introduce me as I am now. As the saying goes, 'the wolf does not worry about the opinion of the sheep.'"

"I don't think I have any choice at the moment, do I?" Ilir said.

"*Babë*, you always have a choice. You can send me away. Exile me to Albania, New Jersey, anywhere you wish. I'll tell you one thing here and now. No one will work harder for you and protect your back as I will. No one."

"Of that, I have no doubt. But where will I put you? What kind of work will you do?"

"Whatever you tell me to do. If you want me to dig ditches, paint apartments, do plumbing, or take numbers, whatever. I will work my way up. I will do whatever you need me to do without question."

"What if I ask you to kill someone? To take back blood? To assassinate an enemy?" Ilir asked.

"I serve at your pleasure," Valbona said.

"My God! I need time to chew on this. And then to digest it."

"I am ready for work this morning, *Babë*. Please don't send me home like a woman. I am no longer a woman. Please respect me as you would any man."

The bodyguards brought in two coffees on a silver platter. No sugar.

Both men couldn't help themselves. They were staring at Valbona when the coffee was placed on the boss's desk. Ilir noticed the uncomfortable scene.

"Arben, Pash, please meet Val Marku. She will be joining us. She will require nothing except to be treated as a man. Understood?"

"Yes, sir," Arben and Pash said in unison. They averted their eyes from Valbona.

Ilir motioned to the door to the bodyguards. When they left the office, Ilir stood from his chair behind his desk and walked over to an ornate, mahogany breakfront. He opened the doors of the cabinet and took out a bottle of homemade *raki* and two shot glasses. He placed the glasses on the desk and pored the clear, distilled *raki* into them.

"Val Marku, I toast to you and your new life. I toast to all the success you can ever dream of. Welcome. *Gezuar!*"

"*Gezuar*! I thank you. I will not disappoint you, *Babë*. On my *Besa*."

"I will call for a meeting of all of our people tonight. I will introduce you as Val Marku as you wish. I will decide in a few days where you will fit into the organization. For now, you report here to me. I want you to learn at my elbow. We have some major problems coming our way with the Russians, and you need to understand every facet of our affairs. Tomorrow morning, we meet with Hamdi and the Miceli family. Carmine Miceli, Jr., and Gino Ranno. You will be there. You will remain silent."

CHAPTER 18

The night that Lloyd Craig had his dreadful dream had turned into a real-life nightmare for two Albanian mob guys who were connected to the Marku Family.

Zef Gjoni and Vasel Gashi, two, up-and-coming soldiers on Ilir Marku's payroll, decided to blow off some steam at the GQ Gentlemen's Club on East Thirty-Fourth Street in Manhattan.

The pair decided to have a big night on the town. They walked into GQ like they owned the joint. As a matter of fact, they knew the owner very well. Arben Baledemij was a distant cousin, a *Kusheri* to Zef Gjoni. Both Gjoni and Gashi had been to GQ on many occasions and scored quite well with the dancers so well and so memorable that they both decided to make it a monthly experience.

After greeting Arben Baledemij with the traditional cheek kisses and shoulder bumps, the duo asked to have a table and bottle service. Rather than the standard five hundred dollars for a single bottle of Grey Goose Vodka, they paid a discounted rate of two hundred, proving once again it's not what you know but whom you know.

They were seated at the best table in the house. Their booth had a round table that would seat at least six people. It was a comfortable, red, leather booth that had several large, decorative pillows and was right next to the stage. The dancers were within just a few feet of Zef and Vasel, enough for the late-twenties gangsters to place single dollar bills in the G-strings of the thoroughbred girls. These two high rollers were not into that scene. Instead, Zef handed three crisp one hundred dollar bills to their waitress and asked for that amount in singles. If they liked how the girls danced and how they worked the pole, they would throw a packet of bills in the air above the stage, showering the strippers with money. This showed the crowded room that there were big spenders in the house. After all, fancy suits, bottle service, and throwing money as if it were confetti was not how the average working stiff behaved. Zef and Vasel were not your average nine-to-fivers who were out for a good time, and maybe get a two-hundred-dollar blowjob.

"Dude, would you look at this redhead? She is magnificent," Zef said.

"I'm too involved with the blonde. She's been looking at me since the minute we walked in," Vasel said.

"Don't flatter yourself, bro. That's her job, to make eye contact and tell you how much she can't wait to suck your cock," Zef said.

"That's fine by me. It's just a matter of where and when," Vasel said.

"They look Russian," Zef said. He threw twenty-five singles in a pack over the heads of the two strippers. The money cascaded all over the stage.

"I don't care if they are Serbian. I'll take her upstairs, and she will come down seeing cross-eyed," Vasel said.

Zef left the table to talk to his cousin Arben, who was sitting alone at the bar.

"*Kusheri*, what's the deal with those two over there? Working girls?" Zef asked.

"They just started a few days ago. I really don't know, but I would say yes for the right price. That's up to you to find out," Arben said.

"Send them to our table when they take a break," Zef said.

"No problem *Kusheri*, consider it done. So how are things with Marku? How is he treating you?"

"I never see him. He mostly stays up in the Bronx and leaves us alone. I'm pulling down three Gs a week, and he gets his envelope like religion through his guy, Hamdi. That's how I want it. For now anyway," Zef said.

"He has a pretty good piece of this place and the place we run on Long Island. Good guy to have as a partner. Nobody ever bothers us. That's how I want it, too," Arben said.

"Your family is good?" Zef asked.

"Yes, very good. Yours?"

"Excellent. Tell these *kurves* to stop by our table for a drink."

"The rest is up to you. Have fun *Kusheri*," Arben said.

The two dancers laid it on thick. They used the pole like they were born to it. As the music to Rihanna, Usher, and Timberland thumped on, so did they. The occasional girl-on-girl tongue kiss and breast lick made Zef and Vasel throw the money in the air like fools. Each time the girls were showered with the bucks, two bouncers scooped the money from the dance floor and placed it into an open box on the side of the bar.

Thirty minutes after Zef spoke with his cousin, Arben, the two girls meandered over to the table. The redhead sat next to Zef, and the blonde sat very closely to Vasel. The men were greeted with friendly kisses on both cheeks. The blonde then kissed Vasel square on his lips with a hint of wetness.

"You ladies are gorgeous," Zef said.

"And the best dancers I've ever laid my eyes on," Vasel added.

"Thank you, my dears. You are not so bad yourselves," the redhead replied. Her accent was thick, Russian, and sexy.

"May we offer you a drink?" Zef asked.

"Yes, but no vodka. It makes our heads hurt," the blonde said. She pointed to the Grey Goose and made a squishy face.

"What is your pleasure?" Zef asked.

"We would like some cold champagne,"

Vasel waived to the waitress who moved quickly to their booth.

"Bring us a bottle of the coldest Cristal you have and four glasses," Vasel said.

Bringing his attention back to the blonde, Vasel put his hand high up on her silky, white thigh. She made no attempt to remove it.

"Where are you beautiful ladies from?" Zef asked.

"Both Kiev. We are here for a few months," the redhead said.

"And you men? Where are you from?" the blonde asked. Her accent was the same as the other girl.

"I'm from Kosovo. He is from Montenegro," Zef said.

"Oh, Albanian?" the redhead said.

"Oh, you can say that," Vasel said. He began slowly massaging the girl's upper thigh as the Cristal arrived in a silver ice bucket with four long-stemmed flutes.

The waitress poured the bubbly, and the four toasted.

"How do they say here? Salute? To your health?" the redhead asked.

"Good for you. God bless America!" Zef said.

"We cannot stay with you very long. We have one more set to do for you then we are off," the blonde said. Her hand was now on Vasel's thigh. She began slowly moving it toward his crotch.

"And then?" Zef asked.

"And then we go home to our apartment," the redhead said. A comely look into Zef's eyes told him she was more than available.

"Can we join you?" Zef asked.

"Of course, if you have the right…" the redhead used the international sign for money as she rubbed her thumb together with her first two fingers.

"Do we look like that would be a problem?" Zef asked.

The girls both laughed and finished their champagne. They made a quick exit from the booth and back to the stage. They worked the pole and each other in a way that had Zef and Vasel drooling.

After their last set, the four were back at the girl's well-appointed rental on East Thirty-Ninth Street.

"We must shower now. Here, try some *real* Russian vodka. That stuff you were drinking is swill compared to ours." The redhead poured the vodka into two glasses on the rocks and handed them to Zef and Vasel.

"We will shower together so no time is wasted," the blonde said.

Vasel got an instant erection. Zef laughed out loud.

After the vodka was drained, the men realized that the shower was taking longer than expected.

"Fuck this, I'm going to watch," Vasel said. He tried to get off the plush sofa, and he realized he could not stand. The room was spinning out of control.

"Jesus Christ, I am so fucked up," Vasel muttered. He looked over at Zef who was now stone-cold asleep.

Vasel pushed himself to stand and wound up falling into a heap on the living room floor.

The girls had played the oldest game in the book. They slipped the men a Mickey, a roofie-call it whatever you want. Zef and Vasel were out for the count…paralyzed.

CHAPTER 19

The morning after Zef Gjoni and Vasel Gashi were drugged by the Russian dancers/hookers, a meeting of the top echelon of the Marku and Miceli families began promptly at nine. Nobody yet reported that the two Marku soldiers were among the missing.

The Marku-Miceli meeting was held in the ballroom of The Pierre Hotel in Manhattan. Bodyguards were a common occurrence at this most venerable of New York City, five-star hotels. Dignitaries from around the globe either stayed at The Pierre or kept apartments there.

Each faction had six men who milled around the ballroom, trying to look inconspicuous with their firearms bulging at their suit jackets. Both families knew the manager of the hotel, who opened the massive, empty room for the meeting that was not to be officially booked. No envelope was needed.

Out of respect for Ilir Marku, Carmine Miceli, Jr., and Gino Ranno arrived first. They ignored the breakfast buffet until Ilir and Hamdi Nezaj came into the room. Valbona Marku trailed the two senior members of the family.

"My dear friend," Ilir said. He embraced Carmine, Jr.. The men kissed each other on one cheek. The same greeting was afforded all around. Ilir noticed the puzzled look on Carmine, Jr., and Gino's faces when they greeted Valbona.

"How is your family, Ilir? I hope well," Carmine said.

"As well as can be expected. A father should never bury a son. Even with time, the pain never leaves the soul. And how is your family, Carmine?" Ilir asked.

"Thank you for asking. Everyone is fine. It's me who has a headache," Carmine said.

"Come, let's have some coffee so we can sit and discuss things," Ilir said.

Hamdi pointed to the buffet. A Marku bodyguard was acting as the waiter for the group. Only coffee was ordered by Ilir, Carmine, Hamdi, and Gino. Valbona stood next to her father-in-law. All five, including Valbona, moved to a large, round table that was set with china, crystal stemware, and a large bouquet of mixed flowers in the center. Carmine, Jr., and Ilir sat next to each other. Valbona sat across from Ilir between Hamdi and Gino.

"Our tradition is the same as yours in many, many ways. But, in some ways, we are very different. Our code allows a woman, at her desire, to take upon herself the role of a man. It generally follows a great family tragedy. In this case, my daughter-in-law has taken a vow to be among the men. This is Val Marku. She is now part of my organization. Her role is not yet clearly defined, but we are supporting her totally," Ilir announced.

"And she will have our support and loyalty always," Carmine, Jr., said.

"Thank you my friend. So you say you have a headache. I hope we can help you," Ilir said.

"I'm certain that you have seen the news about my federal indictment. There are serious allegations against me that may cause a disruption in some of our business dealings," Carmine said. The young Miceli was taught by his father never to show fear or weakness. He looked Ilir straight in the eye and spoke in a matter-of-fact tone.

"Yes, we have heard this news. What can we do?" Ilir asked.

"On the advice of counsel, I have temporarily passed the reigns of the family business to Gino Ranno. He is now the acting boss. I need to make a low profile as I am under a microscope at the moment."

"My friend, you have been under that kind of scrutiny since the day you were born only now the stakes are higher," Ilir said.

"Indeed, they are. The feds have frozen my assets. They are seeking severe monetary penalties as well as many years of confinement. This may turn out to be a long, drawn-out battle," Carmine said.

"I will personally see that you and your wife and children will never want for money," Ilir said.

"Thank you, but that isn't necessary. I have long been prepared for such an event," Carmine, Jr., said.

"God bless your father. He taught his son well," Hamdi said.

"Yes, he did. And he also taught me to surround myself with strong, loyal people. Gino is that person. My father loved him and I'm sure he would have blessed this move. From now on, your dealings will be with only Gino. If I get out of this with the skin on my bones, Gino will remain as my right hand." Carmine, Jr., placed his hand on Gino's arm as a sign of affection and confidence.

"You have made a wise choice. You have our loyalty as does Gino," Ilir said. Hamdi shook his head in agreement.

"Now I'm going to leave this meeting. It's best for everyone that you discuss our mutual problem without me present. I hope you understand and take no insult," Carmine, Jr., said.

"You will be in our constant thoughts, Carmine. Rest your head on your pillow. We are with you," Ilir said.

Carmine rose from the table as did everyone else. Valbona exhaled audibly from nerves. Ilir glanced at her.

"Ilir, I will be absent for a while. Please do not think I'm ignoring you in any way. It's best if we are not together until I clear this up," Carmine, Jr., said, and the men embraced.

"You would never insult me. You were not made that way. We will see each other when the situation allows. Until then, know one thing: we will respect Gino as we did your father and you," Ilir said.

Carmine, Jr., displayed no emotion. He shook Hamdi's hand and then Valbona's.

"Best of luck to you, Val. I wish you all the best."

"Thank you, Mr. Miceli. As I wish the best for you," Valbona replied.

After Carmine, Jr., left the room, Ilir asked the bodyguard to serve some Danish and cookies and refill the coffee cups.

"Next time, we need to have only Turkish and Italian coffee served to us. This American coffee gives me heartburn," Ilir complained. He tapped his stomach and chuckled.

"With respect, I would like to get down to business," Gino said.

"Of course, Gino. There is much we need to discuss," Hamdi said.

"We have a bear to deal with. The claws of the bear can rip us apart, so we must put him in a cage. I see no other option at this point," Ilir said.

"Agreed. How do we proceed?" Gino asked.

"It is not a simple problem. They are ferocious. No honor, no respect, and no fear. They are bold enough to send people to our neighborhood to intimidate us," Hamdi stated.

"And we answered that together. Showing unity was most important," Gino said.

"And we expect them to answer our message. They will come strong as a wounded bear does," Hamdi said.

"Yes, they will. My people have soft, fat bellies right now. I am going to need help from the other side. My man is working on that as we speak. Are your people prepared?" Gino asked.

"Truthfully, they are not. We have lost some fire in our bellies. Many of them have never known what hunger feels like. The younger ones are all show. They need to get out of their soft beds in Westchester and taste the dirt floors. We also will bring in help from Kosovo," Hamdi said.

"Isn't it interesting how one generation's wants become the next generation's needs? We have both lost the edge. The bear can win," Gino warned.

"We cannot ever allow that," Ilir said.

CHAPTER 20

The meeting at The Pierre Hotel continued until almost noon.

Another meeting of sorts was about to take place in an abandoned warehouse near the site of the old, Brooklyn Navy Yard.

Four, black Mercedes E 350 sedans with dark, tinted windows zipped over the Brooklyn Bridge, headed toward Atlantic Avenue. The cars moved in a close caravan as they headed west toward the East River.

Four men of the Petrov *Bratva* were in each car. In the trunk of two of the cars were the semi-conscious Zef Gjonai and Vasel Gashi, both tightly bound and gagged and wrapped in cheap, wool carpeting. The early-morning roofies administered by the smoking-hot, redheaded, Russian dancers, were just beginning to wear off on the captive Albanians. Both the redhead and the blonde were at the United Airline Executive Club at JFK Airport sipping white wine, as they awaited their flight to Los Angeles-first class of course. Their short employment at GQ had served its purpose. Their matching, Louis Vuitton handbags were draped over their shoulders, stuffed with cash.

Two *kryshas*, both enforcers for the Petrov *Bratva*, waited patiently for their cargo to arrive. Anton Trapanov and Oleg Zhvkovsky stood at the buildings loading dock, stomping out their fifth cigarette as the cars arrived.

Zef and Vasel were carried into the warehouse over the shoulders of the heavily tattooed torpedoes.

Trapanov was the more sinister looking of the two *kryshas.* He had dark eyes and hair, was tall and thin, and resembled actor Basil Rathbone. His face seemed to refuse even a glimmer of a smile. Zhvkovsky was the polar opposite to his associate. With short, light blond hair and sparkling, azure blue eyes, Zhvkovsky had a welcoming, almost kind face. The don't-judge-a-book-by-its-cover proverb was never truer than in his case. His violence and sadism had no boundaries.

Zef and Vasel were beginning to be more aware of their situation. The drugs in their systems dissipated, and they both started to become aware that their situation was perilous.

The warehouse reeked of mold and urine. Most of the windows in the warehouse were gone, and the bright daylight illuminated the scene. Brown sparrows and fat street pigeons fluttered overhead. Zef and Vasel were still wrapped in the carpeting.

"I think we should make our guests a bit more comfortable," Trapanov said. He and Zhvkovsky unraveled the rugs from the Albanians, twisting their bound bodies onto the bird-shit-stained warehouse floor.

Zef and Vasel were now aware of whom their captors were. Four torpedoes remained with the two *kryshas.* The others stood guard outside sucking on cigarettes and pretending to wipe the cars clean with their handkerchiefs.

Zhvkovsky readied the tools of his trade, opening a brief-case next to the two tied, prone Albanians.

Trapanov addressed his captives.

"'Morning is wiser than the evening' we say. I love that expression. So now we will get to know each other a bit better. I need information to make this easy on you both. If I get the information, you will die quickly. If I don't, well then things will be, shall I say, uncomfortable for you. My bosses expect results from me, and I've never disappointed them. Remove their gags."

Zhvkowsky took a long, serrated knife from his case, gingerly cutting the masking tape from the back of Zef's and Vasel's heads. He made sure both of the petrified men had a good look at the blade.

"Two of our friends made a visit to Arthur Avenue a few days ago. They never returned. We must assume they are dead. All we want to know is, and it's a simple answer, did the Italians have anything to do with this?"

"I have no idea. We have done nothing wrong to you. Our business is in Manhattan. How would we know anything about this?" Zef said.

"Because you are with that dog, Marku. If his people fart in the Bronx, every one of you hears the sound. Now tell me what I need to know…now."

"Fuck you and your whore of a mother," Vasel said.

"Take that one," Trapanov said. He pointed to Vasel and Zhvkovsky moved in.

Again, the knife was used. This time, Zhvkovsky removed the belt from Vasel's pants. He used the blade to slice open the slacks and underwear from his writhing victim.

"Well, you can call that a cock, I guess. You poor man," Trapanov said. He looked at Vasel's flaccid penis with a sympathetic frown.

Zhvkovsky continued his work with a sadistic grin on his face. He took a long pipette from the briefcase. The slender, quartz tool is commonly used in a laboratory to draw a liquid from one vessel and dispense it into another.

Zhvkovsvky grabbed Vasel's penis and inserted the tube into it. Vasel tried to squirm away from the clutches of his captor with no success.

"You motherfucker. *Po to qijë at nanë!*" Vasel shrieked.

The enforcer tapped Vasel on his forehead and moved slowly to the briefcase. He removed a piece of hard, rubber hose and tapped it several times against his open hand.

Zef turned his head away from the gruesome scene. One of the torpedoes stepped forward, pushed Zef's head toward the action, and held his foot on the horrified Albanian's neck.

Zhvkovsky approached Vasel. Vasel was grimacing in pain while the enforcer had a wide, ear-to-ear smile.

Down came the hard, rubber hose onto Vasel's pipette filled penis, shattering the quartz and sending Vasel's arching body into spasms. Again and again, the Russian slammed the hose onto Vasel's manhood. Blood gushed out and sprayed onto the Russian's clothing and Zef's face. Vasel was sucking in air and exhaling saliva, trying to deal with the pain.

"Well, that is an interesting beginning, my friend. I have another famous saying I would like to impart to you both. 'How well you live makes a difference not how long.' So give me my answer, and this ends. The Italians were involved? Yes or no?"

Blood continued to spew from Vasel's penis. Saliva shot out from his now lip-bitten mouth.

Zef remained silent save for a whimper.

"Okay, act one, scene two, I guess," Trapanov said.

Zhvkovsky slowly turned the tormented Vasel on his stomach. He was humming a Russian lullaby.

The *krysha* put his left foot on Vasel's back for leverage. He grabbed the Albanian's wrist and slowly began to amputate one of his thumbs.

"I think we need to put the tape back on his mouth, boys. They will hear his screams across the river into Manhattan," Trapanov said.

One by one, Vasel's digits on his right hand were gone. His screams became moans through the masking.

"Enough, you sick fuck. Enough. You can have your answer."

"Trapanov waived his now blood-soaked partner away from Vasel's quivering body.

"I'm listening," Trapanov said.

"Yeah, the Italians are with us. It would be smart of your people not to fuck with them. I can tell you as much as I've heard. Your men never left Arthur Avenue alive. Tell your bosses that. Tell them no one will be left alive. All you rat-bastard Russians will be dead soon."

Trapanov glanced at the one torpedo who had his foot on Zef's neck. The sworn killer stepped over to Vasel and put two bullets into his head, ending the man's suffering.

Trapanov kneeled down on one knee next to Zef's head. He spoke as if Zef was an old friend.

"Very good, my friend. We have some more questions to ask you, now that we have your attention. After that, you will be taken to meet a nice man. I am a man of my word. Our good Dr. Abramoff will see to it that you have a painless death.

CHAPTER 21

Valbona had not seen her best friend, Shpresa Metalia, for a few weeks. This kind of thing sometimes happens with close friends until one of them picks up the phone or sends a text. Valbona decided to go the old-fashioned way.

"*Zemer*, my heart, how are you? Where have you been?" Valbona said.

"My Valbona. Sorry, I've been busy. Plus some shit at home."

"Shpresa, you don't sound right. Really, are you okay?"

"I can't talk right now. I've been better," Shpresa said. She was fighting back tears.

"Tonight, at your favorite restaurant or mine?" Valbona asked.

"Mine! What are you doing now?" Shpresa said.

"On my way to meet you at *Zuppa.*"

"I'll be there in fifteen minutes," Shpresa said.

Shpresa arrived at *Zuppa* Restaurant in Yonkers first. The owner, Edi, a dear friend of Rick and Shpresa, poured her favorite drink himself and brought it to her usual table. Water with lemon.

"This is pleasant. I usually see you guys at night. Not for four or five days though. Everyone well?" Edi inquired.

"Yeah, all good. Hey, guess what? I'm meeting Valbona here now," Shpresa said.

"How is she doing, poor thing?" Edi said. The door opened and Edi didn't wait for an answer.

"Hold on. Let me greet and seat this guy, and I'll be right back.

Shpresa sipped her water barely noticing the guy in the suit who walked in.

Edi walked toward Shpresa's table with the guy behind her. Edi had a quizzical look on his face. His eyebrows were almost near his hairline.

Edi steeped aside, not knowing what to say or do. Valbona made her introduction.

"*Zemer*, don't hate me, please," Valbona pleaded.

Shpresa nearly choked on her lemon water.

"Valbona! What the fuck? Is this a new look? Your hair! It's gone," Shpresa said.

"No, not a new look, Shpresa. I've decided to become *burrnesha*," Valbona said.

"All of a sudden? You never said a thing? *Burrnesha*? A sworn virgin? Why? What happened with Adem? I'm blown away."

"Adem and I could never have been. My soul just doesn't want any of that again. I will be working with my *Babë*. He has approved. It's important to me that you do too, Shpresa," Valbona said.

"Of course, I do, *zemer,*" Shpresa said. She finally stood up from her chair and embraced her oldest friend.

"You know, I've read about *burrnesha* and heard it from the old timers, but that was in *Tropoja*. Here? In this country, you must be a first," Shpresa said.

"Nothing will ever change between us. I will love you until the day I die. I'm relieved that you understand," Valbona said.

"I'm with you totally. Understand? Not sure yet. What about sex? That's it? Over? I don't think I could ever do that, Valbona," Shpresa said. She made a funny face and both women laughed.

"Seriously, sex is the furthest thing from my mind. My heart was torn from me. I just want to live and help Ilir with the business. That is my lot in life," Valbona explained.

"How did he take this? By the way, I love the suit," Shpresa remarked.

"It was Lekë's. Ilir was shocked at first. I gave him no choice. You can't preach old school and pick and choose. He knew I was within my rights, and that was that. No bullshit, the look on his face when he first saw me like this was even worse than yours."

"I bet! And what will you be doing? Office work, secretarial?"

"Shpresa, I have the rights of a man. I will do whatever men do. Except scratch my balls," Valbona joked, and both women roared with laughter.

"Okay, Shpresa Metalia. Look at me good, up and down, soak it all in. Call me "Val" please as everyone else will. Then enough about me. What's going on, *zemer*?" Valbona asked.

"I have a million more questions, but okay, my turn. I think Rick is fucking around," Shpresa said. Her lower lip trembled.

"No fucking way. Just no way," Valbona said.

"Yes way. I can't prove it, but I can tell. A wife can tell."

"With whom? Don't say it's a redhead. He always jokingly said he was horny for a redhead."

"That's the funny thing. The *kurve*, if I'm right, and it's her, looks a lot like me. Blonde-ish, *shqiptar* from Montenegro, born there and a Catholic besides."

"Do you know her? Her family?" Valbona asked.

"You know how we always joke that we are all related and cousins and know everyone? Not this time. I think she was from like Worcester, Massachusetts, or someplace like that. Those Albanians came here a million years before we did. I wish I did know her family,"

"Is it serious?" Valbona asked.

"I'm not sure, but, either way, things will never be the same with me and Rick."

"Just stop it. Men are men. That is silly to say. You are just hurt for the moment, Shpresa. First, are you sure? Second, did you confront him?" Valbona said.

"Screw that. I've done everything for him. My life was him, the business, his family, my family, oh, my God. Plus I was a pretty good *nuse*. Okay, maybe not perfect but pretty good. Plus, I made a lot of money for us. And no, I didn't confront him yet. I can't tell his parents, it would kill them. I just need to wait this out and see what happens, I guess," Shpresa said.

"I can talk to him."

"Oh, yeah, he's gonna really listen to you now. Dressed like that he may kick your ass in for you." The women laughed again.

"Let's think about what to do here. I can approach this *kurve* bitch and scare her shitless," Valbona said.

"So, if it's not her, it will be another one. No thanks. I could have scared her myself."

"Right. The issue is with you and Rick. You need to get to the bottom of this with him, I guess. Look who's giving you advice, a sworn virgin. Could you ever imagine this?" Valbona asked.

"Nope. Never. Let's just drop the subject for now. I feel like puking. So what are you going to do for Ilir anyway?" Shpresa asked. She changed the subject quickly.

"Well, I don't know yet. Obviously, I can't say much anyway. Guess who I saw today?" Valbona said.

"No clue."

"Your old friend Gino Ranno."

"I adore him. How is he?" Shpresa asked.

"He's big time now with the Micelies. He is such a nice man. He welcomed me as a man very nicely," Valbona said.

"I miss Gino. I'm going to call him later."

CHAPTER 22

Hamdi Nezaj, a man who has few personal needs, never flowered himself or his family with creature comforts.

Even after his real estate holdings went from a two-family home into a veritable empire after twenty years, he and his family remained in a small basement apartment in the Bronx. When he reached his early sixties, he succumbed to the pressure of success and moved to a sprawling home in tiny Armonk, New York, with the hedge fund and country club crowd.

His association with Ilir Marku added to his wealth and status in the Albanian community.

Ilir chose Hamdi not only for their early friendship in the difficult years when they were broke and poor immigrants but also because of Hamdi's old-school loyalty and work ethic.

Hamdi was a student of the *Kanun* with a full understanding of how the daily life of Albanians was supposed to be comported. Respect, allegiance, and his *Besa* were most important to this quiet, unassuming man.

After their meeting with Carmine Miceli, Jr., and Gino Ranno at the Pierre Hotel, Ilir asked that Hamdi meet him for coffee at his home in Scarsdale. The bodyguards brought Ilir home in a slightly stretched Cadillac. Two cars with his men followed in shiny, well-armed Escalades at a close distance. Hamdi drove himself, in his four-year old *Volvo*, to the Marku estate.

Once inside after he removed his shoes inside the vestibule, Hamdi went straight to his friend's study. Ilir ordered coffee from the housekeeper and then closed the heavy, mahogany door.

"Well, my friend, what do you think about our meeting today?" Ilir said.

"Very interesting turn of events. I'm a bit concerned that my dear friend Gino may not be ready to lead his family during a possible war. You must remember that Gino was a broker and a businessman not a criminal. It seems that he was picked as a moderate leader by Carmine, Jr., as he is a trusted friend."

"Make no mistake that Carmine, Jr., is still sailing the ship for the Miceli family. Gino will be his *consigliere,* yes, but will he be able to lead an army? Time will tell," Ilir said.

"Gino is a smart man and a good friend. He understands the meaning of a handshake. His word is his bond. The rest, we will soon know," Hamdi said.

"And Val. What are your true thoughts?" Ilir asked.

"This is a difficult question and an even more difficult situation. This country has not seen this part of our tradition. We both have known *burrnesha* from the mountains of our fathers. We have known these women who became men and were as ferocious as any man we ever saw. There is a fire in her belly, and in her mind and she wants to prove herself to us. I must say that she is more driven then most of the young men who want to play gangster, dress up fancy, talk big, and throw money around to impress. The truth is, they are mostly spoiled children who are soft in their bellies. I have confidence that she will learn quickly and be loyal to you."

"And when I'm gone?" Ilir said.

"Then your worries will be over, and things will happen as they were destined," Hamdi said.

Coffee was served and drunk quickly. Ilir waited, as tradition dictated, for his guest to drink first.

"So for now, because she is family, I will keep her close to me. The men will accept her in time," Ilir said.

"The men will respect her if you command them and if you treat her as a man. Give her tests as she grows. Let her get her hands dirty. Don't think of her as a woman and pamper her. If you do, you risk losing respect with the men."

"That is sound advice, my friend. Help me to teach her along the way," Ilir implored.

"I will. Now what about if we go to war with these Brooklyn Russians? What role will she have?" Hamdi asked.

"I will take your counsel. She will be treated as any soldier," Ilir said.

"No velvet glove," Hamdi said.

"These hands have bled too much for pampering. Now go home to your family."

Ilir walked Hamdi to the front door. The two friends shook hands and kissed on both cheeks.

"I will see you tomorrow, *Mash'Allah*," Ilir said.

"Yes, God willing."

Hamdi drove the thirty-five minutes from Scarsdale to Armonk, thinking of the time that he and Ilir spent together in San Biaggio, Italy. They were refugees from war. The Catholic Church paid for thousands of Albanians to find refuge. They were housed in abandoned, stone houses with no electricity, running water, or outdoor toilets and little food. They somehow survived the horrors of communist regimes and war in their country. Now he was driving to a home that he or his entire family for generations past could not even fathom.

The traffic on Route 684 was moving well and Hamdi was feeling hungry as he took the Armonk exit. He knew his supper would be well prepared by his wife, still the perfect, Albanian *nuse* after all these years together. He remembered what hunger was like in Albania, Italy, and even here in the great country that took his family in to start a new life. His hunger for his supper now was vastly different than before.

Hamdi drove down the large, tree-lined, stone-paver driveway and parked the Volvo in its usual spot.

As he exited the car, he saw movement in his peripheral vision. Two men in heavy, black jackets came up quickly on him. Both armed with pistols, they fired repeatedly into Hamdi's thin body. He fell to the ground in excruciating pain. One of the men walked quickly to the prone victim and placed a gun to Hamdi's head. He fired two shots. Hamdi Nezaj was dead.

The shooter left a calling card.

A red, bishop, chess piece was placed on Hamdi's forehead.

CHAPTER 23

Gino received a call from the Armonk police about the driveway assassination of Hamdi Nezaj. A police sergeant on the job knew Gino from a shared relative. Armonk was sitting on the news, keeping things quiet until the Westchester County coroner and the county homicide squad did their forensic work. A virtual blanket surrounded the crime scene.

Gino immediately called Ilir from his throwaway cell phone to Ilir's throwaway.

"My friend?"

"Yes, my friend?" Ilir said. He recognized Gino's voice.

"There is terrible news. Your friend upstate is dead. He was murdered at his home. I'm sorry to bring you this news," Gino said.

There was a long pause.

"He just left me. Do we know who did this?"

"They left a message. A red chess piece. There is no doubt who did this," Gino said.

"We must confirm this. He was under *gjakmarrja* from the old country. It goes back to the early fifties. My friend's father was in a battle with another clan. The other man was killed. I'm thinking that could be the cause as well," Ilir said.

"Okay, but it sounds more like those maniacs we know. There were no witnesses."

"I must go to his home immediately before word gets out and the community rushes to his home. That's what we do, my friend," Ilir said.

"I'm aware of that. I think I should lay low for now. We don't want anyone to start saying things about our friendship," Gino said.

"Agreed. There will be time to pay your respects," Ilir said.

Ilir ended the call. No names were mentioned. The conversation, if, by an outside chance, was tapped into by the authorities, would give nothing away.

Ilir summoned his men, including Val Marku, to make the short trip to Armonk. Hamdi's wife and family needed all the support they could get at this moment.

Gino called Joey Clams, C.C., and Mickey Roach. They were told to meet him within the hour. Albert's *Mofongo* House on Broadway and Dyckman Street in the Inwood section of Upper Manhattan was the meeting place.

No one would ever suspect this move. A Dominican Restaurant in an ethnically mixed neighborhood was not on any Russian's radar screen. Any other place would be too risky. Gino had to assume the enemy would be watching his usual haunts. Tonight, Arthur Avenue would be a possible death trap.

Gino was taken by four of his men on the short ride to Albert's *Mofongo*. They drove around the block a few times until everyone was safely inside the place. When Gino walked in with his men, he went to a quiet corner table. Joey Clams,

C.C., and Mickey Roach followed. Gino's men made themselves inconspicuous.

"Hamdi was killed a few hours ago on his driveway at his home. No witnesses, and a calling card was left. We have to check this out but at the same time assume that there is a war right now. I'm fairly certain the Brighton Beach crew did the hit," Gino said.

"Not good," Mickey said.

"I trust you three more than anyone else in the world. Mickey, call out the reserves. And the Sicilians. We need everyone to be on call and ready at a moment's notice. We don't move until we verify. Then Mickey, I need a solid plan of response," Gino said.

Mickey nodded his response.

"I have some contacts out there. Let me make a few calls," Joey Clams offered.

"No, no calls. You and C.C., go see your acquaintances in person. Go heavy. Assume that you are both targets. By now, there is no secret that I am leading the family. They know you two are with me. Every street is perilous for all of us. Don't stick your heads into the bear's nest. These Russians are fierce, so take nothing for granted. In the meantime, we gather our strength, and I will wait to hear from you," Gino said.

"Do you want us to make any noise?" C.C. asked.

"None. Why are you guys still here?" Gino said.

Joey and C.C. got the message and left Mofungo quickly. Mickey awaited further instruction.

"Now make no mistakes here, Mickey. Bring in the best we have, and have a solid plan for me by morning. I want to teach these hoods a real lesson," Gino said.

"What about a sit down with these mutts?" Mickey said.

"That crossed my mind, but they will see this as a sign of further weakness. These Russians understand one thing. Their word is meaningless until they can take control. They will have what they want over my dead body."

"And mine," Mickey said.

Gino returned to his apartment in less than ten minutes. His bodyguards stopped a man as he approached the car in front of the building where Gino lived in the Riverdale section of the Bronx.

"He's one of Marku's men. Says he has a message from his boss for you. He's clean," a bodyguard said. Gino exited the safety of the car.

"Mr. Ranno, Mr. Marku asked that I bring you news."

"What is it?" Gino asked.

"Two of our Manhattan men went missing a couple of days ago. One was found. His body was discovered on a beach in the Rockaways. Most of his internal organs were gone. So were his eyes and most of his skin. He was not beaten or bruised. His blood was gone. There is no sign of the second man," the Marku man explained.

"Anything else?"

"Yes, they left a message. His tongue was clipped off and a star was cut into his forehead," the Albanian messenger said.

"Thank you."

Gino shook the man's hand and turned to one of his guards.

"Call Joey Clams for me. Tell him to come back to my place. This is all the confirmation we need."

CHAPTER 24

The night that Hamdi Nezaj was gunned down at his home in Armonk, there was a crisis of another sort at the Craig residence on Long Island.

Another nightmare woke Lloyd Craig, only, this time, the dream came with or because of a raging fever.

Ericka Craig heard a low moan coming from her son's bedroom. Once inside the room, she could sense that something was very wrong.

"Honey, it's Mom. Are you okay?" Erica approached Lloyd's bed. Her son was soaking wet and thrashing from one side of his bed to the other.

"It's hot…too hot…baby…just stupid…" Lloyd said. The fever had made him delirious.

Ericka called out to her husband. From the sound of her voice, Marty knew there was a problem. He bolted up the wide, curved staircase two steps at a time up to the second floor of their home.

"Baby, what's wrong?" Marty asked. His heart was pounding from the sudden sprint and the abrupt adrenalin surge. The fear that something was wrong with his son was almost too much for Marty to deal with.

"He's burning up. He's talking gibberish and I can't get him to wake up. Oh, my God, Marty, he's shaking like a leaf," Ericka said. Now sitting on Lloyd's bed with her hands holding her son's shoulders, Ericka was crying and in a total panic.

Marty moved his wife away from their son's bed. He needed to take charge of the situation and make some hard decisions.

"Baby, go get a bucket of ice and some bathroom towels. He's pretty hot. We need to get that fever down somehow. Fast as you can, Ericka," Marty said.

Ericka was gone in an instant. She scampered down the stairs to the kitchen. Marty took Lloyd's cell phone from the nightstand and dialed 911.

The moment Marty gave his son's condition and his address, he could hear the shrill sound of a siren in the distance. The volunteer ambulance personnel were alerted that a member of the community was in distress.

Lloyd was still thrashing in his bed. Ericka returned with the ice and towels as her husband was removing the bed covers and the boy's pajama top. Marty then began to wrap the ice into the bath towels.

"We need to cool his body a bit before help arrives. I called 911. Go call Doc G. and tell him we are going to LIJ," Marty said.

Long Island Jewish Medical Center was the closet and best hospital on the North Shore of Long Island. Marty figured, at that time in the middle of the night with lights and sirens, the ride from Sands Point to LIJ would be about fifteen minutes.

Marty put an iced towel under both of his son's armpits and another on his forehead. Lloyd shivered, and his eyes opened wide from the icy feeling.

"It's okay, pal. Mom and I are here with you. We're going to take a run to the hospital and get Doc Gupta to meet us there. Can you hear me?" Marty said.

"I…I can hear you, but I can't see you so good," Lloyd whispered. The sound of the ambulance's siren was getting louder by the second.

"No worries, buddy. We'll get to the bottom of this in a short time. Just hang with me. Let's keep talking for a bit, okay?"

"I saw that girl again, Dad. Who is she? She…she…she said…" Lloyd's eyes rolled back into his head and he started to have a a a seizure.

Ericka was waiting at the door and let the paramedics in. She ran up the staircase and led a man and a woman emergency medical service worker to her son's room. Marty was standing over his son, literally stunned at the scene.

"Excuse me, sir, please let us get to the patient," the male paramedic said. Marty moved away from the bed quickly.

Lloyd's seizure had ended, but he was unconscious. Marty and Ericka embraced one another, Ericka now sobbing into her husband's chest.

Vital signs were taken, and monitors were hooked up to Lloyd's chest and fingers. The doctors at LIJ were already examining the numbers to determine a potential course of action.

"Mr. Craig, anything we should know? Any history of seizure disorder? Drug use?" the female paramedic asked.

"None whatsoever. He had a kidney transplant a few days ago," Marty said.

"Okay. Once we get him stabilized a bit, we'll get him to the hospital. We're in direct contact with the ER doctors. Try to stay calm. He's in good hands," the woman EMS volunteer said.

Pretesh Gupta arrived at LIJ shortly after Lloyd was admitted to the emergency room. The paramedics and ER staff had reduced his fever to almost normal. The young Craig was awake and alert. Mom and dad were not fairing so well. The Craigs and Dr. Gupta went into a staff only room to chat.

"This was totally unexpected. Were there any signs before tonight? Any fever? Problems with urination?" Dr. Gupta asked. Marty and Ericka looked like they were wrung out.

"None of that. No, not at all. The only thing is that he still seems very distracted, very removed, and moody," Ericka said.

"Is this something you see a lot of?" Marty inquired.

"I've done nearly two thousand transplants and have been involved with countless patients who have been the recipients of a new kidney. The common denominator is that there are always issues, always. Our challenge is not in doing the surgery. That is the easy part. The post-surgical issues are what make the surgery a success. We will find out what's at the bottom of this and fix it. Perhaps, the anti-rejection medication needs to be altered, or, perhaps, we need to go in and make a repair or adjustment."

"What do you mean adjustment? An adjustment?" Ericka's tone was aggressive. Her nerves were clearly frazzled.

"Honey, please," Marty said.

"It's a fair question. We are putting the cart way before the horse, but, if certain tests we need to take indicate there is a leak in a blood vessel or the organ itself, we then need to repair the problem. That is a fairly common occurrence," Dr. Gupta said reassuringly.

"I'm so sorry. It's just these last few days have not been easy. Those damn dreams Lloyd is having, and now this. I'm just a mess," Ericka said.

"Perfectly understandable. In a short while, we will be finding Lloyd a bed. Don't panic. I want him in ICU for the moment. He needs to be monitored closely. I will make arrangements for you both to stay the night and follow the process. Thankfully, the head of the hospital and I are very close. I'm not on staff here, but we have a sort of unwritten reciprocal agreement. The chair of nephrology and I went to med school together. Professional courtesy if you will. On top of that, you guys have been very generous here," Gupta said.

"Look, honey, I want to take a walk outside with Pretesh. Go see how Lloyd is doing and I'll be right up, okay?" Marty said.

Ericka shook her head to the affirmative and approached the doctor. She hugged him and kissed his cheek. She left the room, dabbing a tissue at the corners of both eyes.

"Okay, pal. Give it to me straight," Marty said.

"I just did, Marty. No bullshit, no sugar coating," Gupta said.

"I never know when someone is telling the truth or counting my money. Please forgive me for saying that but it's a reality. Maybe I should have not done this thing that I did. Maybe God is punishing me."

"God is punishing you for being rich and generous? C'mon, will ya?"

"Maybe I'm being punished for killing that girl. Now she's haunting my son. This is very fucked up, Pretesh."

"No, what's fucked up is you at the moment. You didn't kill anyone. Some very bad people marked the donor for death. The truth is, she would have been killed anyway in a matter of time. Honestly, the way these animals treat their prey, they may be better off dead anyway."

"I guess you never took an ethics course in med school," Marty said.

"Forget ethics. Forget the moral imperative. That is all fairytale stuff. What's real is that you have money and you did what you needed to do to help a loved one live. Period."

"So why can't I tell my wife and my son?"

"That is a simple question that has a simpler answer. Because you are a man! Sometimes, men have to make hard decisions for the life and well-being of their families. This is one of those times," Gupta said.

CHAPTER 25

The long receiving line of men, all dressed in black and all with a somber expression and pissed-off air, led from the front door to Hamdi Nezaj's coffin at F. Ruggiero & Sons Funeral Home in Yonkers.

A second line of only women all dressed in black mostly crying or cried out and all with black headscarves, snaked around the room where Hamdi's body was being viewed.

Hamdi's sons were on the men's side as tradition dictated; his wife and daughters were with the women.

The traditional silver platter with a selection of American cigarettes stood on an end table near the front door for those who wished to partake.

For such a prominent and respected man in the Albanian community, the line of cars on Yonkers Avenue was now creating a traffic jam. The biggest problem was the everyday drivers unaware of the circumstance leaning on their car horns out of frustration. When a dark-eyed, high-browed, frowning, Albanian approached their car, only a total maniac would continue to complain. The wiseguys were ready to pop. Shooting an asshole who was leaning on his horn was not totally out of the question. The Yonkers police had to be called to keep traffic moving in both directions and to keep the peace. The Ruggiero boys could have had a field day.

Prominent among the visitors and mourners was Ilir Marku. He arrived in his car, which trailed two large SUVs and was followed closely by two others.

Traditionally, the male member of the family pays his respects with the male members of his family. Adem, his illegitimate but recognized son, was in Albania, still broken hearted over being given the gate by Valbona. But Valbona, now Val Marku, would accompany Ilir and stay with the men. What better time to show the entire community that she was now accepted as a sworn virgin by the leader of the largest Albanian crime family in the country?

Beside the bodyguards in the vehicles, other guards awaited Ilir's arrival, encircling the boss and Val Marku with a protective barrier from any would-be assassin. It wasn't unheard of for an Albanian to take his *gjakmarrja*, his revenge for any taking of blood, at a funeral or wedding. Ilir certainly took out some of his enemies over the years in that fashion. This would be a perfect place to make a statement to the community. And the Russians? They couldn't care less where they hit you. Ilir was wise to keep a tight ring around his person.

Ilir shook every man's hand in the receiving line as did Val. They both held their left hands to their hearts as they grasped a hand, a sign of respect and reverence.

"*Zoii ju lasht shnosh,*" Ilir and Val said as they passed along the line. "May God let you be." In effect, may God now leave you alone from more pain.

After they paid their respects to the sons and daughers and wife of Ilir's lifelong friend, Ilir and Val sat for a few minutes with the other male mourners. A steady stream of men continued to file into the large room, which was lined with folding chairs.

"Mr. Marku, you are most vulnerable sitting here. I suggest we leave," Ilir's head of security, Nic Celaj, whispered to his boss.

"Your job just got more difficult, Nic. We must stay for a while. We must not be seen as afraid of anyone or anything. I must be here for my friend's family. I will leave when I think the time is right," Ilir said.

Ilir turned his attention to Valbona.

"Val, go tell the Hamdis' sons I would like a word with them in private. See that we get a quiet room for five minutes and are not disturbed," Ilir said.

Dutifully, Valbona made the necessary arrangements. In a few minutes, followed by Nic Celaj and other guards, Ilir was in the manager's office with the Nezaj sons. Every other room in the funeral home was jam packed with family and friends.

"You all know that your father was a brave and traditional man. He lived by our code of conduct always. I will tell you now that you are to carry on with all of his traditions save one. You are not to get involved with *gjakmarrja*. I will see to that. He is dead because of his friendship with me. The people who did this to you will be killed, have no doubt about that. I swear this on my honor. So now go back to your mother and sisters. Respect them. Tomorrow, we will bury your father together," Ilir said.

As the Nezaj boys left the room, Nic Celaj stepped into the room and again whispered in Ilir's ear.

"Mr. Marku, Gino Ranno is here. He seems awkward. Shall I bring him to you?" Celaj asked.

"No, it is my place to go to him," Ilir said.

Ilir slowly walked to the wide-eyed Gino. Gino wanted to pay his respects to his dear friend Hamdi's family but was unsure what to say. Joey Clams and C.C., acting as bodyguards for Gino, also felt out of place in this foreign world, the world of how Albanians behave when someone is dead. Other men accompanied Gino but did not engage the mourners. Their only thought was protecting their Don. Gino, Joey Clams, and C.C., three Italian kids from the projects, did not want to say the wrong thing for fear of offending the family.

Ilir stepped in and welcomed Gino with a warm embrace.

"So nice of you to come, Gino. It is just terrible. I will walk you in. Our tradition is a bit different than yours, but we share equally in sadness and respect. Walk with me," Ilir said.

Gino remained silent as he, Joey Clams, and C.C. shook every man's hand in the receiving line up to Hamdi's casket. Gino got choked up when he saw Hamdi's children and wife. He remembered them as little boys. The boys knew of Gino from their father and showed him the respect that was taught them. Hamdi's wife and daughters shook Gino's and his men's hands, never making eye contact.

"Now come, and sit with me for a while. When I leave, you leave also," Ilir said to Gino.

"Ilir, Carmine, Jr., sends his sympathy and his regrets," Gino said.

"I know where his heart is. Thank him. You and I have a lot of work ahead of us. After the funeral tomorrow, we must take action," Ilir said.

"We will. This was unnecessary."

"I've told you these Russians have no limits. No code of honor. They disgrace their own parents. Now, Gino, it's time for us to go," Ilir announced.

A phalanx of guards followed Ilir and Gino from the room. It seemed that the room nearly emptied as the two crime bosses moved to leave. The security circle tightened as they approached the exit to Ruggiero's. Out of respect in the Albanian tradition, Ilir walked Gino to the door, allowing him to leave first.

Suddenly, Gino saw a familiar face and stopped in his tracks. Joey Clams saw Gino react and stepped in front of his friend. C.C. was too busy stealing glimpses of the beautiful Albanian women.

Joey Clams relaxed when he saw Gino smile. It was Rick and Shpresa Metalia. They came to pay respects to Rick's cousin, Hamdi, and his family. The Metalias were both somber of course but greeted Gino warmly. Shpresa looked tired through her sadness. Rick seemed distracted. Their greeting was short. Gino's men were getting nervous as they stood in the open door.

Shpresa kissed Gino goodbye and whispered to him.

"I need to talk with you. I'll call you."

CHAPTER 26

Hamdi was buried as he lived: quietly and family only with the exception of his *gumar,* Ilir Marku, along with a protective ring of men sworn to guard him with their lives.

The day after the funeral, Ilir sent his head of security, Nic Cecaj, along with Val Marku and Bekim Selca to meet with some of the Miceli family. Gino had sent word to Ilir requesting to have the joint sit-down. Selca was the go-to member of the Marku crime family whenever bones needed to be cracked or buried. Val volunteered to be part of this despite Ilir's concern that she wasn't ready. Prior to the meeting, Ilir took the opportunity to impart constructive criticism alone with Valbona in his study.

"Val, do you remember your first meeting with the Micelis, at the Pierre?" Ilir asked.

"Every word. Yes, of course, I do," Valbona affirmed.

"You were nervous. And understandably so. After all, it was your first meeting with the Micelis and your coming out to the world as a man. Naturally, you had nothing to add to the discussion. However, you did make a statement. That statement was a mistake."

"I said nothing," Valbona said.

"You said no words, that is correct. But you showed your nerves by exhaling loudly. Your anxiety, your tension told me and the men at that table that this world may not be suited to you."

"Was I that obvious?" Valbona asked.

"If I noticed it, so did the others. You must never, ever show anxiety, stress, or fear in any manner. A man must be strong. *Mos ke frikë,* fear not."

"I understand. I will guard against that in the future," Valbona said. She looked strongly into Ilir's eyes, taking his advice as a man would. She knew she had a lot to learn about being a woman in a man's world.

"To act as a man, you must think like a man. I am confident that you can do this. However, any mistake like this again will set you back in my eyes. Worse, it can cost you your life," Ilir said. "Now go with the other men, and do well. You may be asked to do things that you have never before imagined. My advice to you is to follow my men and do as they say, and do not hesitate. Never show fear again," Ilir said.

The meeting was held in the Bronx. The Bronx is common ground for both the Italians and the Albanians. They were not meeting on Arthur Avenue this time. That neighborhood had too many eyes on it. Maybe the Russians, maybe the feds-Arthur Avenue was just too hot at the moment.

Mickey Roach showed up twenty minutes before the designated time to a small Italian café on Morris Park Avenue. Mickey wanted to survey the street to make certain that they would not be in any danger. He trusted no one. In spite of the current alliance with the Albanians, Mickey looked at them with jaded eyes. With him were two handpicked Sicilians from his hometown, Lercara Friddi. True, Cosa Nostra hit men, who were used by the Miceli family in the past with great success.

Joey Clams and C.C. arrived at the café just before the Marku representatives arrived. Joey also trusted no one. He and C.C. waited on the roof of an apartment building across the street from the café. His surveillance of the area and his gut told him the meeting was safe.

Maria, the proprietor of the café and the widow of a *camora capo* who was killed in Naples, Italy, some years prior, instinctively knew her role: lock the front door, make coffee, hear and say nothing.

Mickey Roach spoke first. The sound of the released steam pressure from Maria's espresso machine filled the small café. The aroma of the coffee immediately permeated the air. None of Maria's homemade *biscotti* or fresh pastry was of any interest.

"We know that every Friday night at about eleven, two of the Petrov *Bratva* higher ups bring their hired girlfriends to a joint called Passages in Sheepshead Bay. They stay until early in the morning, drinking Vodka and Champagne, snorting, and eating everything in sight. They like to dance with their girls. They spread some money around to the waiters and singers in the band. Six to eight men, who stay at the bar and mill around the joint, guard them. By the time they arrive, most of the family people have left, but, sometimes, there are a few stragglers who are feeling no pain by that time.

Our plan is to have two couples who have had dinner, and look like these stragglers planted there. Within a few minutes of their arrival, we will introduce them to the devil," Mickey Roach said.

"How do our people blend in? They are mostly Russians, no?" Nic Celaj asked.

"These two bosses have a weakness. They look at young women as something to be conquered. They cannot control themselves. Our two women will be dancing with each other in a provocative way. Their escorts, Beppie and Claudio, will make themselves busy talking to each other and checking sports scores on their cell phones. This is what most young men do anyway. Joey, C.C., and me will be outside in two cars. One is the limo that our two couples will escape to, the other is a chase car that will block any frigs who try to follow. A third car will follow to get all of our people out if needed," Mickey explained. Beppie Alicata and Claudio Salerno are the two Sicilian button men. If you wanted the epitome of cold-blooded killer, Beppie and Claudio would be tied for first place.

"Pretty bold, going into their place," Joey said.

"It's more than a message. We want to break the *Bratva's* back, force them to react quickly and make mistakes. They will look to come into our streets again. When they do, we will be ready."

"With all due respect, these two Sicilians look like central casting for a gangster movie. They will be watched too closely. And who will be their dates? I'm concerned about how this will look. Where is the element of surprise?" Bekim Selca asked.

"They will blend in. Trust me on that. The women will be perfect. One is a Columbian bombshell who we have used before. She would tempt the devil himself. The other is sitting right here with us. Val, you will dress as a woman, dye your hair blonde and leave nothing to the imagination. It's a perfect set up," Mickey Roach said.

Valbona thought of the advice Ilir had given her earlier. She controlled her breathing, and her face had no tell. Not even an eyebrow moved.

"And how do our people get out?" Nic Celaj asked.

"There are two exits, one in the front and one on the side of the building next to a small bar. There is an elevator that is useless. There are two flights of stairs. The front will be too closely guarded. After the action, our people leave through the side exit. Joey and C.C. will lay down cover from the street. I'll cause a commotion at the front door. Bekim, you are the cleaner. You will be in the parking lot behind the building with me. Anyone who comes out with a gun, or, if, by chance, the two marks escape from the rear, you pop 'em. Everyone leaves together," Mickey Roach said.

"Not a bad plan. Risky, but not bad. We will shock the shit out of them. What about me?" Nic Celaj said.

"You need to stay back with your boss. Ilir will be their first target. Gino their second. Gino will be well protected and out of town," Mickey said.

"Who is our main shooter?" Bekim Selca asked.

"All four," Mickey said.

CHAPTER 27

Shpresa did call Gino on the day Hamdi was buried. They chatted about how terrible Hamdi's murder was and the effect his death would have on his wife and family.

Gino could tell there was something else bothering Shpresa. They made a lunch date for Friday.

On Friday morning, Mickey Roach went to Gino's to advise him of the events that were to take place that evening in Sheepshead Bay. Mickey insisted that Gino leave the city with his protectors for both an alibi and for his personal protection. They decided that Gino would fly to Boston for the weekend. He needed to see the Patriarca family to discuss his elevation as the head of the Miceli family anyway. The timing was perfect.

Gino, not wanting to cancel his appointment with his old friend, called Shpresa to see if they could meet for coffee instead of lunch.

They met at Rocco's Pastry Shop on Bleeker Street in Greenwich Village, Manhattan.

Gino waited in his car with his bodyguards on Sixth Avenue and Bleeker. He saw Shpresa as she walked up the subway stairs and exited his car. Gino's men stayed a comfortable distance behind him.

"Look at you. Gorgeous as always," Gino said.

They embraced and did the double-cheek kiss.

"You look pretty good yourself, Casanova. How do you like being single again?" Shpresa asked.

"If I had any semblance of a social life, I could comment."

"That is one of my favorite churches in Manhattan. What a beautiful, old building," Shpresa pointed to Our Lady of Pompeii Church.

"It is something. My grandmother was baptized and married in that church. My family roots were from this neighborhood," Gino said.

"I wonder what your nana would be thinking now," Shpresa said.

"No idea, but my mother would be pissed. She never wanted me in the life I'm in. She would call me a guinea bastard for sure."

"I thought only my father called you that?"

"Yes, and with great affection."

They walked across the street to Rocco's and took a table in the rear garden. Gino sat facing the front of the bakery, a habit that he always had even as a young man. Lately, it had become an obsession. His back would never be exposed. Gino's men sat in the front of the store, eyeballing everyone who entered.

"We have so much to talk about. Where to start?" Shpresa said.

"You first," Gino said.

"Okay…Valbona…what do you think of that?"

"Shocked at first, then sad, and then I saw how determined she is. I'm not sure what to think," Gino said.

"I almost died when I first saw her. I had no idea she would do this. She was so devastated that I thought she would kill herself a year ago. I guess this sworn virgin thing is what she needs to continue with her life. It's not something that is common in our culture. My dad talked about it, but I've never known anyone who took this vow. I love her and will be there for her forever," Shpresa said.

"I know you do. Whatever I can do for her, just reach out. Now let's get to the eight-hundred-pound gorilla and get him out of the room. How are you and Rick?" Gino asked.

"I guess you can tell."

"A blind man can see it."

"We are having some trouble. I have a hard time talking about it without crying," Shpresa said. Her eyes filled with tears.

"So what do we do when we are sad? We eat. Let me order some goodies," Gino said.

"I'm off wheat."

"*Cannoli's* have no wheat," Gino said. He made a little boy face.

"Of course, they do, Gino." Shpresa laughed out loud for the first time in a while.

"Not these. They are made of a special kind of secret stuff that only a few artisans know. If they break the code of cannoli? *Omerta!* We stuff the baker in the oven."

"You are such a nut. That's why I adore you."

"So do you want to talk about it? I'm a good listener. And my advice sucks, so I'm not going to preach to you like your dad."

"I think Rick is having an affair. It's killing me, and I don't think I can deal with this. If he is, I'm done."

"What makes you think that, Shpresa?"

The waitress came by, and Gino ordered two *cappucini* and two "wheat free" *cannoli.*

"I just know. He's taken a flirtation with this redheaded broker a bit too far. She's twisted his head around. Whore," Shpresa said. Her eyes were burning with disdain.

"Did you confront him?"

"No. I want to stab him. Her, too."

"That wouldn't be good. Use a garrote, much cleaner," Gino joked. He mimed choking someone from behind.

Shpresa almost spit out the water she was drinking.

"You are hysterical. Here I am telling you that my life is over, and you're making me laugh," Shpresa said.

"Because it's all a bunch of bullshit. So he strayed. People sometimes do crazy stuff. If Rick has strayed, it's not because he doesn't love you or that he loves her. It happens to men. We are weak and stupid," Gino said.

"But, if I did it, would that asshole look the other way or forgive me?"

"But he knows you never would."

"Yeah, right. Don't think I never thought of cheating, Gino. Every woman does at some point. And don't think I've never had the opportunity."

"So what are you going to do?" Gino asked.

"I can tell you one thing. I'll never become a sworn virgin like my best friend. Fuck that!"

"So I'll ask again. What are you going to do?"

"I'm going to let it play out. Maybe he wants a divorce. We are in the empty nest syndrome after all. Maybe he wants out. Maybe I want out now," Shpresa's eyes welled up with tears again.

"Nonsense. He loves you like no other. He was made for you and you for him."

"That's what I always thought, until he started this shit. Maybe I need to see what another man is like. I've only been with one."

"And you would never forgive yourself."

"Don't be so sure, Gino."

"Stop it."

"No really, what's stopping me from having an affair? A lot of my friends have. Maybe I should test the waters a bit." She looked coyly at Gino over her *cappuccino* cup.

"What is that look?"

"You know I've had a crush on you since I was a teenager, Gino."

"And I think you are the hottest woman I know, but that will never happen."

"Why not? I could be interested."

"Because you are vulnerable and that would be a scumbag move."

"And if Rick and I split up?"

"You would be a total jerk if you let that happen. Go and work things out with the man you love."

"And if he doesn't want me anymore?"

"And if the queen had balls, she would be king," Gino said.

"Wow, I guess I've been rejected," Shpresa said.

"No, you've been spared from the worst move of your life."

One of the bodyguards caught Gino's eye. He pointed to his watch. It was time to get rolling to the airport.

"Gino Ranno, you are a special man," Shpresa said.

"And you, Shpresa Metalia, are a fabulous woman. But, alas, I have to get going. I need to catch a plane."

"Where to?"

"Can't tell you, but I'll be back in a few days. Can I drop you off somewhere?"

"Actually, I'm showing a condo a few blocks from here. I need the walk. Thanks anyway."

"Okay, it was great seeing you, Shpresa." He hugged her.

"Will I see you again?" Shpresa asked.

"Of course. Next time with Rick…okay?"

"We shall see."

CHAPTER 28

While Gino and Shpresa were meeting, Marty and Ericka Craig had just arrived back at their home with Lloyd. The doctors at Long Island Jewish Medical Center released Lloyd that same morning, with a clean bill of health. At least for the moment.

"Okay pal, you heard the doctors, no sitting around like a mope. They want you to move around and get back to a schedule. I called BL, and they will work out a home study plan all done online so you don't miss too much at school. You'll be back up in Boston with your classmates before you know it," Marty said. Lloyd was still acting sullen.

"What if the new rejection medicine fails? What do I do when I'm in Boston?" Lloyd asked.

"First of all, it's a few months away. By that time, the new meds will be working fine. Doc Gupta said he is confident they found the right stuff. Anyway, Boston has great hospitals and doctors if we need a fall back," Marty said.

"Dad and I will be at the apartment most of the time just in case," Ericka added.

"I'm not a baby, Mom, and I don't want to run your lives," Lloyd argued.

"We are seeing you through this. And we love that city, so it's a win-win," Marty said.

"And these dreams of mine?" Lloyd asked.

"Yeah, what about them?" Marty asked.

"They really haven't gone away. I just haven't said much about them," Lloyd admitted.

"Recurring dreams are common. I've been reading up on this topic. You can ride them out or, as Doc advised, see someone and find out what's at the bottom of this," Ericka said.

"I believe a girl was killed so that I could have her kidney. She keeps telling me she was murdered. What's that all about?" Lloyd asked.

"It's…it's your imagination, son. Your subconscious mind is playing a trick. At some point, you have to let it go," Marty said.

"I feel so terrible for her. They took her eyes and everything," Lloyd said. The boy hung his head, falling further into a depression.

"That's so gory. Look, I read that it might be a good idea to write down every detail of the dream when you wake up. Then we can see someone who may be able to help you over this hurdle. You have so much to be thankful for. No sense getting all down about some silly dreams," Ericka said.

"I'll try it. Right now, I want to go for a swim and relax. I'm feeling a little out of sorts. I need exercise," Lloyd said.

"Cool idea. Just call if you need anything. Mom and I are having a salad. You hungry?"

Lloyd just shook his head and headed for his room.

In the kitchen, Ericka was quiet.

"You okay, honey?" Marty asked. He started to prepare their salad.

"I have a question."

"Sure."

"How did you arrange for Lloyd's kidney?"

"What do you mean? Through Pretesh of course."

"No, really, where did he get it?"

"He has lots of contacts. What are you trying to say?"

"I want to ask you flat out. Is there anything to Lloyd's dreams? Can this girl who comes to him be real?" Ericka asked.

"It's a dream for Christ sake, only a dream."

"So nobody was killed? I read about these organ piracy rings. Is it possible that Pretesh went that route?"

Marty stopped what he was doing. He put both of his hands on Ericka's shoulders and looked right in her eyes.

"Absolutely not. Now let's have a nice lunch."

CHAPTER 29

Passages is a popular Russian nightclub on Emmons Avenue in Sheepshead Bay, Brooklyn. Emmons is the main artery between Sheephead Bay and Brighton Beach.

The famous nightspot is on the second floor of the two-story, stucco-faced building, which looks out on the bay. Along the nearly mile-long waterway are various fishing and small, commercial boats that exit the bay toward the Atlantic Ocean. At night,the lights from Passages and other restaurants along Emmons Avenue cast a slight, eerie shine upon the water.

Along the two-wide lanes in each direction, street parking is at a premium. Cars go speeding by to get to Coney Island to the west, east onto the Belt Parkway toward John F. Kennedy International Airport and the major highways toward the borough of Queens and to Long Island.

Passages has its own parking lot to the rear of the building with a ramp from an adjoining street to the second floor. This is where the main entrance to the nightclub is found.

Mickey Roach sat in the passenger seat of a SUV with tinted windows. His driver was Bekim Selca. Both of them wore dark blue, Detroit Tiger's baseball caps and wraparound sunglasses. Bekim pulled the vehicle into the parking lot at nine o'clock and awaited the action while Joey Clams and C.C. ate clams on the half-shell and fried calamari on the outdoor patio at Randazzo's Clam Bar. There was plenty of time to kill. Joey fixated on the bay. There was something about the water that always soothed him and scared him at the same time. C.C. checked out the local talent walking by with their boyfriends on date night.

To be sure that everything was going as planned, Mickey Roach communicated with everyone who was in on the hit that night via cellphone. He spoke in Sicilian dialect to the two imported mafiosi, and in short, coded words to Joey Clams. At ten minutes to nine, Mickey made a call.

"Tutta posta?" Mickey asked.

"Si, tutto bene," Claudio replied.

"Ei ragazzi, vicinu?"

"Ma chertu, non si preoccupatu. E vicinu?" Claudio said.

Mickey Roach was checking if the Sicilians and the girls were nearby. They were.

"Oh. Is the pot boiling?" Mickey asked.

"Ziti is almost ready," Joey Clams replied.

"Make the delivery later on."

"Sure."

Mickey never would leave anything to chance. He knew Joey and C.C. were staged and ready to execute his plan.

At nine o'clock sharp, a limo dropped Beppie, Claudio, Valbona, and Estella Moscoso, the knockout from Ecuador.

Claudio was the first to exit the car. He offered his hand to Estella. When she stood next to her escort in her body-hugging, red, micro-mini skirt and Jimmy Choo, red spiked heels, Estella resembled a movie star about to walk on the red carpet. Her long, straight, black hair, captivating, violet eyes, high cheek-bones, large, full breasts, and perfect body would make any man or woman stop and stare. And stare they did. Other couples walking into Passages, and passersby along Emmons Avenue slowed down or simply stopped at the sight of the magnificent, one-of-a-kind stunner.

Claudio, his hair styled into a short, like-he-just-woke-up look, had dyed his hair blond for the occasion. His classic, dark, Sicilian, GQ, I-haven't-shaved-in-four-days beard look was replaced by a handsome, Nordic look that disguised the killer well. He held Estella around the waist, the two making close body contact for effect. They had a celebrity air about them with a gaze that said, "everyone is looking at us but we will pretend that there is no one else around us and study the trees and architecture."

Estella was into Claudio. His muscular body and piercing, brown eyes made her role as a prop very enjoyable. It crossed her mind while in the limousine and now, as they were close together, that she wouldn't mind getting under the sheets with him. For Claudio, this was just a job, and she was a prop. Estella was a means to an end.

Beppie alighted the car next. He looked up at the Passages building as if he owned the joint. His look told everyone that he had arrived and was in charge of the entire scene. Shorter than Claudio, Beppie had a Napoleon-like demeanor that momentarily took attention away from the Estella and Claudio show. Now the anticipation of the onlookers was at its peak. What goddess would exit the vehicle next?

Valbona was breathtakingly sexy as she exited the car. Beppie held his right hand out to Valbona while sweeping his left arm toward the nightclub as if he just bought the place and was gifting it to his woman.

She wore a skin-tight, black, leather, short-but not too short-skirt with a tasteful, floral pattern that ran down her backside. Paired with that was a rose-red jacket that complimented the flowers in the skirt over a blouse that all but exposed Valbona's beautiful, full breasts. A strip of double-sided tape helped the fabric cling to her chest. Valbona's heels, spiked, of course, had a strip of thick leather that encircled her ankles that would make the S&M crowd go into a complete frenzy. One large looped, gold earring complimented Valbona's long, creamy neck.

Beppie played his role well, although, like Claudio, he wasn't thinking about getting into Valbona's pants. First, he was told of her role within the Marku family. Any indiscretion, and his mother back in Sicily would never see him again. But above all that, Beppie was a closet homosexual. In his world, that would mean a death sentence. Even Claudio had no clue as to his partner's preference. Their relationship was strictly business. The death business.

Beppie dropped his right hand from Valbona's after she was out of the limo and immediately put his hand square on her high and tight butt as if to tell the world, "this luscious, young creature is all mine, you jealous bastards."

Valbona knew her role. Having a man's hands on her ass sent a shiver through her spine. She wasn't certain if she remembered the feeling and felt a twinge of sexuality or if she was repulsed by it.

The two women embraced, freed themselves from their escorts and then hugged each other closely on the street. The play was now in Act One, Scene Two. Holding hands, walking ahead of the men, Estella looked at Valbona like she could devour her.

"My God, you are gorgeous. Not many of the women can wear the hair so short and look so, how you say in English, *caliente*," Estella exclaimed.

"Thanks. I don't feel very hot at all. If anything, I'm annoyed at this tape that keeps coming off of my chest. I think there may be a wardrobe malfunction tonight," Valbona said.

"That would be fun to watch the men in this place to break their necks to see your *tetas*. I will promise no to laugh, Valbona. Such a pretty name is Valbona."

"Okay, now we make our entrance. You will have the men drooling!" Valbona said.

"What is this drooling? Is like…to cum?"

"No…no…no. They will have water in their mouths over you." Valbona threw her head back in laughter. This moment broke the enormous tension that Valbona was feeling. The words of Ilir rang in Valbona's head, "never show fear."

"Ay…si…mommie. Oh, yeah. They will be doing that when we dance, my beautiful friend, Valbona."

As they exited the elevator into Passages, both Beppie and Claudio began surveying the exits, paying special attention to the burly managers and bouncers and trying to look for the strengths and weaknesses of potential enemies.

The foursome was quickly shown to a prime table to the right of the stage in the main dining room. Next to the table was a large dance floor where fifty people could dance to the beat of Russian pop music as well as Americans like Usher,

Justin Timberlake, and Bruno Mars. The band was comprised of four male musicians and a female singer. The men were dressed in silver sports jackets and black pants. The singer wore a full-length, plum gown and ruby-red slippers to match her lipstick. Her gown had long sleeves with slits on the upper arms, exposing her milky-white skin. A slit up the middle of her gown to just under her *mons veneris* begged for the right move to expose her completely.

The crowd, some families but mostly groups of adults, were enthralled by the singer's voice and good looks. That was, until Estella and Valbona were led to their table with the two camouflaged Sicilians by the restaurant manager, Maksim Savelyev. Savelyev, a thief-in-law, was his own profit center for the Petrov *Bratva*. More than just food and entertainment came out of Passions. There was more going on behind the scenes with the dope trade and prostitution that made the *Bratva* a fatter, blacker, bottom line.

"Please enjoy yourselves tonight, ladies and gentlemen. I am Maksim. My head waiter, Dimi, will take care of you as if you were my family," Savelyev said.

Beppie noticed the tip of a star tattoo on his forehand and something else, another jailhouse tattoo, which was just peeking out from under his tied shirt collar.

"He could be trouble," Beppie whispered to Claudio. Claudio did not react.

"Good evening. May I get you something from the bar before we discuss tonight's specials?" Dimi, the waiter, asked.

"Is there anyone here who speaks Danish? Our men are from Denmark. If not, I will order," Valbona said.

"No, Madam. Russian, German, English and one man can speak a little Norwegian and Swedish, or so he says," Dimi replied.

"Okay, then. What is your best champagne?" Valbona inquired.

"Well, may I suggest a wonderful *Veuve Clicquot*? It is nice with fish and caviar."

"Bring two bottles; keep two on ice," Valbona said.

"Very well, Madam."

"And a bottle of your best Russian vodka. You know as they say, 'When in Rome...'" Valbona said. She smiled at Dimi politely.

"No, Madam, I do not know about Rome," Dimi said.

"Just bring the drinks please," Valbona ordered. She did all she could not to roll her eyes at the unsophisticated Russian.

The group nursed some champagne, danced a bit, and watched the crowd change. At around ten thirty, the restaurant was becoming a real club. The families were all gone, and a steady flow of younger people, all dressed to impress, had taken over.

Beppie and Claudio continued to size up the staff. One guy, who walked around with a reservation sheet in his hand, had to be about three hundred and fifty pounds if he were an ounce. Another shorter, more ferocious looking fellow stood by the entrance door to the club, scanning the crowd.

It was now ten forty-five. Valbona ordered the famous and fabulous Passages seafood tower. Four levels of clams, wilted-looking shrimp, crab claws, lobster tails, and oysters were set upon the table within five minutes. Clearly, the shellfish were opened way before the order was placed. Another prop that was never going to be paid for, Valbona thought. Estella picked at the oysters. No one else at the table ate.

Valbona was keeping her cool, hearing and heeding Ilir's words about showing her fear. She took small breaths into her mouth and exhaled through her nose slowly. Her heart was racing, but no one would be the wiser. She looked at the dance floor and stage, imagining the chaos that would soon follow. Crystal lights hung from the ceiling, and strobe lighting of purple, green, and red bounced off the floor, the walls, and the ceiling. She focused on the ceiling and gave a flower man a ten-dollar bill for two roses so that he would not come by the table again.

The big guy with the reservation sheet walked around, making sure that there were two vacant tables, one was next to Valbona and company's table by the stage, the other across the dance floor abutting the stage.

Suddenly, two couples walked in and were greeted by Save-lyev. The owner walked them toward the table next to the foursome.

Valbona's blood went cold.

One of the two women was young, tall and thin and had full breasts that were not at all bashful. She had flowing, flaming-red hair.

Her escort was Rick Metalia.

CHAPTER 30

Gino was safely ensconced at the Ritz-Carlton in Boston. He planned to stay the night and fly back to LaGuardia Airport on Saturday afternoon.

Vincent Patriarca and his cousin, Salvatore, the leaders of the Boston mafia family by the same name and infamy, met with Gino in his suite. The pleasantries were passed around, and drinks were poured. The three men sat in the living room, overlooking the oldest park in the United States, Boston Common Park.

"How is Carmine, Jr., doing with all this heat on him?" Vincent asked.

"He's holding up, Vinnie. He sends his best to you and your family. I hope you understand that he can't be around certain people right now," Gino said.

"Naturally. We've all had these feds up our asses at some point. Your time will come. Believe me, it ain't easy," Vincent said.

"It's part of the life, I'm learning," Gino said.

"And how are you handling things?" Vincent asked.

"I have a major headache with the Russians. They are very aggressive. They are trying to hone in on a lot of our business affairs. Do you have that problem here?"

"Areyoukiddenmeorwhat? These *morte de fame* are all over the place. Between them and the Chinese, we have to look over our shoulders all day long," Salvatore complained.

"Those two assholes who bombed the marathon came from Russia. Their old man was tortured by the mob in the old country. The Russian wise guys killed the family dog and left its head on their doorstep. Real animals, the whole bunch of them. How do you deal with people like this? I have no idea," Vincent said

"Yeah, this whole Islamic thing is a bunch of bullshit. The media made the bombing look like a whole terrorist-war thing. Nonsense! Those two Tzarnaev brothers who did the bombing were up to their ears in the swag business and other stuff. They came here to be American gangsters. I think they watched too many mob movies over there," Salvatore surmised.

"And these Russians know how to hack computers and shit like that. Our people can't even get on Google, and the Russians figured out how to empty bank accounts and fuck with people's credit cards," Vincent said.

"Cyber thieves," Gino stated.

"Exactly, and our guys are being picked up for taking numbers and football action," Salvatore said.

"The Russians basically print money, other people's money. Gobs of it for Christ sake, and they are getting better and stronger every single day," Vincent said.

"And, to add insult to injury, one of our fucking bosses, one of our own, has turned rat with the FBI. This is not the business of our grandfathers anymore, Gino," Salvatore warned.

"You need to take care of your own house with the rat. So what are we going to do about the Russians?" Gino asked.

"Glad you asked. We are looking to do a meeting of the entire commission, all the families around the entire country. We need your support to put this thing together. Without New York, it just will not happen. The commission will not go for it," Vincent said.

"You have our backing. I give you my word. There will be news in the next few days that will show you that we mean business. When the news gets out, we will need your support, guys," Gino said.

"Totally. And my word is my bond. What do you need from us?" Vincent asked.

"Vinnie, it's like a game to these Russians. A chess game. I don't know if you know anything about chess. There is a word, it's called *priyome*. It's a very obscure Russian term for a chess strategy that counts on the pawns for victory to eventually take down the king. They will use their soldiers to try to control us, to beat us. "

"I don't understand," Salvatore said.

Vincent shrugged his shoulders.

"We have to hit their pawns and hit them hard. Take their soldiers out to allow us to attack their king and win," Gino said.

"When do we start?" Vincent asked.

"I'll need some muscle from you guys. Some of our people don't have the balls, plus, they are lazy and stupid. The Russians can taste blood. They know those damn feds and our own showboating stupidity have nearly smothered us, " Gino said.

"We still have some people who can help you big time. When do you need us?" Vincent asked.

"We are about to go to war. Can you have these people near me next week?"

CHAPTER 31

The look on Rick's face was priceless. At first, he stopped in his tracks, thinking perhaps the sexy lady he was looking at wasn't Valbona. How could it be Valbona? He and Shpresa went back and forth on the topic of her becoming a sworn virgin for days. But it was Valbona in the flesh, dressed as a woman, and she was as hot as hell.

"Is that really you?" Rick asked.

"I should be asking the same question," Valbona said.

"What, I mean I thought you were…"

Valbona put up her hand to stop the question. She pointed to the exit nearest the elevator.

"May I see you over there?" She was showing no distress, her face not giving away the adrenalin rush she was having at seeing her best friend's husband out with his "side-piece."

Rick excused himself from the perplexed redhead and the other couple. He met Valbona near the elevator out of sight from the restaurant and dance floor.

"Valbona, I didn't think that virgin thing would last long," Rick said.

"Your marriage to my best friend may not last long either, douche," Valbona seethed.

"Douche…nice mouth. And why does she have to know about this? Just keep your mouth shut, and I didn't see you out and about either."

"Listen to me. This is no longer the world of the Albanian woman being subservient to the man. I saw you here, and, yes, I will not say a word and stab my best friend in her heart. She already knows you are stepping out on her. It's just a matter of time before Shpresa dumps your sorry, Albanian ass anyway. And, for the record, your girl is a real Russian pig. It's written all over her face."

"And what about you? Pretending to be a sworn virgin, telling Ilir you want to have the rights of a man in the old tradition and here you are, dressed like a slut with some guy who looks like he wants you to jump on him right here," Rick said.

"None of your business. Here is what's going to happen. I'm going back to my table and my friends. So are you, only you are leaving. Don't sit, and don't look at me again. Tell them anything you want, but just fucking leave this place," Valbona demanded.

"Who are you to tell me to leave? I don't run away. Why don't you leave instead?"

Valbona stepped up to Rick and was almost looking eye to eye. Even in the spiked heels, Valbona was shorter. She spoke without emotion in a matter of fact way.

"Things are happening here that you have no business being around. I'm warning you, Rick, leave…leave now. You never saw me, and I never saw you. I am here for my boss. Am I making myself clear? Do you understand me?"

Rick waited for a few seconds, trying to absorb the moment and what he just heard from a woman. Indeed, it sounded like it came from a man…a serious man.

"Ah…okay. Sorry if I offended you. We're out of here," Rick muttered.

Rick shook Valbona's hand and then put his hand to his chest in a sign of respect. He had met his match, and she used to be a woman.

Valbona walked back to her table, giving Rick a chance to make up whatever story he needed to get out of Passion and go off to another nightclub or joint that would make it easier for his girl to pretend she was having fun. Rick was nothing more than a john to this woman. She couldn't care less who was pitching. Rick was simply a wallet that she would be emptying, and then on to the next schmuck with whom she could run her game. Valbona did not make eye contact with the redhead or the other couple in Rick's little shindig.

The four left quickly with Maskim on their heels, asking if something was wrong. Rick threw two hundreds on the table and never looked back.

Valbona sat back in her seat like she had just returned from the ladies' room.

"What was that all about?" Estella asked.

"Oh, nothing, just some guy I dated in high school. He had to leave," Valbona said.

Beppie leaned his head into the center of the table. He signaled with his eyebrows and eyes for the others to do the same as he had something to say.

"It is almost the time. *Informa*, be ready,"

Valbona checked her watch. It was five minutes to eleven.

CHAPTER 32

A brand new, shining, gold-colored Mercedes C550 sedan pulled into the parking lot at the rear of Passages at ten minutes after eleven. The valets jumped to attention and ran to open the vehicle's doors. The car and its occupants were well known to the attendants. Mikhail Andratova, the brigadier of the Boris Petrov *Bratva* was the driver. In the seat next to him was his twenty-four-year-old, steady girlfriend on the side. When he opened the passenger-side door, the young valet made certain that he averted his eyes when the girl in a skimpy mini-skirt placed her long, shapely legs onto the pavement.

A few months ago, one of the boys told the other valets that Andratova's girl was not wearing panties. He graphically described her clean-shaved vagina. Jokingly, the daring young man called her The Commando. A few days later when word got around about the valet, he found himself with multiple bone fractures on the powdery sands of Brighton Beach. Two weeks later after the youngster left Coney Island hospital in a full body cast, his family had to send him back to Volgograd to spare a second beating. And probably much worse.

Andratova couldn't care less about the thirty-four-year difference in age or his fifty-inch waist. What people thought meant nothing to him. Exiting the rear of the car was the *Bratva's Sovietnivk*, the counselor to the head of the family and loyal friend of Boris Petrov himself. With him was a raven-haired, blue-eyed beauty who looked more like his granddaughter than his girlfriend. Her red dress, shoes, lipstick, and tight, red, silky evening gown were showstoppers.

In a car behind the two senior members of the *Bratva* was a guest whom Mickey Roach did not expect. One of the two *Bratva* spies, Oleg Zhvkovsky, would be joining the two couples for a drink…or five.

When they entered the nightclub, the fog machine had engulfed most of the dance floor with a fine vapor, which made the multi-colored lights bounce off the patron dancers in a psychedelic haze.

The band was playing a popular Russian tune that made the girl singer reach all of the high octaves. The patrons would throw their hands in the air when a high note was sung, making the fog and light show seem almost eerie.

Andratova and Kuklowski were greeted with a warm hand-shake and hug from their fellow *Bratva* member and club owner, Maskim. The girls followed behind the men as if they were walking on a fashion runway in Milan as Maxim led them to their stage side table.

Valbona felt as if she would vomit at the first sight of the three men and two girls but not because of the visual of these girls servicing these men. Valbona was, in a short time, going to be involved with killing other human beings. Twenty minutes ago, Valbona confronted Rick Metalia and insisted-no, demanded-in no uncertain terms, that he and his sidekicks leave the club. Now she was about to take the ultimate test of a man.

Valbona could feel her heart beating and hear the pounding of her blood pressure in her ears. She began her unnoticeable breathing routine to settle herself.

The band began to play to Bruno Mars' "Uptown Funk."

"Let's dance, Valbona…just me and you, mommie," Estella said.

"Let's give them a real good show, one they will never forget," Valbona agreed.

Beppie and Claudio, ice running through their veins, knew that the time was near for them to move into action.

The music was ear-piercingly loud, much too loud for anyone to have a conversation. Andratova noticed Valbona and Estelle move to the dance floor. Suddenly, his young chippy was fungible. Andratova saw something he liked that was better than his lady. He nudged Kuklowski and brought his comrade's attention to the two beauties dancing together.

Estella moved like she were born to dance. It seemed as if she moved all parts of her body at the same time. Valbona moved nicely but not nearly as sexy and sensuous, and alluring, as the Ecuadorian.

As Estella moved into Valbona and began running her hands over Valbona's curvaceous hips and tight thighs, Andratova and the other two men at his table were mesmerized. The men didn't even blink for fear of missing one bump or grind. The Russian girls at Andratova's table looked at each other, rolled their eyes, and smiled.

"*Uptown funk you up…uptown funk you up,*" the girl singer and her two male backups intoned. The more they repeated the verse, the sexier Estelle and Valbona moved and the more the Russian mob guys loved the show.

The DJ segued into another American hit, giving the band a needed respite, and Estella and Valbona went with it.

Martin Garrix's "Don't Look Down" blasted from the speakers. The lights strobed in a helter-skelter circular motion, and the fog blasted from the floor units around the dance floor.

Is your head spinning?

Is your heart racing?

Is that fire in your veins?

Estella got behind Valbona and grinded her slowly, touching her shapely butt with both hands. The sweat now forming on the girls' necks and backs, the fog, and the bouncing light show gave the *Bratva* men an erotic stimulation that was almost unbearable.

"I must meet these two. I will not be happy until I see their dresses on the floor of my fucking bedroom," Andratova demanded. He pulled Kuklowski into him so he could be heard and their girls could not hear them.

"Tell our girls to join them. Maybe this could be a night to remember," Kuklowski said.

"Good idea. I was thinking the same," Andratova agreed.

"Ladies, why not join those two out there? They seem to be having a good time. Maybe we join you later out there," Andratova said.

When he asked his girl for something, it was more like he was telling her. She took a shot of vodka and pulled Kuklowski's girl onto the dance floor.

The four of them danced together for a long set of club music that had the entire place captivated. Hands were touching asses, tits were rubbing together, and, at one point, Estella kissed

Kuklowski's girl square on the mouth, holding her head in both hands. The Russian girl was into it.

"Look, Val, look, they are tonguing each other. I swear to God I saw it. I saw they did that. Who are these fucking bitches?" Andratova asked.

"They will tire, and we will soon know," Zhvkovsky said.

"We? We? There is no we. There is no us. You can watch, but you can't touch. You brought no sand to this beach, Oleg," Andratova growled.

"I should leave after this drink then. What use is eating out my heart? I have my rounds to make anyway," Zhvkovsky said.

A minute later, the four girls wobbled back to their respective tables. Beppie and Claudio were using their phones as props, pretending to be texting and not watching the girl-on-girl show.

Andratova called for his waiter.

"Send them champagne. Tell them their night is on us."

The fog dissipated, but the music was still blaring. Russian pop music now filled the floor with dancers, many of them lip syncing to the tune.

The waiter brought the champagne to the table as instructed and poured the bubbly into four crystal, stem glasses.

Andratova raised his glass in a salute to Valbona and Estelle. Everyone raised a glass and toasted.

Beppie and Claudio were smiling broadly.

"Salute, *cornudu*," Beppie said mockingly, possibly the worst thing a man can call another man in Sicilian. Its meaning is something along the lines of a man who pimps out his wife. The Russians had no idea what was being said, only that the guys were friendly and maybe, hopefully, into some kind of kinky orgy.

Kuklowski waived at the table for Valbona and the others to join them.

"Here we go. Let's do this thing," Valbona said.

"*Ma certo*," Claudio said.

Estella and Valbona draped their purses over their shoulders as Beppie and Claudio buttoned their suit jackets in a sign of respect. They walked across the dance floor along the stage where there were no dancers impeding their movement.

"What great dancers you are. Come, join us," Andratova said. The three men stood, the Russian girls sat.

"You are too kind," Estella said.

Estella and Valbona simultaneously flipped open their purses and filled their right hands with Berretta, 40mm pistols. Estella pumped two shots into Andratova's chest. Valbona put two into the chest of Kuklowski.

The dance floor went into pandemonium. The patron rush to the front exit was like a heard of wildebeests fleeing a predator. Others took cover under their tables. The DJ, unaware of the shots being fired, kept the music blasting. The light show continued.

Claudio took an automatic pistol from the small of his back and shot the unwitting Zhvkovsky in his forehead. The spray of blood and brains seem to be sucked onto the ceiling.

Beppie shot Kuklowski in his head and turned and fired three times into the gut of the oncoming, huge guy who used to hold the reservation list. Now his hands were full of guts and blood. He held a gun in his hand, but Beppie was too quick for him. He never got a shot off.

"*Andiamo*, follow me," Claudio directed. The four shooters headed as planned to the side exit. The street was full of screaming women and frightened men.

Two of the *Bratva* men followed Claudio and the others, shooting their pistols wildly as then ran.

"Here they come, C.C. Don't hit our people," Joey Clams shouted.

"Fuck that, I want these fucking Ruskies," C.C. said.

Claudio, Beppie, Valbona, and Estella made their way to the escape car. Beppie fired his pistol in the air to clear a passage toward Emmons Avenue. Joey Clams and C.C. laid down cover fire, both with M16 automatic rifles, reminiscent of their days together in Vietnam. The *Bratva* men returned fire but knew they were outgunned and took cover.

Maskim, brave in the face of death, the big earner and up and comer in the Petrov *Bratva,* ran out into the street with a sawed-off shotgun that he kept behind the bar.

Mickey Roach, waiting patiently for his opportunity to put a cap on this piece of work, dropped Maskim where he stood, right on the double, yellow lines of Emmons Avenue.

Everyone got away as planned.

The war had been taken to another level.

CHAPTER 33

Gino Ranno arrived as planned at LaGuardia Airport the afternoon after the massacre at Passages nightclub. Joey Clams, C.C., and Mickey Roach, along with four other bodyguards, whisked Gino within fifteen minutes back to his apartment in the Riverdale section of the Bronx.

"What should we expect from the Russians?" Gino asked.

"Nothing today. They are in shock. Now they will make their plan or ask for a sit down," Mickey Roach said.

"I agree, Gino. After last night's hit sinks in, they will formulate a plan. Right now, it's all about surprise, panic, and blame in Brighton Beach. We should see some action next week at the earliest," Joey Clams added.

"By that time, we will have our people ready for a fight. Boston is sending some muscle to help," Gino said.

"What's in it for them?" Joey Clams asked.

"It's a mess in New England. The Russians are steamrolling our friend Vinnie's family as bad as or even worse than we have here, if that's even possible," Gino said.

"And if they ask to sit down?" Mickey Roach asked.

"I'm not sure. I guess we have to play it out," Gino replied.

"Look, they hit the Albanians. They know we were with the Albanians on that piece of work in the restaurant. If they have any balls, we are next in line," Joey Clams said.

"I'm not sure they will do that, Joey. They still have some regard for us," Gino pointed out.

"I agree with Joey. Gino, they have no respect for anyone. The worst for them is running back to their country and coming back as another group of low lives with a different name and ID. Maybe not here but somewhere where that they can chop up little kids for money. Life is not so sacred to them," Mickey Roach argued.

"C.C., you've been quiet. What's on your mind?" Gino asked.

"I say we hit them again. Show them we mean business. We hit them high, now let's hit them low," C.C. said.

"Do you play chess, C.C.?" Gino asked.

"He can't even play checkers," Joey Clams teased. Everyone laughed.

"C.C. may be on to something. Let me tell you all about the Russian *priyome* strategy," Gino said.

That evening, Claudio and Beppie were on their way back to the safety of Palermo on an Alitalia flight out of JFK Airport.

That morning, Estella flew back to her family in Ecuador in time to celebrate the First Holy Communion of her niece on Sunday.

The New York Daily News late edition headline shouted:

MOB HIT IN BROOKLYN

The New York Post headline was just a bit tacky. It read:

BLOOD BORSCHT!

Both tabloids had photos of the murder victims being brought out in body bags and loaded into a coroner's van. The Passages' neon sign was visible in the pictures' backgrounds.

The Daily News and the Post agreed upon one thing that was typical of the Brighton Beach crowd:

"None of the patrons or the staff of Passages was able to give a description of the shooter or shooters."

Valbona couldn't sleep after the hit. She paced around her bedroom suite at the Marku estate in Scarsdale. At six o'clock the morning after she killed Andratova, she went down to the kitchen to make herself coffee. Ilir Marku was waiting for her, freshly shaven in a suit and tie.

"How are you, Val?" Ilir asked.

"I was unable to sleep last night. Today will be a long day."

"I understand the job was done without loss to us."

"Yes."

"And you did well," Ilir added. He studied her face closely, looking for a sign of distress as Valbona sipped the hot coffee.

"It was not my first time firing a gun. I did it many times back home in Albania," Valbona said.

"But never into the body of another. There is a difference," Ilir said.

"I had a job to do. I had to prove myself. I will do it again if need be."

"Yet, you could not sleep. Are you upset that you did what you had to do?"

"No, I felt nothing. I couldn't sleep because I'm excited."

"Excited, *nuse*? What do you mean?" Ilir asked.

"I'm eager to get to the next steps with these Russians. If we don't stop them now, they will bury us all. Our way of life will be gone forever. Our people will be scrubbing floors for these animals," Valbona said. Ilir showed nothing. He was unsure of where Valbona was going with the conversation.

"Were you afraid last night?" Ilir asked.

"Afraid? Would you ask one of your men if he had fear? With respect, Babë, that is a question for women."

"Yes. I apologize. I meant no disrespect."

CHAPTER 34

"He was like a son to me. Today, he is dead at the hands of those dirty, Albanian bastards and stinking Italians who have stabbed us in the back. My blood hurts," Boris Petrov said. He was speaking to what remained of his inner circle. The meeting took place in the rear of Café Arbat on Avenue U in Brighton Beach. Ten of the *Bratva's* bodyguards, the *Byki,* and four *Shestyorka,* the lower ranking associates, stood guard outside of the café. Not one person could pass this Russian wall of flesh.

"How we will answer this?" Anton asked. Trapanov, a handsome Ukrainian with hands that resembled two fresh hams and who was much younger than the late *Brigadier,* made a commanding presence.

"We will answer. Make no doubt about that. Now I need to gather my thoughts and digest this poison."

"Perhaps, we should reach out to these Micelis through our mutual Brooklyn friends. After all, we made out well together in the gasoline business," Trapanov suggested.

"They all drink from the same trough. They will never turn on their own. That business is over and done with, and these Italians have amnesia. If we ask to meet, we will be showing weakness. And weakness is very costly, Anton."

"But so is war," Trapanov pointed out. This remark was bold and could have been taken wrong. It was very clear that

Trapanov wanted Andratova's spot. Trapanov thought his boldness would fare him well.

"Anton, I appreciate your sentiments. My instincts tell me to strike them in their stomachs. They will be thinking that we will attack their leadership. So we shall hit them on the street. Take out their pawns, then their kings, and then that Marku and the Miceli kid will be exposed," Petrov said.

"Miceli is out to pasture at the moment. His lackey is in the boss's chair," Trapanov said.

"Carmine Miceli, Jr., is still the head of the family. Don't be deceived by the smokescreen. Miceli still pulls the strings. He is our ultimate target. The other guy is only a figurehead with little experience in matters such as this."

"He has war in his veins. A true Sicilian. I would not take his inexperience as a flaw," Trapanov said.

"That is old thinking. The New York Sicilian mafia is not what it once was. We have seen them shrink to a shadow of their past," Andrey Aleksandrovich said. He also was vying for the job of *Brigadier*.

"Never underestimate your opponent, Aleks. When a rat is cornered, what does he do? He will strike. He has nothing to lose," Trapanov said. His remark was said through his clenched teeth. The veins on his full neck were engorged.

The positioning was obvious.

"In a day or so, I will make my decision. I will appoint my new *Brigadier* and *Sovietnik* and spy. We will gather our strength and replace our losses. These men will help me decide what road we take. Until then, we keep our guard up, we stay quiet…and mourn our friends."

CHAPTER 35

Marty Craig had just finished a grueling, hour-long session with his personal trainer at home. He headed for the pool to cool off. His tee-shirt, gym shorts, and hair were sopping wet with sweat. His wife waylaid him before he could take the refreshing plunge.

"We need to talk," Ericka said.

"Okay, let me take a few laps, and I'll be right with you," Marty said.

"No, Marty, we need to talk right now."

"Okay, what's the big problem?"

"The problem is that you lied to me," Ericka said. Happy wife, happy life was not in the offing at the moment.

"Lied? About what, honey?" Marty said. He grabbed a pool towel and started to sop up the water that was running down his face.

"About Lloyd's kidney. You looked me in the eye and bold-face lied to me."

"What are you talking about, Ericka?"

"I'm talking about your personal checking account. Three days before his surgery, you withdrew two hundred and fifty thousand dollars. I checked with Wells Fargo. You withdrew cash. Now think of another lie, and make up some bullshit before I lose it."

"Now you're checking up on me? In all the years we are together, you never questioned one thing that I've done. I don't deserve this."

"So tell me what you did with a sum like that. I don't see a new car in the driveway."

"It's really something I would rather not discuss with you," Marty said. He dropped the towel onto the pool deck.

"I really don't care what you'd rather not discuss, Marty. Have you noticed your son lately? He is sinking, Marty. He is still having dreams about that girl. I found him mumbling to himself yesterday, like he was talking to someone who wasn't even there. I want the truth. I did my research. There is a six-to-eight-year wait for a kidney. How did he get one so fast?" Erika demanded. She was fuming and in her husband's face.

"Look, I did what was necessary. That's all you need to know."

"Are you fucking kidding me? All of a sudden, you are the boss, and I have no say when it comes to our son? I have no rights as his mother? Try again."

"Why are you so pissed off? Some things are better left alone, honey."

"Don't you dare "honey" me! Lloyd is suffering emotionally. The psychiatrist will not even discuss him with me. A HIPPA violation he said. HIPPA, my ass. I want the truth, and I want it now."

"Just leave it alone. What's the end game here?" Marty said.

"The end game is simple. I find out what happened with this kidney, and if I think you are lying, you and I have an even bigger problem."

"I did what I had to do."

"That's not an acceptable answer. Tell me what you did, and tell me right now, Martin Craig."

"Look, I knew the wait time for a kidney. Lloyd was failing quickly. Dialysis four times a week or worse. He could have died. His future was grim what with school and his eye and hearing issues. He's still not out of the woods."

"So you went on the black market and got a kidney?"

"Yes. Yes, I did. And I would do it again. I would use every penny we have to save our son. I would do it for you, our daughter, myself for that matter."

"Was the donor someone you knew? Was it voluntary? Did she do it for the money?" Ericka asked.

"I honestly don't know."

"Liar!"

"And what if it wasn't voluntary?"

"So you had someone murdered so our son would have a better life? And Pretesh blessed this killing? I thought doctors took an oath never to do harm?"

"You're being over dramatic. The kidney is working, that's all that matters at this point."

"Bullshit! You committed an immoral act. What you did is mortal sin in the eyes of God. Someone died so that you had what you wanted. Is this what money does to people?"

"Ericka, what was I supposed to do? You should have just left this alone instead of acting like Sherlock Holmes," Marty said. He took his tee-shirt off. Marty was getting ready for his swim.

"Don't you dare dismiss me like that."

"Okay, what do you want me to say? Yes, I did what you are saying. Yes, someone died to save our son. Don't you think I will go to my grave haunted by what I've done? That girl would have been killed anyway! If not for Lloyd, for someone else."

"And that is how you justify murder? You are no better than the people who killed her."

"So what now? I turn myself in and go to jail? Don't talk that shit to me, Ericka. What's done is done."

"We have to tell Lloyd. He needs to know."

"Why? Why does he have to share in my misery? Have you lost your freakin' mind?" Marty shouted. He picked up his sweat soaked tee shirt and slammed it back onto the floor.

"Because he is already haunted. That girl's spirit is all around him. I guess you never counted on that, Mister Rich Guy," Ericka said sarcastically.

"I do plenty of good with our money, and you know that."

"So that permits you to be an accessory to murder?"

"Stop it! That is so unfair."

"Unfair? What about her? What about her family? Did they get a fair shake?"

"I hear you. It troubles me every day, and I really don't believe in this spirit mumbo-jumbo."

"So explain his dreams. She basically told Lloyd that she was killed. She told him about her whole life. How can that be explained? He already knows, for Christ sake."

"And who knows how he will react to the truth?" Marty said.

"He deserves the truth. Maybe the truth will set him free from her."

"You hope. We are treading on thin ice, and you know it."

"Then let fate take its course. If you don't tell him then I will."

CHAPTER 36

Gino went to see Carmine Miceli, Jr., at the Seventy-Ninth street townhouse. Joey Clams and C.C. dropped him off two blocks away on Madison Avenue. Gino walked alone to Carmine, Jr.'s, home so as not to bring attention to his arrival. Walking with two men, two big tough-looking guys, to protect him would not look so good if any law-enforcement agencies were keeping tabs. Carmine, Jr., knowing that Gino would visit, had his house electronically swept that morning just in case there were any eavesdropping devices planted.

"Gino, how are you making out? You look a bit tired," Carmine, Jr., said.

"I'm fine. Just a lot of hours the past couple of days is all," Gino said.

"What's the latest?"

"We hit them hard. Unless they ask to meet, which I highly doubt, they will attack in force. I'm worried for you, Carmine. You probably will be their next target. I'm pretty sure they will strike back at us soon. I need to get you away from here for a while."

"Maybe you're right. That piece of work in Brooklyn probably has them climbing the walls."

"And we don't know how the next crew will react. Sometimes, the devil you know is better than the devil you don't."

"You sound like my father. I wish he were still here. So what are you thinking?" Carmine, Jr., asked.

"A nice trip with the family to Sicily. Lercara Friddi with the family will be the safest place."

"Can't do it. The judge took my passport away, don't you remember?"

"Shit, sorry, I forgot all about that."

"And I don't want to be a prisoner here. Think about another place," Carmine, Jr., said.

"Private jet out of Teterboro to the place in Puerto Rico. The place is well fortified, and our contacts there will see to it that you are all safe. Plus, our people will be there around the clock."

"How long?"

"Not sure yet. Two weeks? A month? The hearings don't start for a while, and you are entitled to a family vacation. It would be great for the kids, too."

"I love that place. Haven't been in a while. I like this idea, Gino."

"I'll set it up. Can you be ready tomorrow?"

"Let me talk to my boss. I think she would love it."

"Gino, you are up to your ass in alligators. What's the big-picture plan?" Carmine, Jr., asked.

"Your father, may he rest in peace, always said, 'man plans, and God laughs,' so any plan we have is really not our own. That being said, I've been studying the Russians for some time now. They think a lot differently than we do. The Russian mob has a different sense of right and wrong. Not saying we are saints, but the Russians have no limits. To them, our world is a game, like a chess game where your opponent can capitalize on one mistake and the game can be lost quickly," Gino said.

"Educate me, my friend," Carmine, Jr., said.

"Even when I was in business and now that I'm with you, I look at three things that are necessary to win. First and foremost, know yourself. Know your strengths as well as your weaknesses. Second, know your opponent's strengths and weaknesses better than he does. Last, make your victory greater than the moment. Make winning not only for now but for the future as well. Momentary satisfaction is for losers. I'm guided by that," Gino explained.

Carmine, Jr., paused and looked at Gino for a long moment and sat back in his chair.

"Not that I ever doubted you, but I now know for sure that you are the right man to sit in my chair," Carmine, Jr., said.

"I never claimed to be the smartest guy in the room," Gino said.

"In my eyes, you always were the smartest guy around. My father thought so, too. Now tell me about our frailties and our strong points."

"We are not nearly what we once were. In your father's time, a man's word meant something. Until Joe Valachi, there were no rats. Those old timers would never make a deal to save their own asses. They would have done thirty years rather than roll over on someone. *Omerta,* the old, Sicilian code of silence, was very real back then. Today, the cowboys we have among us would rat out their mother to get out of six months in jail. The old timers took care of one another. A made guy's family would not want for money. Now there is nothing like that, so there is only fear among these guys. They are afraid for their families and what would happened to them if they go inside or die. Right now, it's quick money and gone; that's all we have today. Our power is fleeting because of lack of honor and respect. The Albanians have their *Besa* and if they go against their word, their life is pulp. Maybe forty years from now, they will evolve into what we've sadly become. Right now, the Albanians are strong together. The Russians…they have their own code. A Russian mob member denounces his family before he joins the life. If he dares to breach the *Bratva's* trust, he goes, and his entire family goes. But his family goes first and not in a pleasant way. That is the core of our problem," Gino said.

"Go on," Carmine, Jr., said.

"We have men. They have men. We have guns; so do they. That is basically called a stalemate. Just like with the nukes, nobody wants to fire a missile first. In their game with their way of thinking, the Russians will sacrifice their pawns and look ahead to take the stronger pieces. Our people are all here-and-now thinkers. We've gotten fat by being in this country for so long. The Russians still have fire in their bellies. They know what hunger is. We've lost that edge. Instead of being smart and quiet, our guys walk around in five-thousand-dollar, *Brioni* suits, holding court in the open, and pissing on the shoes of the feds. We can learn an awful lot from our opponents. The Russians have the right idea. This life is a game. Stay in the game long enough to win," Gino explained.

"Can we fix this?" Carmine, Jr., asked.

"This whole made guy, burning the saint, and swearing an oath is purely Hollywood, Carmine. We have to make the life worth living and, more important, worth sacrificing for. There is no backup for our people. They think it's better to talk, make a deal, go into witness protection, and live out a meager existence. We need a better plan, like a profit-sharing plan and a retirement plan. Look at the guys we have in their late fifties through their eighties. Almost to a man, they are broke and poor. They still live scheme to scheme, deal to deal, pissing away everything. They live hand to mouth and have pressure to earn just to line the pockets of our capos. It doesn't work anymore. What worked for your father cannot work for you or anyone after you. Otherwise, the life will be someone else's."

"So what do we do, call in consultants? We're not Microsoft or Apple," Carmine, Jr., said.

"Not at all. We need to take a look at changing our model. Instead of having a *post mortem* and analyzing why we lost, we need to use our skills to help us win. Our people will get back their inherent power by having more skin in the game. Make them successful not flashy. Make them not want to lose their position, their status. Make them more upwardly mobile."

"Make them legitimate?"

"Sometimes, yes, but tie their success closely to us. Their tribute may be smaller at first, but it will be steady.

"You sound like a socialist, Gino. Share the wealth with the comrade next to you."

"Call it what you will. Redistribution of wealth among our people may not necessarily be a bad thing. We need more thinkers and less gangsters, Carmine. Otherwise within the next five years, the Russians will put us into checkmate. Game over!"

"The game has changed, Gino," Carmine, Jr., agreed.

"Now we have to change but not until we master their game of chess."

CHAPTER 37

Three days after the hit at Passages, Ilir Marku called a meeting at his office in the Morris Park section of the Bronx. Still largely Italian and Albanian, any outsider was easily spotted upon entering the storefront-lined community that ran from Pelham Parkway through Williamsbridge Road to Morris Park Avenue. This neighborhood changed very little since the nineteen-fifties, and its residents were bound and determined to keep it that way. The police would often advise the Italian and Albanian community leaders as to who from the neighborhood was "acting up." Justice was dispensed quickly, and the guilty party received the appropriate street justice. The cops looked the other way when someone was found broken and battered on a sidewalk or in a playground. The system worked marvelously.

Ilir was to name the successor to Hamdi Nezaj. In normal times, he would have waited a month or so until Hamdi's *pamje,* the traditional, Albanian, mourning gathering, was completed. These times where not anywhere close to being normal. Ilir expected the Russians to have retaliated by now.

The streets around Ilir's real estate office were like an armed camp. The police in the Four-Eight precinct patrolled the main thoroughfares, occasionally driving down a side street to bring both warning and comfort to the locals, depending on which side of the law they leaned. Two uniformed men in each patrol car and two unmarked detective squad cars scouted the area at a veritable snail's pace. No stop and frisk happened on these streets. Unless, of course, you were a black or Hispanic and were just happening to be walking through the neighborhood. That's just the way things are.

Ilir's men looked as ominous as they were. Dark hair, darker eyes, wearing sports coats or suits that looked rumpled and in bad need of a dry cleaning, and their shoes all screaming out for polish, these men would kill any and everyone who came near their leader. A cloud of cigarette smoke hung over the Marku Realty building, which took up two apartments on the first floor of the property.

Valbona, dressed as a man, quietly sat in a metal, folding chair behind Ilir's desk. Several other men, all smoking cigarettes and drinking Turkish coffee, *cognac,* or *raki,* silently awaited the boss of their clan to arrive and begin the meeting. Ilir had busied himself reviewing financial statements on his buildings and property for sale listings. His massive real estate portfolio had suffered in the last year. Ilir had not bought a building since the death of his son. His heart was simply not into expanding his business. There was no longer a driving purpose.

"Pashko, I'm thinking of selling off some of my properties. These here are selling for twelve times rent roll. Why not test the waters?" Ilir asked his friend, Pashko Luli. Ilir handed Pashko a multiple-listing page of Bronx buildings for sale. Pashko, like Hamdi, was a *kumar* to Ilir. They were friends since childhood in *Tropojë.*

"It is always good to know what is going on around you. Do you think this is the right time, Ilir, with the Russian bear breathing down our backs?" Pashko asked.

"Selling, buying, killing. It's all the same to me. I get no pleasure from very much these days, my friend. I must admit, I have been excited about this dispute with those Brighton Beach creatures. If I had a crystal ball, I would love to see the end result of this quarrel."

"We are all waiting for you to pronounce your new right hand, Ilir. We must be ready for possibly the fight of our lives. Preparation is needed right now. We need guidance," Pashko said.

"Deda Doli, do you want to be my right hand, or you, Agim Balaj? Who wants this job? Fiton, do you want this? How about you, my *kumar*? Anyone who wants this job is an insane man. Just raise your hand, and it's yours. Why do I need only one advisor? I have all of you to agree or disagree with me. You all have good minds. Some skilled with our gambling business, others better with a knife or gun. Some of you have skills selling merchandise that comes to us. George, Henry, Val? You have proven yourselves as loyal men to me. Why is any one of you better than another? If I name one of you, I hurt the others. You don't get more money for Hamdi's place next to me. We will have a circle of men as in the old clans. Age and experience will dictate the respect you deserve. Now let's discuss our next move," Ilir said.

One of the bodyguards entered the office and pointed to his own ear, signaling to Ilir that he needed a word with him. Ilir excised himself and went into the next room.

"Mr. Marku, we have some news that is distressing. Two of your men have been gunned down not very far from here. On Boston Road. Our guys were getting gas, and four men walked up to their car and assassinated them," the bodyguard said.

"Do you have names?" Ilir asked.

"Gjovalin Shkreli and Tony Camaj. Young guys, it's a shame."

"Witnesses?"

"We just got the call. One of the detectives on our payroll said they were both shot multiple times. That's all I have at the moment."

Ilir walked slowly back into his office. His head was hung low.

"The Russians killed two of our men just now. They were new associates of ours. They were not very long in our family. Right here in the Bronx," Ilir said.

"They are showing us that no Albanian is safe even in our own backyard. I suggest it's time for us to garner our forces and be ready for another attack," Dedi Doli said.

"It's curious to me that we hit them on the head and they get us at our knees. I would have expected them to try for Ilir or one of us," Agim Belaj said.

Ilir rotated his chair from behind his desk and faced Valbona.

"What is your opinion, Val?" Ilir asked.

Valbona was surprised at the boss's question. She was caught momentarily off guard but recovered well.

"This is typically Russian. They will pick away at us, making our ranks jumpy and out of sorts. This message will send rumors throughout our group," Valbona said.

"What do you suggest?" Ilir said.

"I propose we not respond as they think we will. We should follow their lead and hit their lower ranks as well. I would go with Frankie Aloshi and Frank Ujkay. Again to Brooklyn in the

Russians backyard. I will work with the Italians again and take out one of the Russians income streams. I have a good place in mind," Valbona said.

"Keep that place close to yourself. Why the Italians again?" Ilir said.

"For one, they are expert at executing a plan. This attack will also signal to the Russians that we are joined at the hip. It may force them to the table," Valbona surmised.

"I like this thinking. Anyone have any other thoughts or objections?" Ilir asked.

"When will this take place? Those Russians are not stupid. They will be expecting that we become defensive. I agree with a counter attack," Deda Doli said.

"The two young men who were killed today will be buried quickly as is their family custom. We pretend that we are devastated by the loss. A big, one-day wake and then a Muslim funeral. Put the word out that both boys were cousins to me. The day after tomorrow, we follow Val's plan. I will review the plan with Val. And speak to the Miceli family. Use whomever you wish in our family Val, just make sure it makes a very big noise," Ilir directed.

"They will hear this from Brighton Beach to Moscow," Valbona promised.

CHAPTER 38

The evening of the day that Ericka Craig confronted her husband, she decided to put some space between her and Marty. Ericka spent a restless night in one of the guestrooms in their home. Marty didn't get much sleep that night either, knowing that his wife was determined to tell their son the truth about his new kidney. It was the first time that the Craigs ever slept apart in their home.

In the morning, Ericka went down to the kitchen to make some coffee and again discuss the troublesome issue with Marty. Her husband was usually up early, starting the day with his ritual workout. This morning, Marty was not in the gym. Ericka found Lloyd sitting at the kitchen table, staring at his laptop. She noticed, for the first time, dark circles around her son's eyes. Lloyd, his hair disheveled, wearing a Boston Latin tee-shirt and boxer briefs, looked as though he hadn't slept much that night.

"Lloyd, honey, are you okay?" Ericka asked.

Lloyd did not respond to his mother.

"Lloyd, what are you doing? What are you looking at?"

Ericka went behind her son to see what he was so intent on looking at. On the screen of his laptop was the photograph of a pretty, young, blonde girl whom Ericka didn't recognize.

"Who is she, Lloyd? Someone you are interested in? She's a very pretty girl," Ericka asked.

"Just a photo I found online. She looks a lot like the girl who comes to me," Lloyd said. The teen never took his eyes from the photo.

"Did you dream of her last night?"

"Mom, she is with me right now. It's not just in the dreams. I see her most of the day."

Ericka's expression went from sympathetic to shock. It took her a moment to compose herself.

"You mean you see her during the day, Lloyd?" Ericka asked.

"For the last few days, it's as if we were boyfriend and girl-friend, without the benefits of course."

"What do you mean?"

"We are getting very close. She understands me, you know, what I've been through with Alport and all."

"Lloyd, this is not real. You are talking as if this girl were real. Don't you understand that, sweetie?" Ericka asked. She felt and heard her voice quiver.

"Mom, but that's the thing. I know she is dead; I know she is in my imagination, but she is as real to me as you are right now. She is so sweet and nice. What they did to her was so fucked up. Sorry, Mom, I didn't mean to swear."

"Tell me more about her. What else do you know?" Ericka asked.

"She had this baby with this boyfriend and had to sell the baby. She didn't want the baby, but she didn't want an abortion, so she sold the baby. She got involved with this bad guy, and… well…she did some more stupid things. There really isn't too much more to tell. Anyway, some of the stuff we talk about is personal."

"What about this bad guy that she was involved with?" Ericka asked. Her shaky voice was gone, and she was now focused on what her son had to say.

"Some Russian dude. She thought she loved him, but he used her. Then another Russian dude raped her. She went to a doctor, and that was it. Then, somehow, I got her kidney. Now her spirit is roaming, and she's here with me. Mom, she thinks you are beautiful," Lloyd said.

"So why are you looking at this photograph if you can see her?"

"It's just a game we play. I try to find actresses and random girls, and we look at them. She pretends that her life could have been different and that we could always be friends."

"Lloyd, sweetie, we really have to go see someone about this. You have your whole life ahead of you. There will be other girls, and, who knows, one day…"

"Mom, right now, I want to help Barbara. She needs closure so she can go to the next level," Lloyd said. He closed the laptop and now focused on his mother.

"Closure? What does that mean?" Ericka asked.

"Those men who killed her need to be brought to justice. They killed her and plenty of other people. Mostly kids and young people, who had their lives taken from them."

"Has Barbara asked you to come with her?" Ericka asked.

"No way. She knows that I'm here and she's there. Maybe one day, we can be friends like that but not for a long time,"

Marty Craig came down to the kitchen. He wasn't carrying the confidence that he normally displayed.

"Hey, what's up, guys? Mother and son private conversation?" If anything, Marty looked a bit sheepish.

"We are just discussing a few things. I think Lloyd needs a rest now. Maybe some breakfast?" Ericka said.

"I'm starved, Mom. Yeah, that would be a good idea."

"Great, after that, a nap, and then we can have a family discussion about things. What do you think?" Ericka said.

"I really would like to go to the mall today. I need a few things," Lloyd said.

"Deal! And then we will have a nice lunch at Peter Luger's. Feel like steak?" Ericka said.

"Dad, how about it?"

"Sure, I'm game," Marty said.

Lloyd went out of the kitchen, smiling with a bounce in his step. The talk with his mother seemed to be good for him.

"Marty, we need to talk again. Either Lloyd is delusional, or there is something to this spirit-world stuff. We have to find out what we can do to help him. I don't know what the right thing to do is at this point. He sees the dead girl right now as if she were a friend. Not only in his dreams," Ericka said.

"Maybe it will pass? I have no idea about this kind of thing. I feel like it's all my fault," Marty admitted.

"Let's not go there right now. Let's just concentrate on helping our son. Then you and I have to make a decision. I'm not sure that I can go on together, knowing what you've done."

"Jesus Christ, Ericka, it's not like you caught me cheating on you!" Marty exclaimed.

"What you did was far worse. I could maybe forgive you if you had a one-night stand, but murder? I don't know."

"I didn't murder anyone. She was as good as dead anyway. If it weren't me, someone else would have paid to get whatever they needed. It was just a matter of timing."

"That's the kind of bullshit story you use to make what you did right. Sometimes money can't buy everything. It certainly hasn't bought my soul, Marty Craig,"

CHAPTER 39

Mickey Roach's favorite button men from his hometown town of Lercara Friddi, Sicily, had been Gabriel Luzzi and Pietro Salerno. Unfortunately a little over a year ago when the Albanian and Italian mobs was doing battle, these two hit men were used to attack Ilir Marku's office, killing a number of Ilir's men. Mickey was forced to use the "B" team for obvious reasons.

Franceso Lucania and Cristofo Rodio were called by Mickey to assist him when needed to work for the Miceli family. They had been in New York for over a month. Mickey always planned ahead.

Younger than Luzzi and Salerno, Lucania, who is a distant relative of Lucky Luciano and Rodio, both twenty-eight, had experience in using a variety of tools to hone their murderous trade. Rodio, who spent time in the Italian army and was an expert on bombs and incendiary devices, and Lucania, who was an electronics expert who could use a knife as well as anyone, were both ready for action. They both fit well into the plan Valbona Marku had devised.

Mickey Roach and the two Sicilians met with Valbona at Maria's Café on Morris Park Avenue. Mickey, superstitious as are most Sicilians, thought the café was a good-luck charm. Maria served her perfect coffee and homemade biscotti. Mickey Roach translated Valbona's words to Lucania and Rodio.

"The human chop shop that the Russians have on Bath Avenue is our target. Two of our people have been monitoring the comings and goings of this place for the last few days on my order. It seems the activity in this building takes place at night," Valbona said.

"How about security?" Mickey Roach asked.

"Aside from the cameras and alarm, there are two Petrov muscle men in the building. They act as the cleanup and disposal unit. No doubt that they are armed. We have no idea of the kind of weapons they have inside. We must assume they are heavy," Valbona replied.

Rodio was smitten by Valbona. Even though Val was dressed as a man and one of Marku's inner circle, the young Sicilian could see her feminine beauty. When she spoke, Rodio gazed at her face, imagining her in his bed.

"How many people in total?" Mickey Roach asked.

"Eight to ten at the most. They have three or four females, probably nurses, and two doctors. A couple of assistants and two soldiers, depending on activity.

"They all die," Valbona said.

"Agreed. They are all part of the organ piracy ring. This will choke the Petrovs right in their pocket. The building must be totally destroyed."

"Naturally. That is the easy part. Is there a rear entrance?" Mickey asked.

"Yes. That is where the bodies generally leave. That door also is monitored," Valbona explained.

"But it's not on the main drag?"

"No. It's secure for us. No one can see the activity. There has been a black hearse with tinted windows backed up to the door. It has a funeral company nameplate on either side of the rear windows."

"Pretty smart. Cops don't usually stop funeral cars."

"Correct. No cop wants to see the body bag or casket. Bad juju," Valbona said.

"Okay, the cops: how often do they drive by?" Mickey Roach asked.

"Their routine patrol takes place more during the day, but you should all know the Six-O precinct house is close by."

"So we need a diversion."

"I would suggest that, yes," Valbona said.

"We can use Coney Island. Make some kind of ruckus so the cops go running there. I got it!" Mickey Roach exclaimed. Valbona could see Mickey's wheels turning.

"You should plan a quick attack. In and out. Take side streets away from the building rather than the Belt Parkway. Here is a map of the area."

"I have guys who know Brooklyn very well. They will be there with us," Mickey Roach said.

"Anything else?" Valbona asked. She put thirty dollars on the table for Maria.

"Yeah, when?"

"Tomorrow night. Gives you a chance today to have these two look things over." Valbona pointed to the Sicilians.

"Not much time, Val."

"I know. We need to play their game. The Russians will never suspect this place to be hit. Then the fun begins."

"You coming?" Mickey asked.

Valbona didn't smile.

"Wouldn't miss it for the world."

CHAPTER 40

Valbona returned to Ilir's office right after meeting Mickey Roach and the two Sicilians.

Selection of the team of Albanians to assist Mickey Roach and his men was foremost on Valbona's mind. Valbona no longer felt the pressure of having to prove herself as a man. Killing Andropova settled any question about Val Marku's bravery. Physiologically, there were no balls in Valbona's pants. Emotionally, she had them bigger than any man. Her blood ran as cold as the waters of the river in the *Tropojë* district of northern Albania after which she was named.

Shpresa Metalia had called Valbona twice and left messages on her voicemail that morning. The first was in English, the second, in Albanian. The Albanian had a sense of urgency.

"Valbona, kom nevoj me u taku me ty! Ku ti me kum sot?" Shpresa said.

Valbona knew her best friend needed to talk, but there wasn't much time to get her plan completely buttoned up. She texted her friend.

Shpresa...wtf...French Roast Crnr 85th Broadway. Forty-five min?

Shpresa replied:

C U there thanks.

Valbona, dressed in a smart, blue blazer, tan slacks, and an open, button-down, collared shirt, arrived before Shpresa, and sat at a corner table by the window facing Broadway. She ordered an American coffee. The waitress, a tall, gorgeous African with skin-tight, black leggings gave Valbona a coy smile and a wink. Valbona snarled back at her, ending any possible girl-on-girl potential hook up.

Valbona gazed out on the people passing the restaurant. Her mind was a borough away in Brooklyn, reviewing the plans for tomorrow night's hit on the Russian organ mill. Shpresa pulled up in her red Mercedes. She had a passenger with her.

"I need to get used to seeing you like this, Valbona. I guess we need to spend more time together," Shpresa remarked. The two old friends embraced and kissed on both cheeks.

"Valbona, you look good. Nice jacket," Rick said. Valbona showed no shock at seeing Shpresa's husband. She and Rick embraced as they always did.

"You two look great. No work today?" Valbona asked.

"Took the day off, and we're just doing some errands. Rick and I wanted to tell you the good news," Shpresa said.

"Oh, my God, don't tell me you are pregnant," Valbona said. They all laughed at the same time. Rick had a nervous, sheepish look on his face.

"Pregnant? Oh, my God, not nearly. We just wanted to tell you that everything is fine with us. I can't tell you how important you are to me, to both of us. Rick knows that I confided in you, and we wanted to tell you in person that we worked things out. Too many years together to throw things away at this point," Shpresa said.

"I acted like an asshole. Never again, I swear on my life," Rick said.

Valbona took a sip of her now-cold coffee. She looked at Shpresa and smiled.

"I'm so happy for you. For both of you. You have no idea what it's like to lose someone you love," Valbona said.

"Thanks so much, Valbona, for being there for Shpresa. I wish I had a friend like you who I could confide in. I guess men don't have that luxury as much as women do…I mean…jeez, I'm sorry, that came out wrong, I guess," Rick said.

"Rick, I'm still a woman. I just have the rights of a man. I understand what you mean. Thank you," Valbona said.

"Excuse me, I have to find the men's room," Rick said. He moved quickly toward the back of the restaurant.

"He seems nervous," Valbona observed.

"For the past week, he's been pacing around the office and the house. Totally distracted. I forgave him, but I'm still hurting. I'm wondering if that red-headed *kurve* is trying to get him back. Anyway, he's been asking me every day about how you're doing. I figured it was a good time for us to see you."

"I'm glad you called. It will all work out. Just learn to trust him again. Try not to smother him," Valbona said. Rick returned to the table.

"So how is Mr. Marku doing? I heard he might be selling some of his property," Rick said.

"I have no idea about that. I'm not involved with his business affairs," Valbona said. She looked at Rick with an incredulous glare. Rick averted his eyes.

"Now I have to find the little girls' room. Be right back," Shpresa said. She stood, kissed Rick on his cheek, grabbed her purse and headed toward the door with the sign reading *Dames*.

"Valbona, I…I…"

"Forget it, Rick. An Italian friend of mine has a favorite expression: 'a fish dies by its open mouth.' Understand?"

"I got it. Not a word will be spoken. And Mr. Marku? Am I all right?"

"Yes. Just remember what I just told you, Rick."

"I hear you loud and clear," he replied.

"And, if you hurt my friend again, I will rip your heart out with my bare hands.

"I got it. I'm so sorry, Valbona. It will never happen again. Trust me on this," Rick pleaded.

"The only person I trust is myself."

CHAPTER 41

The Klinger Pavilion had an active evening planned. One "intake" was scheduled, and the staff was moving rapidly to meet the demand for fresh organs. The schedule at Klinger was always soft. A lot could happen to the buyer as well as the donor in the waning hours before surgery. Dr. Mickele Abramoff demanded flexibility, and his staff knew there was no whining accepted. The Klinger workforce was so well paid in cold cash that there would never be the slightest complaint. The surgical team's lives depended on their full cooperation and total silence.

Buyers came in at a steady pace. Donors were readily available from the Petrov stables. The supply and demand curve was in perfect economic equilibrium.

As fate would have it, Ari Mamantov did his best Romeo work since Barbara Black. This time, a sixteen-year-old, African American girl, a crack addict from the Oceanhill-Brownsville section of Brooklyn, would be the kidney donor to a wealthy, sixty-eight-year-old, Philadelphia slumlord. The recipient of her young organ was in the first stages of renal failure. Blood match was perfect, tissue match was close enough. Her corneas would be going to a nearly blind mother of three in Cleveland. They were willing to pay a premium for additional anonymity. Her husband was a member of the United States Congress and an heir to a fortune. Money was no problem, but leaks could bring the flow of cash to a trickle.

The black girl's second kidney may or may not have a home, depending on the buyer, who was acting silly, trying to negotiate a lower price. The Petrov *Bratva* had no patience for offering lower prices. They would rather leave the organ to rot or burn up in their victim's final destination.

Skin, ligaments, and the teenager's other body parts could be held longer than soft tissue, and this added to the overall profit margin for the *Bratva*.

Romeo was keeping his prey quiet and high, watching as Freddy the Rapist had his way with the teen. They would move her to Klinger when the good Dr. Abramoff arrived.

As the surgical staff prepared themselves and the operatory's machines and implements, Valbona Marku did a final check with her team. Mickey Roach was driving another vehicle, a Dodge Caravan with New Jersey license plates. The Dodge, complete with a family of stick-figure people on the rear window and a bumper sticker that read, "Proud Parent of a Paramus High School Honor Student," was a perfect soccer-dad prop. Four murderous, Italian mob soldiers were with him.

Valbona was sitting in the front passenger seat of a black Cadillac Escalade on Cropsey Avenue. Her goal was to destroy the entire building, to leave it in ashes. If anyone were inside, they would be a bonus. As Klinger personnel began entering the building in the dark, it was clear to Valbona and to her people that there would be a bonus round tonight.

Sejdi Rukaj, Ilir Marku's top man in Brooklyn, knew the local streets like the back of his hand. He drove the Escalade. In the rear of the vehicle, the Sicilian button men, Francesco Lucania and Cristofo Rodio, waited patiently to execute Valbona's plan. They had closely studied the building the night before and early that morning. They went through the plan *ad nauseam* until Valbona was convinced it was perfect.

In Sicilian dialect, Rodio spoke with Lucania in a whisper.

"I wish she were sitting back here with me instead of you. I could make her change her mind, really," Rodio said.

"Would you stop? You have talked about her since we met in the café. Have you lost your mind, Cristofo?" Lucania asked.

"Look at her ass. Even through those men's pants, it moves in two different directions at one time. Perfect."

"She will shoot you dead."

"I will lick her until she calls the saints. Believe me, I know what a woman needs."

"And Mickey will cut your throat like a young sheep."

"Don't you see how she looks at me? She is in love, I can smell it. Woman like her give off a certain scent when they want to make love. She is drenched in the aroma of love. Just one time and she will take those silly men's clothes off and get into a nice thong for me. Nothing else, just that thong, a red one," Rodio went on.

"You are struck by the thunderbolt. You have no chance. Anyway, she likes me better," Lucania said.

"My ass. She will make a perfect woman for me. I will marry her one day. Wait, and see," Rodio promised.

"Silence, we have a job to do. Idiot."

A few more of the surgical staff entered the Klinger Pavilion by using the voice-and-fingerprint recognition keypad on the building's entrance. Valbona's headcount was six. She texted Mickey Roach.

Six?

No, eight! Two before you arrived.

Mickey texted back.

We move in two minutes.

Mickey removed the Smith and Wesson 45 from his shoulder harness. He slid the action back. Two of his men did the same. One took an AK-47 Kalashnikov assault rifle from the floor of the vehicle and loaded the clip. He placed the Kalash on his lap.

Mickey Roach typed a few words into his cell phone. He texted some of his men who were at the famous Coney Island Amusement Park. Their job was to start a fight with the locals at Nathan's Famous Restaurant. Within minutes, three Six-O squad cars went speeding down Cropsey Avenue toward Coney Island. The diversion was a success.

Two minutes were up, and Rodio, as planned, made his way to the door to bypass the electronic entrance device. He would take out the cameras as well.

"How do you say in English? One piece of cake," Rodio told Valbona the night before.

As he walked across Cropsey Avenue to the Klinger entrance with a red, white, and green knapsack on his shoulder, a car pulled up in front of the building, ignoring the no-parking sign.

"Vatine...Cristofo...vatine," Mickey Roach said into Rodio's earpiece, warning him to back off.

Rodio made a forty-five degree turn and walked alongside the parked car along the avenue.

"What the hell is this?" Valbona asked.

"Everyone stay calm…*stati calmi*," Mickey Roach said into the microphone in the sleeve of his jacket.

Two men who were sitting in the car's front seats exited the vehicle, none the wiser about Rodio. They went to the rear passenger side, opened the door, and helped a young, black girl out of the car. They both took the girl under her arms and walked the staggering youth to the door. In a moment, they disappeared into the building.

"Okay, now there are ten plus that girl. *Dieci e ragazzu*," Mickey Roach said. The crew heard the count in their earpieces.

"We move in two minutes. Try not to harm the girl," Valbona said.

Mickey didn't translate her command. He would prefer no witnesses. The girl was in God's hands in Mickey's mind.

Rodio returned to the Escalade and moved on Valbona's command. He approached the entranceway again, and, in seconds, the door was open, and he was inside.

The others moved quickly. Valbona and her crew moved to the back of the property. All, that is, except for Lucania, who followed his fellow Sicilians into the front door with Mickey and the rest of his crew.

Rodio killed the alarm on the back door, opening it for Valbona and the others. Everyone was inside.

"Looks like they are on the next floor up," Mickey said.

Rodio placed his knapsack and some plastic explosives with charges strategically on the first floor.

The others moved quietly up the staircase. Freddy was sitting in the hallway, reading a Russian girly magazine. Lucania dispatched him with a swipe of his stiletto. The rapist died much too easily. One down.

Mickey and his men could hear the clanking of what sounded like pots and pans being moved around. It was the medical trays and surgical instruments being prepared for the black girl's evisceration. The sound of music was wafting into the hallway. It was Van Morrison's "Moondance."

Well, it's a wonderful night for a moondance with the stars up above in your eyes....

Mickey gave the signal, and his men moved into Operating Room Number 1.

The surgical staff, startled by the sudden intrusion stepped away from what they were doing. The operating table was empty. The girl was not yet in the room. Dr. Abramoff was last to notice the raid.

"What are you doing here? This is a surgical ward. Get out immediately," Abramoff demanded.

Mickey Roach dropped the doctor where he stood with a 45 headshot. Abramoff's head exploded onto the wall behind him. The low-hanging lighting was covered with blood and brains.

The Kalash burst into action. The Russian-made rifle cut down the other doctor and three assistants, including the sexy Sonja whom Abramoff lusted after and the bad-toothed anesthesiologist.

"Six down," Mickey said into his sleeve.

Ari Mamantov was in another room. Hearing the shots ring out, Ari ran for the stairs, taking them three at a time. He ran until he was face to face with Val Marku. She lifted her Glock 40 millimeter pistol up and waited. She wanted to see his face before she fired.

"Please, don't shoot," Ari pleaded.

Valbona didn't listen.

"Seven," Valbona said into the mic attached to her jacket lapel.

That left three.

Three nurses preparing the drugged, sleeping girl for surgery moved to the back of the room where they was about to meet their doom. Lucania moved quickly. He buried his knife into the chest of the nearest surgical-blue-dressed woman. Two of Mickey's men shot the other two dead as Valbona entered the prep room. She didn't flinch at the carnage.

"Val, now what? It's not good to leave a witness," Mickey Roach said. He pointed at the black girl on the gurney.

"Witness? She saw nothing. Carry her down to the car. We will drop her along the way," Valbona said.

Mickey Roach shook his head in disagreement.

Three of the men took the child like a ragdoll from the gurney.

"Everyone out to the cars. No running. Take the girl to the back door. I'll bring the van," Mickey said. He was as calm as if he were picking up groceries.

Valbona walked out of the building to the Escalade with Lucania and Sejdi Rukaj. Less than a minute later, Rodio followed, smoking a cigarette.

Rodio stomped out the butt and entered the vehicle. Calmly, he took an electronic device from his jacket pocket. The explosion rocked the entire neighborhood. The blast and fireball shattered all of the windows from the Klinger Pavilion onto the sidewalk and pavement of Cropsey Avenue. The building was engulfed in flames. Secondary explosions rocked the cars.

"Now drive away slowly. Follow me until we get to the designated street. Then we scatter," Mickey said.

Valbona smiled at the two Sicilians in the rear of the Escalade.

Rodio smiled from ear to ear. He whispered in Lucania's ear.

"See, I told you she liked me."

CHAPTER 42

The explosion at the Klinger Pavilion shook Brighton Beach, but it reverberated to Moscow, Kiev, and all other cities in the former Soviet Republic where the Russian mafia flourished.

The next morning, the NYPD placed a Mobile Command Unit at the scene. Uniformed police from the Six-0, Brooklyn Borough Command, fire inspectors, forensic teams from NYPD headquarters, and several coroner's office vans blanketed the scene. A dozen men were combing through the rubble. The NYPD photography unit was taking video and still shots of the wreckage and what looked like human remains. Two backhoes and a demolition team were waiting further instruction to start sifting through the ruins of the masonry.

Only three of the many news trucks equipped with satellite dishes on their roofs remained at the scene since the night before. It was a media circus just after the explosions.

Most of the Russian families, both here and in the old country, began questioning Boris Petrov's leadership and naturally so. Once there was an interruption in business when cash flow was diminished, the pawns may be to blame, but the bosses are totally accountable.

The morning after the slaughter on Cropsey Avenue while Mickey Roach debriefed Gino and Valbona was explaining the outcome to Ilir, Boris Petrov was licking his wounds.

Petrov, Anton Trapanov, Andrey Aleksandrovich, and a small army of the *Bratva* were at what used to be their cash cow, the Klinger Pavilion. They all stood outside the yellow police lines on the closed Cropsey Avenue asphalt. Some of the tar had melted and rehardened from the incredible heat given off by the fire.

"Gone, nothing to salvage. How do we start to rebuild? To find someone like Abramoff and the others is not a simple task," Boris Petrov lamented.

"To say nothing of the building and the equipment. Tens of millions," Trapanov added.

"How did we allow this to happen? Why wasn't this place better secured?" Petrov demanded.

"Who could have predicted this as a target? It was simply not considered. The place worked well without any problems or visibility for years," Alexsandrovich said.

"How many of our people were in that inferno?" Petrov asked.

"We have no idea how many were here on the team. Two of our people are missing and presumed dead," Trapanov said.

"Have the police been able to find remains?" Petrov asked.

"Bits and pieces. It will take DNA testing if the families are lucky enough to find some bones, some teeth," Trapanov said.

"Once again, we are not certain who our enemy is. Is it the Albanians alone, or are they together with those Bronx Italians? The fucking Chinese?" Petrov said.

"Not the Albanians. At least, they were not alone. They are not smart enough to pull this off. It looks like a combined effort to me," Trapanov said.

"And so now how do we respond? We are thinking *priyome*, a chess move to go after their pawns and they take a bishop. This does not make us look good to our partners, Boris," Alexsandovich said.

"Screw those old-country guys. They have no idea what we are living with over here. What would they advise anyway? Make peace; war is no good for the bottom line. That is what they would say. If we do that, we may as well go back to Russia and wait in lines for meat and toilet paper," Trapanov replied.

"So your advice is to hit back, Anton?" Petrov asked.

"And hit them hard. No more going after their pussy-ass pawns. We go for the king, we make a move to win, and we hit Miceli, his wife, his mutt kids, the fucking dog, all of them. And we do it yesterday. No more waiting, mourning, acting like scared children," Trapanov insisted.

Anton, you are acting out of emotion. Some of my men have been watching the Miceli home in Manhattan. He and his family, yes, and the dog, are gone. They've been gone for days. We have no idea where they are," Alexsandrovich said. His smarmy tone, meant to upstage Trapanov in front of their boss, infuriated his nemesis.

"Then the underboss. That Gino is an easy target. We take him and his crew out without mercy and show these pigs who we really are," Trapanov said. He was furious at Alexsandrovich to the point that he entered into the smaller man's personal space.

"So now we are fighting in the street with each other like dogs. Anton, stop it now. We go after their so-called leader and send yet another message to the Miceli family. We will bring Miceli out of hiding and to the table after his friend is gone," Petrov said.

"And if we fail?" Alexsandrovich asked.

Trapanov composed himself. He knew he had gotten his way with Petrov. He pointed a crooked finger at Aleksandrovich.

"Failure is not an option."

CHAPTER 43

Ericka and Marty Craig were still sleeping in separate beds.

"It's because Dad is snoring," Ericka told Lloyd, but the teen wasn't stupid. He could tell that in, the last few days, things were icy feelings between his parents. Lloyd had no idea he was the cause of the rift, so he stayed out of it.

The night of the Klinger Pavilion bloodbath, a major change took place in Lloyd's relationship with his dead friend.

Lloyd knocked on his mother's bedroom door

"Hey, Mom, can you come downstairs. I have to tell you something," Lloyd said.

Lloyd walked down the hall and called out to his father.

"Dad? Are you up? Need to chat about something."

Ericka and Marty came out of their respective rooms and saw Lloyd walking down the massive staircase. They followed.

"What now?" Marty said. The remark was almost under his breath.

"Be prepared, Marty. Now may be a good time to admit what you did," Ericka urged.

"I doubt it."

Lloyd went into the kitchen. It seems that most important family discussions take place in the kitchen.

"What's the matter, sweetie?" Ericka asked. She was biting her lower lip ever so slightly, awaiting more craziness from her son.

"Barbara is gone," Lloyd said.

"Gone? What do you mean, gone?" Ericka said. Marty was about to ask the same question.

"She went to the next place. She just came to me and said goodbye. It's amazing. I know she's dead, but she was as vivid and alive as you two are right now. Then she just vanished just like that," Lloyd snapped his fingers to show that, in an instant, things were over.

"What did she have to say?" Ericka said. She glanced at her husband. Marty never bought into the spiritual thing, and he hadn't become an overnight believer. The smirk on his face was telling.

"Barbara said that her spirit was freed, that justice was served. She said that the people who killed her are all dead. All killed. She was going to see her mom and dad before she went on. One final time, probably in a dream or a sign or something. They have no idea she's even dead."

"Okay, so you can move on now, too?" Marty asked, the tone of his voice more irritated than sympathetic.

"Marty, please!" Ericka shouted. "Go on sweetie."

"Funny thing, Barbara turned on YouTube on my computer to show me a news story. There was an explosion in Brooklyn. Barbara said her murderers were all killed in that explosion.

A random explosion," Lloyd explained. He seemed like his old self for the first time in a long time.

"What else did she say, sweetie?" Ericka asked. Marty cleared his throat.

"She was really pretty, all dressed up in a nice outfit, and her hair was real nice. She was smiling a lot."

"So she said nothing else?" Ericka said.

"She did. Dad, don't get all pissed off at me. Barbara said that I shouldn't be upset with you, and she said to tell you that too, Mom. She said Dad did what he had to do to help me. Dad, Barbara told me the whole story, how you paid for my kidney, how they have done this many times, and to many people. She is happy they are where they are. Barbara said it wasn't in a good place," Lloyd said.

"Anything else?" Ericka asked. Her husband was staring at Lloyd, his mouth agape.

"Oh, yeah, she said her life was pretty screwed up and that she was happy that her kidney and other stuff would help other people. I was closest to her age, and that's why she came to me. But I can tell you both something I haven't said before. I'm glad Barbara is gone. I'm glad that she went on to the next step. I was really thinking that I wanted to be with her a few days ago. I mean, really be with her. I never felt like that ever before, and I hope I never get to that point in my life again ever."

"Will she come back, ya' think?" Ericka asked.

"No, never, she said that was it. She thanked me and told me to take care of her kidney, and, bam, she was gone."

Ericka looked at Marty to see if he was still making the disbelieving faces and rolling his eyes. He wasn't. Not because he believed in any of this Barbara talk; he was just happy that it was over.

"Let's celebrate. How about some cocoa and cookies?" Ericka suggested.

"Sure, I like those Toll House ones you have, Mom," Lloyd replied.

"I'll pass on the cookies. How about a yogurt?" Marty chimed in.

The three Craigs talked for about an hour, never mentioning Barbara Black again. They spoke mostly about Lloyd's online studies and his return to Boston Latin.

They all went to their respective bedrooms. Ericka to hers, Marty to the guest room, and Lloyd to his bedroom.

Marty was almost asleep when he felt his wife snuggling up behind him.

"Wow, that's nice," Marty said.

"Marty, I love you. Just one thing, okay?"

"What's that?"

"Never do anything like this again."

"I never will."

CHAPTER 44

Rick Metalia received a telephone call from the redhead. In spite of his admonition never to call him again, the Russian sexpot was not having his brush off.

"I want to see you. I have something important to tell you," the redhead implored.

"I have nothing to say to you. I almost lost my marriage because of my own stupidity, and that's not happening again. I love my wife. I told you that from day one. "

"Your wife has a friend. He is in great danger."

"What, what are you saying? Who?"

"You know, I would rather tell you in person."

"Not happening."

"You know this Italian, Gino? I had, let's say a friend, last night who got very, very drunk. He said some things that I never wanted to know."

"And?"

"And they are going to get him tonight. I don't know where, but he said they have a snitch. They know where he is hiding, I just wanted you to know, and that's all."

"So I'm supposed to believe you? How do I know that you are not giving me some bullshit? That you aren't being paid by those slick friends of yours?" Rick said accusingly.

"Because I hate these fuckers. What they did to my sister in Russia, I will never forget and never forgive. This is my gift to you, Rick."

"Gotta go. Please don't ever call me again."

Rick hit the off button on his cell phone. He thought about blocking and deleting the redhead's number but decided not to, just in case her call was legitimate.

Rick scrolled down on the address book on his cell phone to Ranno, Gino and hit the send button.

Rick's name came up on Gino's cell screen.

"Rick Metalia, to what do I owe this honor? How are you, pal?" Gino asked.

"You around? I just got a strange call that you may want to know about," Rick said.

"Sure, don't say anymore right now. Do you know that place where we had lunch with your bride last time? In an hour?" Gino said.

"I can be there in twenty minutes," Rick said.

"Done."

Gino adored Rick and wasn't at all bothered by Rick and Shpresa's problems. That was life, and Gino was not able to throw that first stone. Despite his personal feeling and trust toward Rick, Gino was not in a position to trust anyone. After the Cropsey Avenue annihilation, no one associated with the Miceli family was safe. Gino had already relocated from his Riverdale apartment to a well-guarded and fortified house along the water in the Throggs Neck section of the Bronx.

Joey Clams, C.C., Mickey Roach, and Gino left the sanctuary, followed by two cars carrying eight men, fully loaded, who were there to protect Gino. The meeting place was a small restaurant on Tremont Avenue less than a mile away.

Louis Restaurant is a small, family place that is not at all fancy. Almost a cliché of *The Godfather*, everyone minds his own business, and the veal is the best in the city.

Four of Gino's men took a table inside the restaurant, while four of the others stayed close to the storefront. Joey Clams parked across the street in the Sisto Funeral Home parking lot, awaiting Rick's arrival. Rick parked his red Benz in front of Louis Restaurant and found the meter machine to pay for street parking. Rick went inside and found a booth.

Joey Clams, C.C., and Mickey Roach walked across Tremont Avenue with Gino. Gino found Rick; the others sat at a table nearest the door.

"You brought the whole army, Gino," Rick said. They hugged closely. Gino always felt awkward hugging much taller men. Not because he was unaffectionate toward male friends, he just felt silly or self conscious when tall guys had to bend so low.

"No choice, pal. I'm in the hot chair at the moment. The Brighton Beach crowd wants to make me a memory," Gino said.

"I'm glad you are aware of that. Here is what I want to tell you. This Russian broad I know…"

"I'm up to speed on that, Rick. I hope you know what you're doing," Gino said.

"No…listen. It's not about her. She's out of my life, but she called to warn me that they are planning a hit tonight…on you."

"That just sent a shiver up my spine. I wouldn't lie about that," Gino admitted.

"Her friend said they know where you are. Evidently, you have a leak somewhere."

"Or this call to you is a set-up," Gino surmised.

"I thought of that. She is a lot of things but not a liar. I'm convinced she has a grudge for these guys. They turned her twin sister into a prostitute. When the girl tried to get out of that life, she disappeared. Likely another one of these chop-shop girls. I think she is sincere, Gino," Rick said.

"Better to be safe anyway, right?" Gino said.

"If they know where you are, they are probably watching us now."

"I suspect you're right. I appreciate you calling to warn me."

"Gino, look, my wife told me she confided in you when I was off the deep end. She was vulnerable. Another man would have taken advantage of this situation. You are a good friend and a good guy. I hope you aren't judging me for…"

"C'mon, Rick. No way. Who am I to point a finger? That's not me, and you know it," Gino said.

"And the night I ran into Valbona in Brooklyn?" Rick asked.

"Never happened."

"What can I do to help you, Gino? Just say the word."

"There is something. Just don't feel obligated, okay? If you don't want to get involved, I totally understand."

"Okay, tell me."

"We have some men coming down from Boston. They don't know shit about the area. They need to be moved to a place where they can set up and be ready for a fight. Maybe five days, maybe a week. Any ideas?"

"I have it covered. I have a townhouse in The Village, owner is in Europe, and I can sublet it. Safe place, my pocket. A gift to you," Rick said.

"That's very generous. You won't come out second with me, Rick."

"I can arrange to have them picked up, fed, the whole thing. Just one question. When?" Rick asked.

"Day after tomorrow, noon. La Guardia shuttle."

"Done. Another question, what about guns and stuff? I have a guy. Anything you need?"

"My guys, Joey and C.C., that's their thing. Nobody better. I appreciate your loyalty, Rick," Gino said. He stood to shake Rick's hand and embrace him.

"So Rick Metalia isn't a wimp after all?" Rick said.

"Never thought you were. You have that quiet bravery that comes with the territory," Gino said.

"Territory?" Rick asked.

"Yeah, you're Albanian, remember?"

CHAPTER 45

Ilir Marku had not been feeling well for the past few weeks. There was a dull pain in his stomach that, at times, became a bit sharper, especially after he ate a full meal. Thinking he had aggravated a long-ago stomach ulcer, Ilir made a rare visit to Dr. Mark Kaplan who had been his physician for more than twenty years.

Kaplan, a no-nonsense man with a clinical approach to his patients, had a special place in his heart for Ilir. Marku reminded him of his grandfather, who escaped Nazi Germany and the Holocaust and made a magnificent life for himself and his family in this country from less than nothing. Kaplan's medical school bills were all paid for by an endowment, left by his grandfather. Twelve other family members received their education or started their businesses from the funds left to them by their concentration-camp-survivor grandfather.

Kaplan visited Ilir at his home to discuss the results of tests that were taken. The doctor was sensitive to Ilir's security and had been following the news of mob trouble in the area. Mark Kaplan made no judgments.

After the usual Marku greeting and discussion about the doctor's family, the two men got down to business-but not before they were served Turkish coffee made by Ilir's staff and *Rugelach* brought by Dr. Kaplan.

"So tell me, my friend, will I live to be one hundred like my great-uncle in Albania?" Ilir asked.

"Well, there is nothing I see on these tests that would tell me otherwise. The tests all came back good. Except for a fatty liver and a marker for a potential problem in your pancreas, I think that diet and medication will send you on your way to a nice, old age. There are a few more tests that we need to take," Kaplan said.

"You know I have never taken medicine, not even aspirin. What makes you think I'm starting now?

"Because you are in the big leagues now, you old bull. Not for long; six months, and then we check your blood again. I'm not suggesting this, Ilir, it's an order."

"Why would I want to live long anyway? I have lost my desire to do very much. I have really not much to live for."

"That doesn't sound very much like you," Kaplan said.

"Since Lekë died, there is no fire left in me. I think, if you told me I were dying, I would go to Albania and wait to die. No big deal. I will leave everything to my wife, my son in Tirana, and his mother with a little for some others who are special to me. That's all I have left, just money."

"And your other business interests?"

"The vultures are at the door as we speak. Soon, another war, then quiet, then another war. I've lost my stomach for such things, my dear friend."

"I would say you are suffering from depression. I won't prescribe medication for that because I am not that kind of doctor and you are not that kind of patient. My suggestion, if you don't mind hearing it?" Kaplan said.

"You will tell me even if I say no."

"Correct. So here goes. Why not retire? Who knows how much life is left? Why not go to Tirana, spend time with your son, see him flourish, and do good things with your money? Or stay here, eat yourself alive with sadness, and die miserably," Kaplan said.

Not many people with maybe the exception of Ilir's friend and confidant, Hamdi Nezaj, would speak this bluntly to a man of his character and background.

Ilir stared for a long twenty seconds before responding.

"You studied your psychiatry books well, Dr."

"That was never my thing. I study people, and I know when someone has checked out. You have all but checked out of this life. First, pains in the stomach then your head, and you will talk yourself into being a sick man. That is not you, Ilir. Take my advice, and start a new life."

"It's not as simple as that, my friend."

"Tell me why? You first select those around you whom you trust. That will be good to your people, and that will not flush your legacy down the damn toilet. Then you empower them all the while you are packing up and making the move back to the land of your father. There is a lot that can be done in Albania. Besides, you don't really know your son. Sorry, I've forgotten his name."

"His name is Adem."

"So he may not be the son who wants to be in your world, but my friend, he is still your son. It's not too late," Kaplan said.

"My father often said that the Jews were smarter, that I should respect and learn from them," Ilir remembered.

"And my grandfather often told us of how the Albanian people hid and protected him and so many other Jews from the Nazis while they were fleeing out of Europe."

"And here we are together, planning a new life for me. If those old men didn't survive, we would not even have known life," Ilir said.

"So here is my prescription. I'm writing you a script for the medication that you will take, and my handshake that I will visit you and your son, Adem, in Tirana this year."

"You will be impressed by Adem," Ilir promised.

"Of that, I have no doubt, my friend, no doubt at all."

CHAPTER 46

Gino and his crew of guys left Louis Restaurant unscathed and headed back to the now not-so-safe house.

At end of the bustling, storefront-laden, largely Italian neighborhood of Tremont Avenue, a huge catering hall, the Marina del Rey, stands in front of the glistening waters of the mouth of the East River. The river bends under the Throggs Neck Bridge into Little Neck Bay, where hundreds of pleasure boats are docked and sail the usually calm waters.

About three quarters of a mile to the right of the Marina del Rey, Schurz Avenue winds into Pennyfield Avenue. A quick right on an unnamed lane and two blocks straight to the water is where Gino had taken temporary refuge. A thousand yards from the State University of New York Maritime College and the large, docked ship that dominates the campus, the house is a figurative million miles from the Bronx. Not many Bronx addresses have a bucolic feel at their front entrances or their own beaches at the rear.

"So what do you think, pal o' mine? Do we move again before they hit?" Joey Clams asked.

"Not so sure, Joey. Let me hear myself think for a minute. I say we meet them here on our own turf. After all, this is the Bronx, our home, and our stomping grounds. Let them do battle on our side of the chessboard. We have plenty of help, right?"

"The Boston group won't be ready," Joey Clams said.

"What about the Albos? Ain't they in this with us?" C.C. asked.

"Of course, Charlie. It's a call away. Ilir Marku will send the best he has if I ask. Then these Russians will know once and for sure that they are battling both factions. Then let's see how they react," Gino said.

"Gino, you have to be concerned about the water. The Russians can make a two-pronged attack on us. They know you are here, and they will do anything they can to take you out," Mickey Roach pointed out.

"See, Mickey, you do play chess. You're thinking two, maybe three, or even four moves ahead. So what's your plan?" Gino asked.

"We meet them on the street and on the water. They won't be expecting us on the water," Mickey replied.

"Bingo. The element of surprise! Once you take out their pawns, the big pieces are exposed. Then we strike hard. They think they have the advantage of surprise, and we nullify their surprise with our own…beautifully played," Gino said.

"It's sort of like shock and awe," Joey Clams said.

"I'm happy that we are finally drawing the line in the sand with these Russian fucks," C.C. said with passion.

"Charlie, they are just our current opponents, nothing more, nothing less. There will be others if we win here. Of that, I have absolutely no doubt," Gino said.

Gino sent Joey Clams to see Ilir Marku. The Albanians were ready for action and moved quickly to defend their Sicilian mafia friends.

Ilir called Valbona into his office, which was more like an armed camp than a workplace.

"Val, you are making quite a name and reputation for yourself," Ilir stated.

"It is not a reputation that I am after, *Babë."*

"What then?"

"First, respect; I need to have your men look at me as one of them. So one day if I am called upon, I can lead them," Valbona said.

"Quite a lot to ask for someone in the business for only a short time, don't you think?"

"*Babë,* with all respect, I was in this life the moment I met your son until the moment he was taken from us. I lived this life with him. He shared everything with me. It may be a lot for you to understand, but Albanian women today are different than we were years ago in the old country. We may not carry water in jugs from the river to the village, but we share our men's burdens completely."

"Times have changed," Ilir agreed.

"Yes, and they will change again, with my…" Valbona stopped, and tears welled into her eyes.

"I have counseled you before about wearing your emotions on your sleeve, Val, and here you are, showing me tears."

"Some tears even a man can have, no?" She managed to keep the tears from flowing down her cheeks.

"You were about to say that things would change for your children. Are you planning to adopt?" Ilir said with a sarcastic hint to his voice.

"No, for a weak moment I forgot my place."

"Valbona, I am now talking to the woman not the man; forgive me this one indiscretion. Your sworn oath may not last forever. You are still young, and there may still be a chance for you to be a real woman, to have children, *Mash'Allah*. That is the last we will speak of this," Ilir said.

"What did you call me for, *Babë?*"

"Gino Ranno needs us in force tonight. I must still be protected. After all, they have once before after Lekë died tried to attack my home. Nic Ceca will see to my protection. You will go with our people, as many as we can spare, to meet these Russians. This skirmish may be the turning point in this war, and who knows who will come out ahead after tonight? You will be in great personal danger, but, if I left you here, then I-and you-lose face. Do you understand?"

"Completely, *Babë*. I will do my best. I am not at all afraid. It is the Russians who should have fear."

"Trust me, Val, they are fearless. If they lose, there are worse things than death, and they are aware of that more than any people on earth. Do not underestimate their ferocity."

CHAPTER 47

The evening darkness slowly fell over Throggs Neck. Along Tremont Avenue, the restaurants, pizzerias, ice cream joints, and bars were teaming with patrons. The dazzling Marina del Rey had an event that jam-packed the catering hall's sprawling parking lots. The neighborhood was alive and thriving.

If Rick Metalia's redhead had her information right, pretty soon, Throggs Neck would be lit up like the Macy's Fourth of July fireworks show way down on the other end of the East River. If the information was bogus, so what? It was good practice.

Two thirty-foot, cabin cruisers were borrowed from friends in the contracting business, made guys who weren't afraid to do an insurance job if their boats came back all shot up. The boats were quiet and still in the East River waters about two hundred yards away from the house where Gino and his men were holed up.

One cruiser, a Sea Ray Pursuit 365 Sci, was just out of the showroom. The three hundred and fifty horsepower Mercury engine made this boat formidable if the Russians came with anything less. The other, a Malow Mainship 32, was slower, but it could do the job that was needed tonight.

The boats, carrying four men each, all armed with automatic weapons, were barely visible from the house in the evening darkness save for a silhouette against the huge Maritime College ship. The men were lying low, anticipating any approaching vessel.

Mickey Roach orchestrated the Italio-Albanian defense both on the water and on land in front and to the sides of the fortified house. Twenty-two men or if Valbona Marku was considered a man, twenty-three, were breathlessly awaiting a Russian assault team. M16 automatic rifles, one AK 47, and a dozen or so Uzi submachine guns were in the hands of the people protecting Gino and the Miceli family name.

Joey Clams and C.C. placed three M18A1 Claymore anti-personnel mines with M57 firing devices and M4 electric blasting caps. Vietnam-War trained, Joey Clams and C.C. used these mines for two full tours against the Viet Cong. There was no way of knowing how many enemies died at the hands of C.C. and Joey Clams in two years.

Still in use today by the United States Military, the Claymore is a command-detonated and directional mine. Simply put, the device is remote controlled and sprays metal balls into a kill zone. No passenger car or person could penetrate a one-hundred-and-ten-yard area in or around a Claymore.

The frontage of the house that was the Miceli Family safe house was only seventy-five feet wide. The Russians had nothing to counter these mines unless they drove a tank down Pennyfield Avenue.

Valbona and Mickey's two Sicilians, Rodio and Lucania, were stationed in the front living room of the house. They stood to the sides of a twenty-five feet bay window that was identical to the window that overlooked the water in the house's rear kitchen. Three Albanian bodyguards manned the kitchen window while three, beefy, Miceli men lay armed and camouflaged on the small, sandy beach along the river shore. If anyone got past the cabin cruisers, they would be cut down before they could enter the house.

Only an armed helicopter could penetrate the defense that Mickey Roach had laid out. That kind of attack was highly unlikely as the house was in the flight path of both LaGuardia and JFK Airports. Just in case, Joey Clams and C.C. had an "Arash" in their arsenal. An Arash is a twenty-millimeter, anti-helicopter, shoulder-fired weapon that the Iranians developed. Gino's people were well prepared for any assault.

Gino was surveying the manpower and firepower. He stopped at the Arash.

"Joey, where and how did you guys get your hands on this freakin' thing? And those mines?" Gino asked.

"Me and C.C. picked them up in Miami last month, and we carried them on the plane as a personal item," Joey Clams joked.

"Why was I dumb enough even to ask that question?" Gino asked.

"Don't worry, Gino, if they don't work, we can return them for a Craftsmen mechanics tool set," C.C. added.

"Another comedian. Same as when we were kids. Ask a question, get your balls broken," Gino said.

Gino himself was armed with a sawed-off shotgun and a fifteen-shot, 9mm pistol.

"Gino, better you stay away from anything mechanical. I heard you once got hurt by a stapler in your office," Joey Clams said.

"Not true, Joey, it was a girl in the office who slammed it on the side of my head. That was thirty years ago," Gino exclaimed.

"Lucky for you she didn't staple something else," C.C. jeered.

All three old friends were like kids again. They broke out in hysterical laughter.

Valbona saw no humor in the situation. The two Sicilians couldn't understand a word that was being said, and Mickey Roach just shook his head.

Suddenly, lights from a vehicle, the first of the evening, were bouncing off the adjoining homes on the pitch-black street. Mickey had his men sever the wires on the streetlights near the safe house.

"*Zittita*, quiet. *Attenzione*," Mickey ordered.

"It's just a kid and his girlfriend looking for a place to park," Valbona said. She used the curtains on the bay window to hide herself.

"Wrong. That was two guys. One had a wig," Joey Clams said. Joey was using infrared specs.

"How so sure?" Mickey Roach asked.

"The Adam's apple. Plus, he was a real ugly broad. That was a scouting expedition. They think the place is prime for a hit. I think we outplayed them," Joey Clams said.

"Any movement out there?" Mickey Roach inquired. He was talking into his mic to the guys on the boats.

"We are watching a light that's heading in this direction. Couple a thousand yards away, but it's definitely bouncing on the water," a voice informed him.

"Be ready, we've already had some surveillance in the front," Mickey Roach said.

"Roger that."

Rodio was standing to the side of Valbona. He had all to do not to bite his hand. Val was dressed in a pair of black, chino slacks, a cut-off sweatshirt, and turned-around, Yankee baseball cap. Nothing that would say sexy to any normal man. The very proximity to Valbona was simply driving the testosterone-laden Sicilian crazy. Lucania, from the other side of the bay window, noticed his partner's near swooning. He put his two fingers and thumb together on his right hand in the typical Italian expression of "what the hell is wrong with you?" Lucania waived his hand at Rodio, who seemed to snap out of his love stupor with his friend's momentary intervention.

"Just about a thousand yards and heading our way." A voice came over Mickey Roach's earpiece.

Just then, several vehicles, lights off, could be seen moving in the distance down the unnamed lane, directly in front of the safe house. The attack was now. Rick's redhead was dead-on accurate.

"Here we go, lock and load," Joey Clams said.

The distinct sound of metal clanging echoed through the house. Joey Clams stood ready to initiate the Claymore mine if anyone or anything came near the front yard. He didn't have to wait very long.

One of the vehicles slammed over the concrete curb on the street and came to rest a few feet onto the small, grass lawn, just twenty feet from the center Claymore. The car's four doors swung open. Four stocky men with ski masks and AK-47 rifles exited the car and started walking toward the front of the house.

The assassins had a nonchalant cockiness that seemed almost choreographed. Joey Clams snapped the Claymore blasting cap, sending thousands of lethal metal balls into the flesh and bones of the oncoming Russians. All four men were killed instantly, their car riddled with the destructive balls, which sounded like a hail of metallic rain. The explosion and pellets of the first Claymore imploded windows on cars and houses within three hundred feet. Dogs barked and howled from blocks away.

A second car drove by, spraying the front of the house with automatic fire from three weapons. The wooden front door of the home was shattered to pieces, and the bay window was a memory. Glass and wood shards sprayed throughout the first floor, sending everyone ducking for cover. Rodio was hit by flying glass and wood on the left side of his face and neck. He dropped to the floor and was motionless.

The car drove into the driveway of the house next door. The gunmen exited the car and assaulted the side of the safe house, peppering the windows on both floors with hundreds of bullets. Joey Clams let loose with the second Claymore, which scattered the steel and brass pellets in a sixty-degree spray. The assault ended on the left.

The waterside assault fared no better for the Russian hit squad. The boat was a motorized catamaran that exposed its four occupants. The speed at which the attacking vessel approached the tiny beach would have been enough to ground the boat, allowing the four assassins to storm the house and murder the unsuspecting mob boss, namely, Gino Ranno.

They never came close.

As the Russian neared within fifty yards of the anchored cabin cruisers, the four men on each boat stood and riddled the catamaran with automatic fire. No shots were returned. All four of the Russians were dead; the pathetic vessel came to an easy rest on the safe house beach.

Police sirens could be heard in the distance as two more killers ran to the shattered front door. Mickey Roach dropped one in his tracks while Valbona and Lucania shared the second kill, cutting the assailant nearly in half. The assault was finished. Lucania turned his attention to his fallen friend, Rodio.

Joey Clams and C.C. quickly gathered as many of their weapons as possible, especially their prized Arash, which was never fired. It may be called up for another day, but right now, the boys had to get their guns onto the cabin cruisers and away from the grasp of the soon-to-arrive NYPD.

Valbona ordered her men to leave and return to a designated social club in Morris Park. The other bodyguards disappeared into the darkness of the night.

Gino, Joey Clams, C.C., Mickey Roach, Valbona, Lucania, and the bloodied Rodio waded out to the waiting cabin cruisers for a trip to a friendly dock on City Island.

As they approached the cruisers, there was a problem that they hadn't thought of.

"I can't swim, you stupid bastards," Gino yelled.

"What, swim? You can almost walk out to the friggen boat, Gino," Joey Clams said.

"You can walk, you big fuck. I'll drown, you idiot," Gino said.

"Charlie, grab the midget. I'll take the guns," Joey Clams ordered. C.C. complied and grabbed the boss under his armpits.

Valbona, taught never to show her emotions, began laughing so hard she had to be helped to the boat by Mickey Roach.

"He called me a midget! Did you hear what he called me, Charlie? That's not right."

CHAPTER 48

Eamon Fitzpatrick III, the federal prosecutor in New York City, met with his assistant and a few of his lackey, stone-faced, federal lawyers at the federal plaza building.

"Okay, so what do you get when you cross a Sicilian with an Albanian?" Fitzpatrick asked.

All he got back were blank stares from around the conference table.

"An even crazier motherfucker."

Only Don Wilson dared to chuckle at the boss' joke.

"Look at today's Post headline...MARITIME MURDER... And the Daily News... BRONX MOB SAYS...NOT ON OUR BEACH.

"Any minute, that phone on my desk will ring and the attorney general of the United States of America will ask me what is going on in Dodge City. Then he will ask where we stand with the Miceli case. Then he will call me to Washington as if I'm a child and reprimand me for not moving quickly enough. Then I will come back in a sour mood and fire a few of you bastards," Fitzpatrick said angrily. To say his Irish was up is a total understatement.

"Mr. Fitzpatrick, Miceli's lawyers have us walking into walls. He is good, and he knows it, and our case is not exactly open and shut. We are really forcing the RICO predicates here," Wilson said.

"We are the United States Government…they are piss-ant criminals who deserve never to see the light of day. What am I missing here?" Fitzpatrick banged his red-haired, large, freckled arm on the table for effect.

Fitzpatrick stood over six feet six inches tall and used his height, ample weight, and booming voice to intimidate anyone and everyone in his path.

"Sir, we are trying to meet with Miceli's main counsel this week to come to terms on a few issues," one of the lawyers said.

"Scranton," Fitzpatrick said.

"Sir?" the lawyer responded.

"You will be working in Scranton, fucking Pennsylvania, before the week is out. What is this shit? Trying to meet? Discuss issues? Is anyone here on my page, or do you all need to get thrown to the hick towns? This is New York City. This is where the shit hits the fan. Now listen, and listen well. I want this case put on the fast track. And I want that Gino Ranno nobody wannabe wise guy fuck questioned on this mess up in the Bronx. Go in with NYPD, go in with the fucking Salvation Army if you have to, but I want action from this office… UNDERSTOOD?"

CHAPTER 49

The same morning that the New York tabloids blabbed about the continuing mob war in the city and Federal Prosecutor Eamon Fitzpatrick III had his temperamental hissy fit, Gino Ranno and his group came together to discuss their next move.

This time, Gino called upon his friend Rick Metalia for a temporary lease of the townhouse he managed in Greenwich Village. Seven thousand dollars a week was a bargain. Rick wouldn't take a commission and Gino knew that he would make his friend whole at some future date. Right now, living just off Bleeker Street near Sixth Avenue was like turning back the hands of time.

"Again, I am living in the shadows of Our Lady of Pompeii Church. My great-grandmother and grandfather lived around the corner. My grandmother, my Nani, received all her sacraments in this church, including her marriage to my Sicilian Nono. They found some sanctuary of sorts in this parish, and now look at me. I'm finding shelter here myself, being guarded by my closest friends, a few Sicilians from the old town, and some Albanians, one of which is a woman who is a man. Who could ever imagine this kind of craziness? I was a nice guy who made an honest buck," Gino said.

"Seriously, Gino, and I can say this to you because I know you our entire lives. Nice guy? C'mon, the exterior may have been *sympatico,* but you always had the instinct to get whatever you needed to get. You could be ruthless with a ballpoint pen," Joey Clams said.

"But now lives are on the line. It was different for me to be in business," Gino said.

"Six of one, half a dozen of another," Joey Clams said.

"I never understood what that meant, that six-of-one-thing," C.C. said.

"That's because your mother and father dropped you on your head a lot when you were a baby. Just clean the guns C.C., and let the grownups talk," Joey Clams jested.

C.C. flipped him the bird and went back to his oiling and wiping.

Valbona arrived at the new hideaway and was let in by two of Gino's men. Gino gave strict instructions to keep a low profile in this house. No SUVs parked on the sidewalk, no secret-service-looking, two-way communication.

"Just act like we belong here," Gino said to everyone.

Valbona walked in and paid her respects to Gino and Mickey Roach and the boys. She shook everyone's hand but kissed Gino on both cheeks with the sign of respect.

"Gino, with your permission before we talk, I would like to see Cristofo. All night, I was concerned about his wounds."

"By all means, Val," Gino said. He looked at Mickey Roach, who got up from his seat and went to get the Sicilian who was shooting pool in the downstairs family room.

Out of Valbona's vision, C.C. looked at Joey Clams and slowly and silently mouthed the word...C R I S T O F O. Joey bit his upper lip to prevent a disrespectful laugh.

Rodio walked into the study where the others were sitting. Valbona walked up to the patched-up Sicilian. She greeting him with a handshake and the kiss on both cheeks. Rodio nearly dropped to one knee.

"You were very lucky," Valbona said.

Rodio understood some of what Valbona was saying. When he didn't, he looked at Mickey Roach for the translation.

"Grazie...yes, thank you," Rodio replied.

"Are you in much pain?" Valbona asked.

Rodio looked at his boss. The translation came back a bit different.

"Can I play with your dick?" Mickey Roach said in Sicilian dialect. Gino nearly fell from his chair. Rodio was momentarily stunned.

"No, Val, he's all right. He is what we call in our language, *testa di scheku*, the head of a donkey. Nothing can penetrate that hard head of his," Mickey Roach said.

"*Allura signiorina giacondu pool?*" Rodio invited Val to shoot some pool. He really wanted to get Valbona downstairs, perhaps alone."

"*Dopo, dopo*, maybe later. Now we have men's business to discuss," Gino said.

Valbona nodded her head at Gino, thanking him for saving her and for his compliment.

"Okay, so how is my dear friend Ilir? Is he up to speed with our latest chess move?" Gino asked.

"He sends his respects and regards, Gino. He applauds your bravery. Ilir wanted me to tell you that he knows your family and his family will win so long as we are together against the bear," Valbona said.

"And please tell him that his Val Marku is braver than five men," Gino said.

"Thank you."

"Does he have any suggestions at this point?" Gino asked.

"He thinks that a wounded animal will strike from instinct. We must be on our guard. Three more of our soldiers were hit early this morning in Queens. Much like the two we lost earlier," Valbona reported.

"Just like I thought, they are now attacking our pawns again," Gino said.

"May I speak, Gino?" Mickey Roach asked.

Gino gave him an approving look.

"It may be a good time for us to try for a sit down. They lost last night. They know this morning was just a symbolic jab. I think they would welcome the chance to talk, a chance to save face,"

"Are we risking face here? Will we seem afraid?" Gino asked.

"It will show that we are smarter than they believe us to be. The cops are all over the place, looking for anyone on either side to fart in their pants. Business will come to a halt. The last thing the Russians want is for the Chinese mobs to move in on the action. Money speaks loudly to the Russian people. They have a history of starvation and death."

"Val, what do you think Ilir will say to a sit down?"

"I will have to ask him that question. I cannot speak for him," Valbona said.

"Then what do you think, Val?" Gino prodded.

"I would prefer if they were all dead, but that is not reasonable. Trying for a cease-fire and talks makes sense," Valbona said.

"Please go back, and get his approval. We can work out the logistics and security. I don't trust these Russians as far as I can throw any one of them. Right now, my orders will be to lay low. Having said that, Mickey, make your plans for a frontal assault on their king."

A similar meeting was taking place at Tatiana Restaurant in Brighton Beach.

"They pushed our noses into their shit. We looked like amateur gangsters, like a bunch of *suchka*, like little bitches. I am ashamed," Boris Petrov said.

"And we attack them by slapping them on the wrist this morning, like a *pizda* who was upset with her boyfriend. Now all the cops and the feds will be all over us. A disaster," Andrey Aleksandrovich added.

Petrov glared at Aleksandrovich. The vile word *pizda* he used hit the right button. How could anyone refer to the Petrov *Bratva* as a cunt? Petrov turned his attention to Anton Trapanov.

"You said failure was not an option, Anton. This was your doing. They won, you lost."

"They had to have discovered our plan. Someone inside our circle had to have warned them. They were prepared for our next moves. Someone whispered in the ear of that Ranno," Trapanov insisted.

"So that is your defense? Someone at this table or near to me stabbed us in the back? That is your best argument?" Petrov demanded.

Petrov cocked his head toward Trapanov while looking at three of his enforcers who stood in the wings. Trapanov was given a death sentence.

The enforcers took Trapanov out of the rear door of the closed nightclub. Petrov made sure the condemned man heard his next words.

"Andrey, you are the new brigadier, my right hand. Make sure you don't follow your comrade out the same door."

CHAPTER 50

Anton Trapanov's body was discovered within an hour of his summary execution. Discovered would be the wrong term to use. The location of his body was called in to the Six-0 Precinct in Brighton Beach. Trapanov was lain under the boardwalk one block away from Tatiana Nightclub. Two bullets were put into the back of his head. Clean, simple, efficient, and a warning to any and all *Bratva* members: *If you fuck up you will be eating the sand.*

Boris Petrov was still playing the game. He was not yet ready to concede defeat, although he was getting weary of the questions he was getting from others in his capacity both here in the states and in Russia. Petrov needed a way to save face. A draw at this point would be a victory for him.

Allowing the NYPD to fast track the discovery of Trapanov's body was designed to let Petrov's opponents know his feelings. A brilliant tactical move, it gave a a "tell" to Ilir Marku and Gino Ranno without the luxury of them seeing Boris Petrov's face.

The tabloids jumped all over the story, remote news trucks swarmed Brighton Beach, the New York City Mayor and Police Commissioner scheduled a joint news conference, and, as expected, Eamon Fitzpatrick III was summoned to Washington. The proverbial shit was now hitting the fan.

Valbona returned to the Greenwich Village safe house with Ilir Marku's thoughts on a sit down with the Russians. As luck would have it, Rick and Shpresa Metalia were visiting the property to check on Gino and see if he was satisfied and comfortable with his new digs.

"Now everyone is here, and we can go out for dinner," Gino said.

"Gino, not a good idea," Joey Clams warned.

"Why not? If you think I'm going to hole up in this place like John Dillinger, you're nuts," Gino said.

"Ahh, boss. Dillinger went to the movies and was shot dead," Joey Clams argued.

"Okay, so I used the wrong gangster. I'm taking my friends for dinner. You guys can follow us to Monte's. If we make a big fuss, we will have a problem, otherwise, three guys and a lady are going to dinner. The streets are packed with people, cops everywhere. I'll be fine," Gino stated.

Joey Clams knew that there was no negotiating with Gino when he made up his mind. Mickey Roach, C.C., and Joey Clams would keep a reasonable distance from the four friends as they walked to the neighborhood, basement-level restaurant.

Once inside, the conversation started off light-living in the Village, the taxis versus Uber, the great jazz clubs and restaurants all around, and the great pizza at John's.

Then onto the Yankees and the Orioles-Rick was a birds fan, Gino was true to his school.

"You're not really a Yankees fan, Gino," Rick observed.

"What are you talking about? I've been a Yankees fan since before you were born,"

"Define fan," Rick said.

"Rick, cut it out," Shpresa admonished.

"No, really, define fan," Rick continued.

"I've been going to Yankee Stadium since 1958. That's a fan."

"And if the Yankees lose?" Rick asked.

"If they lose, they lose. That's the game."

"When the Orioles lose, I can't sleep. That's a fan."

"Do you still trade baseball cards like I did when I was twelve?" Gino.

"No, but I bleed orange."

"Then I guess I'm no longer a fan. Let's call me an observer. And I'm going to observe the Yankees kicking the Birds' asses. Just check me in October, my friend," Gino taunted.

"And Yankee Stadium will be dark again. Mark my words, Gino."

"I have to admit, that is a very depressing sight. The great stadium, dark and quiet during the playoff and World Series," Gino said.

"And Shpresa and I will be at Camden Yards. Loser pays for the tickets?"

"Rick, you are such an ass," Shpresa scolded.

"No, no, Shpresa, the bet is on. And I will force your husband to wear a Yankee hat and sit over the Yankee dugout," Gino said.

"Pigs will fly," Rick retorted.

"Val will be my guest. Val, you like the Yankees, right?" Gino asked.

"I have other things to do with my time. I don't follow sports anymore," Valbona said.

A brief, uncomfortable silence fell over the table. She and Lekë Marku never missed a Yankee home game.

"So how do you like the place, Gino, really?" Shpresa asked. She needed to change the subject.

"What's not to like? Actually, when this whole thing is over, I want you guys to sell my apartment in Riverdale, and I want a nice place down here in the Village," Gino said.

"By the way, your Boston friends are in town. I got another place for them to stay, not very far from here," Rick told him.

"Good. Let's go over later and say hello," Gino said.

After dinner, the four friends strolled back to the safe house. Gino and Valbona walked ahead of the Metalias, followed by Mickey Roach and the boys.

"Ilir is all for that meeting, Gino," Valbona said.

"Any advice?" Gino asked.

"He has two thoughts. Making an agreement with those maniacs will be difficult. They must be told that their days of chopping up people for money in our city are over," Valbona explained.

"And his second thought?"

"He is very concerned that they will use the meeting to attack him and you," Valbona added.

"I agree with that," Gino said.

"So we need to make a fail-proof plan."

"Our Boston people are here. You get together with Mickey and come up with something. I have to figure out a way to let the Russians know we are willing to talk," Gino said.

"No problem, I'll get with Mickey now. And, oh, one more thing," Valbona paused for a moment.

"What's up?"

"A package was delivered to Ilir's office in the Bronx. A scalp was in the package. A red-headed scalp," Valbona said.

"What's that about?"

"Rick's redhead, Gino. The Russians figured out their leak."

CHAPTER 51

At dawn the next morning, Gino had urgent business to attend to. He was called to a one-on-one.

"We're all painted by the same friggen' brush, Gino. My people are getting their balls broken left and right. The cops who are with us have orders to squeeze us dry, and this ain't even our fight," Jimmy Nardone complained.

Nardone, a capo in the Gambino crime family in Brooklyn, was pissed off. Nardone ran Brooklyn, Staten Island, and most of Queens with an iron hand. He and Gino met at Battery Park for a walk-talk. They both wore jogging shorts and tee-shirts so no foolish recordings could be made. The trust factor from the days of Sammy Gravano was gone.

Joey Clams and C.C. stayed close behind but not within hearing distance. Nardone's driver was lurking nearby. Walking was not Joey's thing; Vietnam injuries had turned into arthritis in his ankles and knees. C.C. was in a daze from the young women joggers, skaters, and bike riders along the promenade near Bowling Green.

"I thought you guys were going to support us with this thing," Gino said.

"Support is one thing, but starvation is another. Our business is way off, my friend, and our guys are getting very antsy. This is not good. My boss wants to see Carmine, Jr.," Nardone said.

"That's not happening now, and he knows that. We have more heat on us than you can imagine."

"Yeah, but you guys started this *conzone*. And over what? Let the Russians do what they gotta do."

"Jimmy, please! If you think we have heat now, wait until the word gets out that these jokers are chopping up kids and their human trafficking stuff. This will kill us all. If you guys don't understand that, I don't know what to tell you," Gino said.

"Can't there be a compromise? C'mon, this war is chewing us all up," Nardone reminded him.

"What compromise? There are plenty of things that they earn from. Nobody says a word about the drugs, credit card fraud, stock fraud, insurance fraud, girls, swag, and the rest. We are not pretending to be the Vatican, the moral leaders of the underworld. This thing they do has got to stop in this city. That's it," Gino said firmly.

"You already put a stop to it. You took their building out for Christ sake. No discussion, bam, gone."

"We tried to talk with them," Gino argued.

"Maybe you did; maybe you didn't. And what about these Albanians? We think they pushed you into this war," Nardone said.

"That's nonsense. They asked for our help. We had a choice to jump in or sit it out. How do you get the word pushed from that?

"Regardless, we need to find a way to stop leaving blood all over the place."

"I don't disagree Jimmy," Gino said.

"You willing to sit down with them?"

"Let me think about it. How do we get something like that done? Don't forget, Jimmy, I'm new to this. I don't actually have Petrov's phone number."

"I can reach out, Gino. All we want is peace and quiet so we can do what we do."

"Okay, just one thing I ask," Gino said.

"What's that?"

"Just remember your blood. It's the same as mine."

CHAPTER 52

Gino got into the car with Joey Clams and C.C.. They were on their way back to the safe house.

"Joey, make sure no one is following us," Gino said.

"Way ahead of you, pal. See this thing? It tells me if anyone planted a GPS on the car. Clean as a whistle," Joey Clams said proudly. He showed Gino a hand-held, electronic scanner that prevented anyone from tracking the car back to the safe house.

"Great thinking," Gino said.

"How's that for four moves ahead?" C.C. said.

"I'm starved. You guys hungry?" Gino asked.

"Always," C.C. said.

"I could eat," Joey Clams added.

"Let's stop at that bakery on Sullivan Street and get some bread. I'll make us a nice, potato and egg frittata," Gino said.

"You trust that guy, Gino?" Joey Clams asked. There was something about Jimmy Nardone that Joey just didn't like.

"Absolutely not. He's a snake. For all I know, he has a piece of the Russian organ business," Gino surmised.

"You are up to your ass in alligators, my friend," Joey Clams said.

"It's all part of the game, Joey. Let's see if I'm really any good at it."

"And if you're not? Then what? A friggen' severance package?"

Back at the safe house, Mickey Roach, Valbona, and the Sicilians were pouring over maps. Valbona took notes so no detail would be missed. She stayed the night, sleeping in a guest room. Rodio knew better than to make a move on her. Mickey would have slit his throat. If she were interested, it would have to wait for another time. She wasn't.

"So I'll make breakfast for everyone. Then we have to wait for a call from our friends in Brooklyn," Gino said.

"They gonna broker a meet?" Mickey Roach asked.

"Yep. I can't wait to hear their plan," Gino said.

"Fuck their plan. They go with our plan, or there is no meeting, period," Mickey Roach asserted.

"Absolutely. What do you have so far?" Gino asked.

"We have to assume the worst. They may really want to talk, but if they want revenge for their last try, they got a problem. Then it's all over; we have all-out war," Mickey Roach said.

"I have a feeling they are having the same conversation as we are right about now," Gino conjectured.

"So we need to think four moves ahead, Gino. Like you said, in the chess game, four moves," Mickey said.

"Where?" Gino asked.

"City Island just outside the Bronx. Only two ways in and out, one road and the water. We meet them at a restaurant that Val's cousin owns. There is a dock there. They have a nice, wine cellar room down below, so there are no windows. The meeting can be in that room. We will sweep it for bugs. If we have to get you out of there in a hurry, the place has a dock. We escape on the water. We can go to a few places from there that will be manned and safe," Mickey Roach explained.

"No way will they want to come up there. Isn't that the place where one of the Albanians was hit when we had that thing with Ilir's son?" Gino said.

"Yeah. Ancient history," Mickey Roach said.

"We have no problem with the place. My cousin who owns the place is actually Ilir's brother's son. My husband and I had our last meal together there," Valbona added.

"No problem for you, Val?" Gino asked.

"Like Mickey said, ancient history." Her icy stare confirmed her resolve.

"What if they say no? They may want to meet in a neutral place," Gino said.

"They are wounded. We ain't gonna give them a choice. You will have me, Val, Joey, and C.C. with you. Petrov can bring four of his people. Meantime, there will be more Russians on City Island that day than in the history of that turd-of-shit island. Their people will be all over the place, we can't prevent that, but our friends will be packing the island, too. The Boston crew, our people, and the Albanians. And these two will be waiters in the joint," Mickey Roach said, referring to Lucania and Rodio."

"Even with those bandages?" Gino asked.

"Coming off. He's fine."

"Ilir's bodyguard will not leave his side," Valbona stated.

"So then we let them bring an extra guy. No problem," Mickey Roach agreed.

"What about Jimmy Nardone? I got a feeling they will want him as a mediator," Gino said.

"Lucania will watch him closely. One wrong move, and he visits the devil. That guy always rubbed me the wrong way. I just can't put my finger on it," Mickey Roach said.

Gino looked at Joey Clams and smiled.

"Then it's unanimous. He's a real scumbag, but, unless he proves otherwise, he is a friend of ours.

"Let's have a nice breakfast. C.C., go around the corner to Rocco's and get some nice pastries and cookies. Bring back the newspapers. The frittata will be ready in ten minutes. Then we go to our Boston friends and fill them in," Gino announced.

CHAPTER 53

Gino's cellphone rang. The screen read UNKNOWN NUMBER. Gino knew who it was. All the wiseguys were using throwaway cells these days.

"I need to see you," Jimmy Nardone said.

"Sure. I'm a bit busy right now. When are you thinking?" Gino asked. He was playing a tactic that he learned from his business days. Don't show too much interest, even when you can't wait to hear if the deal is ready.

"Tonight. An hour."

"Too soon. Where you thinking?" Gino asked.

"Same place."

"Nah, too predictable."

"How about the clam bar? Two hours." Nardone sounded impatient.

"See you there," Gino confirmed. He pressed the red button on his phone.

"I'm meeting Nardone at Vincent's on Mott Street in two hours," Gino declared.

"No, you're not. I'll meet him there and bring him to Katz Deli on East Houston Street, where you will be waiting. Katz is always packed, and a lot of cops eat there. Nobody will start anything there. If Jimmy doesn't like it, let him go see who he has to go see," Mickey Roach said.

"But I haven't had Vincent's hot sauce in years," Gino said.

"Maybe you should just get a nice chicken salad, Gino, you're not young anymore," C.C. said.

"Listen, we're not going there to eat. Quick, in-and-out meeting. The longer we stay, the bigger the target," Joey Clams warned.

"Yes, sir. I'm glad you guys don't want to eat. I'll need a second job after feeding you two for so many days," Gino joked.

"Wait a minute. They have take-out. Now I have a *woolie*. You know, when you can almost taste something and you just have to have it. I have a *woolie* for their hot dogs," C.C. said.

"Try having a *woolie* with work, Charlie. Double check the weapons. We may need them sooner than you think," Joey Clams cautioned.

Two hours later on the clock, Jimmy Nardone walked into Vincent's with his driver. He spotted Mickey Roach and walked over to the table where the Roach was sitting. Jimmy's hands were outstretched to his sides.

"Where is he?" Nardone asked.

"Somewhere else. Not too far. I'm gonna take you there," Mickey Roach said.

"I don't like this one bit. Here I am, doing you guys a favor, and you insult me. This is our neighborhood; what are you afraid of?" Nardone asked.

"Your neighborhood? Look around. You see one Italian face on this street? It's fucking Chinatown now. The chinks took over this place years ago. The neighborhood died when Gotti left. Go see the old hangout. The Ravenite is now a fucking shoe store. Get off your high horse, Jimmy. Let's go; he ain't gonna wait all night," Mickey Roach ordered.

Nardone followed Mickey out to the Roach's car. The capo's face was as red as a smacked ass.

Gino was sitting in the rear of the massive, iconic eatery. Joey Clams and C.C. were spread out, sitting at different tables, each with a hot dog and a Dr. Brown's Cel-Ray soda.

Nardone took the mandatory seating ticket and walked to where Gino was waiting. He was still red faced and pissed off.

"You make me come like a stranger to a Jew joint? This ain't right, Gino," Nardone protested.

"Relax, Jimmy, sit down please. I have to be careful where I park my ass these days. You understand that," Gino said.

"And that Roach fuck. He better watch his mouth," Nardone went on.

"C'mon, Jimmy, he was a made guy when you were in diapers. He's just doing his job. Everyone is antsy these days. You said it yourself."

"Petrov will meet. But he has conditions."

"Conditions?" Gino asked. Gino made a smirk as if to say, "Who the hell is he to have conditions?"

"He wants restitution on his loss. They lost millions on the building, plus the loss of their business. That's gotta be a big number. You have to pay a tax, Gino. Carmine, Jr., would understand," Nardone said.

"I'm in charge, Jimmy, not Carmine; get that straight. Petrov gets nothing. Let him file an insurance claim on his building, I couldn't care less. The only tax we will pay is to you for your time and help with this thing."

"Another insult. This is a favor we do for you, Gino. Don't you see how peace helps us all?"

"And their loss of business? Petrov has to know that he is out of that business. If they want to chop kids up and sell their parts, let him go back to Putinville and do it there. He has no choice on our streets," Gino said.

"Gino, how do I go back and tell him this? These Russians are crazy. They will go all out to destroy you," Nardone warned.

"I hope you meant to say us, Jimmy? They will go all out to destroy us. I thought you guys had our backs here? What was that word John Gotti always used, a *borgata*? Another word for family, am I right? I thought we were all part of a bigger *borgata*...no?" Gino asked.

In the battle of the wits, Jimmy Nardone was unarmed. Gino could smell him from a mile away.

"Yeah, yeah, us...all of us...together. That's what I meant."

"So go back, and tell Petrov we don't accept his conditions or we don't meet. And, if we don't meet, so be it, and I will see his ass kicked all the way back to fucking Kiev or wherever he's from. Remind him that they will fry his ass in oil, and he already knows that."

"Let me go back and reason with him, I'll do the best I can. I just don't know what he will say," Nardone said.

"He has twenty-four hours. Then the real party begins, Jimmy."

"Give me two days, forty-eight hours. I want to make some moves. A ceasefire for two days. Can you do that Gino?"

"Jimmy, if you can guarantee a two-day ceasefire, out of respect for you, I will live to it. But, if one of my guys or Marku's guys gets diarrhea, or a head cold, we will turn Brighton Beach into a Kinney parking lot. I swear this on all the saints."

CHAPTER 54

Eamon Fitzpatrick III came back to New York from Washington, loaded for bear. The attorney general, on orders from the president, let Fitzpatrick know that his work on the New York underworld was being examined carefully. Words like "national security," "unacceptable," "retirement," "replacement," and "future appointments" were being thrown around like so many nickels.

Fitzpatrick was back in the pressure-cooker conference room at Federal Plaza in Manhattan. The assistant attorneys general was referring to the room as "the snake pit."

"Wilson, I want to be very clear to you and to everyone in the room that we need to move on this mob war shit without delay. I am not going down alone on this one, boys. Conversely, if I look good, we all look good, and those of us who rise to the occasion will be remembered. I got my ass handed to me in D.C., and you all know how that feels. What do you got so far, Wilson?"

"Mr. Fitzpatrick, Gino Ranno will be here in an hour with counsel. We called him in for a friendly talk, and he agreed. Ranno knows we are on to him, and he would rather not have the publicity, I suppose," Don Wilson said.

"I want to be in the room," Fitzpatrick said.

"Absolutely, sir."

"You start the meeting, and I'll just happen to walk in."

Jim Rem and Gino arrived on time and were shown to the snake pit. Wilson let them cool their heels for fifteen minutes. No coffee, no water, and no nothing was offered. The room was warm and uncomfortable by design. A photograph of the president and the attorney general loomed over the table as if they were both looking down on the events that took place in the sterile conference room.

"Mr. Ranno, I'm Assistant Federal Prosecutor Donald Wilson. This is my associate, James Troy. I know Mr. Rem."

"Mr. Prosecutor, it's been a while. My client agreed to meet. I'm pleased to see that there is no record of this meeting being taken," Rem said.

"Our intent is to have a reasonable conversation about current activities that your client may have knowledge of," Wilson explained.

"Mr. Ranno is a retired businessman. We are not aware of how he may be of help to you. He is aware of his rights, and that's what I'm here to assure. I will assist him in the protection of his rights as an American citizen."

"Thank you, Mr. Rem. Our concern is for the safety of the citizens of this city. It has come to our attention, Mr. Ranno, that you are filling in for Mr. Carmine Miceli, Jr., while he is under federal indictment on a variety of federal charges."

"Mr. Miceli is a lifelong family friend. Filling in is a pretty broad characterization of my relationship with Mr. Miceli," Gino said.

Eamon Fitzpatrick III walked into the conference room and sat down at the head of the table.

"So you deny any involvement in the Miceli crime family, Mr. Ranno?"

"I know nothing about that, Mr. Wilson. As I've said, Mr. Miceli and I have known each other our whole lives. My family and his family came to this country from the same, small town in Sicily, many years ago," Gino said.

"We are aware of your history, sir. Our goal here is to understand where you fit in with the various Miceli interests in and around this city," Wilson said.

"So, because I have an Italian surname and am a friend of the family, your call did not come as a surprise."

Fitzpatrick cleared his throat and placed his two beefy arms on the conference table.

"Mr. Ranno, we know who you are and what you are doing these days. We also know that you have been immersed with the mob for the past few years, maybe not as a made man but certainly as an associate. Now, suddenly, your name is on everyone's lips. Every two-bit, mafia hood, every wiretap we listen to, all the gangsters on the east coast are singing your name like minstrels. It's not like years ago, Mr. Ranno. You guys stopped that code of silence of yours many moons ago. The days of loyalty among you Italian bad boys is over. You know it better than we do," Fitzpatrick glared at Gino with his piercing, blue eyes.

"And your point?" Gino asked.

"My point is very simple. You are not just a friend of Mr. Miceli who only eats macaroni on Sundays with him. You are fully entangled in the nefarious dealings of the Miceli crime family. Do you deny that?"

Jim Rem placed his hand on Gino's arm, a signal for him not to answer the question.

"Mr. Fitzpatrick, my client was asked and has answered that question. He has no idea what you are talking about," Rem said.

Gino felt the heat rising up into his head. The need for revenge and contempt for authority is a chain in Gino's DNA.

"Let's be frank, counselor. The federal government will not tolerate this mob war going on right here in this city right now as we speak. Our intelligence indicates that Mr. Ranno is acting boss of the notorious Miceli crime family."

"I have no idea what you are referring to, sir. What mob war?" Gino said.

"The one between the Russian mafia in Brighton Beach, Brooklyn, and the Miceli Family and the Marku family, the Albanian mob that has aligned with you," Fitzpatrick seethed. The prosecutors red face kicked up a notch to scarlet.

"Aligned with me? The Russians? This is like a work of fiction," Gino said.

"Yes, the Russians who tried to kill you the other night up in the Bronx, those Russians," Fitzpatrick said.

"Absolute nonsense. Where do you get this stuff?" Gino asked.

"It's all a puzzle, Mr. Ranno. We have put the pieces together very nicely indeed. The Russians can't find Carmine, Jr., so they went after you. We want it to stop," Fitzpatrick said. The huge man stood for emphasis. His sheer size was supposed to intimidate Ranno and Rem.

"Sir, with all due respect, please take your seat, and guard against such theatrics. We came here in good faith to listen to what you have to say. So far, the allegations you have made are totally false and unfounded," Rem stated.

Fitzpatrick straightened the necktie around his bulging red neck and sat.

"Look, the Italians are one thing. We've locked up hundreds of your friends and associates for decades. In the last twenty or so years we have locked up more of you then we can remember. Carmine Miceli is the next to fall under the RICO act. We will add your name to the indictments if you so wish," Fitzpatrick said.

"Bullshit. If you had any proof to substantiate my client's involvement with criminal activities, you would have already done that. Now I'm insulted and my client will not sit here and take these scurrilous and outrageous insinuations," Rem snapped.

"Insinuations will become charges, Mr. Rem, in due time. I want it to be known to you and your client that he will be under a microscope. The Italian mafia has seen its day in this country, and especially in this city. The Russian mafia is another story altogether. As a group, they are heartless, ruthless, unscrupulous, and soulless sharks, feeding on the sea of humanity. The Russian Mafia didn't come to be part of the American dream, gentlemen. They came to steal it," Fitzpatrick charged.

"Thank you, sir, for the civics lesson. My client is a law-abiding taxpayer and citizen. My client has no other comments to make. This meeting is over. You know where I can be reached.

Gino and Rem stood and left the room without personal contact with the three prosecutors.

Fitzpatrick fumed. He waited for the door to close behind Gino and Rem. He looked drained, and he folded his fat fingers on the table and spoke to his hands.

"I'm going to get that little, fucking, guinea bastard if it's the last thing I ever do."

CHAPTER 55

Andrey Aleksandrovich walked along Brighton 6th Street in the mid-day, blazing sun toward the beach.

Aleksandrovich enjoyed walking on the shore as close to the water as possible to breath the fresh, salty, sea air, which helped clear his mind. The newly appointed Petrov *Bratva* brigadier removed his heavy, black, Russian-made shoes so he could feel the sand and water on his bare feet.

After a mile walk down the wet sand, Aleksandrovich, as planned, met with an associate to discuss pressing business matters.

"I could never believe such a beautiful place like this would be found in New York City. It really does remind me of Odessa in many ways. Our life is very hard. This place gives us all some relief," Aleksandrovich said.

"I've been coming here from when I was a kid, this place and Far Rockaway. Once in a while, we took a short train ride to Long Beach. Have you been to Long Beach at all?" Jimmy Nardone asked.

"A few times. That is the best I have seen so far."

"So you said it was important that we meet. I was surprised that you wanted to see me privately. Petrov agreed to the cease-fire and the sit down with Ranno and Marku. All we need to do now is figure out if we can all live together," Alexsandrovich said.

"The Miceli family will never agree to allow the organ business to continue here in Brooklyn. They have no idea how much this hurts your pocket," Nardone said.

"And they have no idea that it hurts your pocket as well."

"It's none of their business how I earn. They have no right to dictate terms to Petrov. Who the fuck do they think they are anyway?" Nardone fumed.

"And Petrov will agree to these terms. He will take some concession, more gambling, more of whatever the Italians and Albanians are willing to give up to justify their high morality."

"That's what I wanted to talk about. I understand Petrov is getting heat from Moscow and some other *Bratvas* in this country. Do these friends of yours agree that Petrov should fold up this business? That's the most ridiculous thing I've ever heard," Nardone said.

"All they want is their tribute, the same amounts as before. They couldn't care less how the envelope is filled so long as the flow continues. Petrov could sell his mother and sister as far as they are concerned."

"And how do you feel about them blowing up your building and killing your people?" Nardone asked.

"I want our business to be our business. We have enough to worry about with the police and the feds breathing down our necks. What if we were to say we think gambling is wrong? Would the Miceli family shut down their operations, stop taking sports betting, having card games, numbers? We both know the answer to that."

"I agree completely. So do the people on top of me. Until the Micelis brought up this organ bullshit, it wasn't even thought of."

"So, what are you asking?"

"Petrov…is he just going to roll over and let them win?"

"I believe Petrov is showing weakness. You and I have made great money together in that business. I would wish it to continue. Jimmy, there is an old expression: 'once you have had wine, the water doesn't taste so good.' Petrov will make the water taste like this ocean to me."

"As his underboss, you have no advice for him?" Nardone asked.

"Petrov is a very stubborn man. He has dug his heels into the sand. He believes that a war on two fronts with the Italians and the Albanians will ultimately destroy him."

"What is he afraid of?" Nardone asked.

"The man has no fear, not even death. His belly is fat now. Petrov is willing to suck dicks to make his life easier at this point."

"And you? How do you watch our mutual business be taken away like this?"

"That is a very good question. I want to hear what this meeting with the Italians and those mongrel Albanians brings. Then I will decide what my role is. At the moment I am simply a worker, even though I am brigadier. Our *Bratva* has been weakened. You understand how that feels, my friend. Your family no longer has the teeth it once had. I have to see how the game plays out."

"Know this, Andrey, our branch of the service drinks from the same well as you do. We will support you if you need to make a move."

"And I am to trust you? Remember we are from two different worlds, my friend."

"That's where you are wrong. We are both from the same world. The world of money."

CHAPTER 56

Valbona called Shpresa. She needed to talk with her best friend. Valbona asked for Shpresa to meet again at the French Roast. She asked her to come alone this time. They took the same table by the window facing Broadway.

"I need to hear myself think, Shpresa. I have a lot on my mind," Valbona admitted.

"You look as if you are a thousand miles away. Are you okay?"

"I'm not nearly okay. Look, I took this sword virgin vow because I thought it would be my entranceway into the man's world. I think like a man, act like a man, dress like a man, but I'm not sure this world is for me. There is more to life for me I think."

"Do you mean the world that Ilir is in?"

"No, the world in general. I have done things that I would never have imagined I was capable of, things that will haunt me for the rest of my life, I'm sure. I can't tell you specifics, Shpresa, so please don't ask."

"I don't want to know, Valbona, I can only imagine."

"One thing happened that has been haunting me," Valbona said. For a moment, Valbona's façade, the emotionless, man role that she was playing, slipped. Her eyes filled with tears, and her lower lip trembled.

"Drink some water. Try to relax," Shpresa said. She handed a glass of ice water to Valbona, who took small sips.

"There was this young, *zezack* girl. She could have been a witness to a very bad scene. Someone wanted to, how can I say this, they wanted to put her under."

"Oh, my God," Shpresa said. Shpresa sat back in her chair, not certain if she wanted to hear the rest.

"I stopped it. For a moment, I was a woman again. I thought of the poor girl as a baby, a tiny baby in her mother's arms. I thought of my own child, who never had a chance at life. In a way, I gave this girl life. I gave her a chance to live a life for better or for worse."

"You did the right thing, I guess," Shpresa said.

"And I felt in my soul that I want to give life again, to nurture a child and watch him or her grow. I want to be able to leave something in this world. Shpresa, I am so confused," Valbona confessed.

"You want a baby?"

"I guess so. I also want this life that I have found myself in. I want to act like a man yet still be a woman. How screwed up am I?"

"Why can't you do both? Why are you so black and white, Valbona?" Shpresa asked.

"How many women can be in that life and raise a child properly? How many women are in that life at all?"

"How many women dress like a man and do what you have done? It's crazy just as it is," Shpresa pointed out.

"So what are you saying? Give this whole thing up, meet a guy, get pregnant, be a *nuse* again, and pretend what happened to me never happened?"

"I'm not saying anything. Only you can decide what's right for you, Valbona. You need to decide what is most important to you. Work or family...or both. You need to find yourself. Remember, this is not the country and life of our fathers. Times have changed so much that it seems our old ways are slipping away. How will you feel in ten years? How will you feel as an old sworn virgin?"

"What do you mean?"

"How will you feel if you never have kids and live on, remembering a tragedy every hour of every day in your life? Will you be able to deal with that?" Shpresa asked.

"I don't know. That *zezack* girl is haunting me every day. I would have loved to take her as my own, adopted her, and raised her to be a woman."

"She would never be your blood."

"I know, and that would never be enough for me."

"You need to make a decision and work toward fulfilling your destiny as a woman, a woman without children or a mother who will really know the beauty of what we do."

"And what kind of man will have me? Damaged goods, a wife who can make homemade *pite* during the day, and kill someone at night. How pathetic am I, Shpresa?" Valbona asked. The tears and trembling returned.

Shpresa's eyes now filled with tears, feeling the pain of her best friend. Shpresa composed herself before she spoke.

"Valbona, *zemer*, in our own way, we are all pathetic."

CHAPTER 57

The two-day ceasefire was in its second day. The sit down of the Russian, Albanian, and Italian bad boys was scheduled for that evening as requested on City Island. Surprisingly, the Petrov *Bratva* did not recoil at the selected location, a true sign that they wanted a real resolution to the differences between the mob factions.

Early that morning, Ilir Marku was taken by car to see Gino at the new Greenwich Village safe house. The meeting was at Ilir's request. Valbona was with her *Babë*.

"Gino, how is your family?" Ilir asked.

"Everyone is fine, Ilir, and yours?"

"Thank God, and how is my friend Carmine?"

"All is well with him and his family. He will be returning soon although we don't yet have a definite date. He sends his best regards to you," Gino told him.

"I look forward to seeing him soon. Now, at the risk of being rude and in the interest of time, I would like to discuss some business matters with you."

"By all means, Ilir."

"Gino, as you know, life is very short. We are all here, borrowed to each other for whatever time is allowed to us. I have come to the time in my life when I want to enjoy what I have accomplished and, as you say in this country, to smell the flowers. After this mess we have with the Russians is settled, one way or another, I will be retiring from all of my business affairs. I wanted you to hear this from me before you heard from someone else. Only my wife and Valbona know of my plans so far," Ilir admitted. His voice was clear and strong, his gaze as powerful as ever.

"This does come as quite a surprise, Ilir. I didn't imagine a man like you would ever retire. You are still full of life."

"I would never have considered full retirement, but circumstances have pushed me into this decision. I want to spend time with my son in Albania. I didn't know him while he was growing up. Now we can know each other as men."

"Will you miss this life you have worked so hard to build?"

"Naturally for a while anyway. In time, my new life will take over, and then, of course, the inevitable," Ilir said.

"From my heart, and I know I speak for Carmine, Jr., we will always have a place at our table for you. You are a great man who will have our respect and loyalty forever."

"Thank you, my dear friend. You must know that I will not walk away until this problem we are sharing is resolved. There is still time to break bread and drink some good wine," Ilir said.

"And *raki*. Let's not forget your homemade *raki*."

"Needless to say."

"May I ask you a sensitive question, Ilir? Please don't take my inexperience as a sign of disrespect," Gino said.

"Ask me anything. You don't know how to be disrespectful, Gino. You were raised the right way."

"I know of no one who could fill your shoes, but have you thought about a successor?" Gino asked.

"That is all I've been thinking about since my son, Lekë, was taken from me. I am not quite sure yet who will sit in my chair. Certainly, there needs to be a boss. In our world, there always has to be a boss. Men desire to be led. I wish my Hamdi were still here. His counsel is needed right now."

"You have a strong team behind you. Certainly, the cream will rise to the top."

"I wish it were that simple. Men who seek power can act foolish when they attain it. I would not want to see what we have built destroyed by a reckless ego. In this regard, I have not done a very good job. Thinking Lekë would have taken over for me one day was where I put all my thoughts. And then, in an instant, the plans I made were smashed into pieces. I have no obvious successor," Ilir said.

Gino let his guard down in a moment of frailty. He glanced quickly at Valbona. Valbona shifted nervously in her chair.

"My friend, your eyes tell the story. Val has proven many things to me in the short while she is with us. Bravery is among her best qualities, but there is so much more for her to learn. Time is the common enemy, my friend," Ilir said.

"When Carmine, Jr., asked me to sit in his chair for a while, it was as if I were being baptized by fire. And look now with this war. I am not sure my decisions are right for this family, but I do know one thing for an absolute certainty. This life is in my blood. Finding someone who has the business in their veins is the hard part."

"And there are other issues to be concerned about that I will save for another discussion," Ilir said.

"Babë, I have sat here quietly. May I speak?" Valbona asked.

Ilir nodded his approval.

"The issue you are referring to, Babë, with all due respect, is that, at the end of the day I am still just a woman. You are concerned that the men in our life will always view me as a woman in spite of my vow, and our tradition. Men use our code to their own benefit. They always have, and they always will regardless of the situation. I am not sure I would even be willing to be in that kind of hypocrisy for the rest of my life," Valbona expressed.

Ilir did not reply. Gino bit his lower lip, regretting that he put Valbona and Ilir in such a tense moment by virtue of a quick glance.

"So how about a glass of grappa?" Gino asked.

"I am delighted to drink with you, Gino," Ilir said.

Gino looked at Valbona more to check her vital signs then to take her drink approval. Valbona sat straight up in her chair and squared her shoulders before she spoke.

"Sure, make mine a double."

CHAPTER 58

The City Island Bridge connects the one-and-a-half-mile City Island with the Bronx. Mickey Roach was correct. There is one main road. City Island Avenue is the only way in and the only way out except by boat on the murky waters of Long Island Sound.

Anyone thinking of making an assassination attempt against their opponent on City Island would be forfeiting their life.

Unless, of course, they have nothing to live for. A Russian rogue member of the Petrov *Bratva* was the concern of Ilir Marku's men Nic Celaj and Bekim Selca and Gino Ranno's mafia warlord, Mickey Roach.

In the car on the way to City Island, Gino and Mickey Roach were alone. Mickey was jumpy, Gino as cool as he could ever be.

"Numbers don't mean shit, Gino. There are dozens of our people spread out over this piece of shitty island. We have all the Boston crew waiting on each side of the bridge, and they ain't makin' as if they are undercover. Anyone who wants to play around will never make it out of there alive. We have our own crew, ready, willing, and able to kill more Russians than World War II. Plus, the inner circle will be near you. My two guys will make sure you are as safe as can be. With all that security, if one guy is willing to lose his life to kill you, their ain't much that can be done," Mickey Roach warned.

"And that's the risk the Russians take as well. That's called a stalemate, and, in their world under these circumstances, they view that as a win. I don't think one shot will be fired, Mickey," Gino replied.

"I'm not willing to take that risk. I'm not going to rest until you are safe and sound in bed tonight back in the Village," Mickey Roach said.

"You are worrying too much, Mickey. I'm playing the percentages. I'm playing their chess game."

"Little boys and girls play games. I'm an old man who stopped playing games when I saw what happened in Sicily to men who let their guard down. Not on my watch, boss."

"And that's why you are still here and why I feel so safe."

Mickey Roach drove his car slowly over the City Island Bridge. No car was following him. The Boston crew was in the strategic locations that Mickey planned and re-planned.

Just after the bridge, on the right of the main drag was the designated meeting place, *Portofino Ristorante*, which was owned by Ilir Marku's cousin Benny. Just off Portofino's dock fifty yards into the water, four heavily armed, Miceli men were pretending to fish. The cabin cruiser that was used to cut the Russian assassins to pieces a few days ago in Throggs Neck was called back into action.

Gino and Mickey Roach were the first to arrive. Mickey walked into the restaurant first, his keen eye surveying the room for anything out of the ordinary. Lucania and Rodio busied themselves, wiping wine glasses at the table where the meeting was to take place. Mickey breathed easy, knowing that everything was set up according to his arrangements. Gino sat at the round table in the corner overlooking the water. Rodio served a bottle of *San Pellegrino* water with some bread, cheese, and olive oil.

Moments later, Ilir Marku arrived with Valbona. Bekim Selca was behind the bar. His automatic rifle was tucked neatly out of view.

The usual greetings ensued, and Ilir and Gino sat, patiently awaiting the arrival of the Russians.

"This meeting will determine the fate of both of our families, Gino," Ilir said.

"With all due respect, my friend, I am not at all concerned about which way things will go tonight. There will be some bumps in the road, but I'm convinced we will come out with what we want. Let's see how the first few minutes go," Gino answered.

"And if they don't go well for us?" Ilir asked.

"Then we punt."

"Punt? What is punt?" Ilir asked. The head of the Marku family was not aware of the meaning of the American idiom.

"Just an expression that means we will react as we need to. We know what we want, and we know that they will spar with us. I will follow your lead, and you will follow mine. The important thing is that we are both together, whichever way the wind takes us."

Boris Petrov and Andrey Alexandrovich stood in the entranceway to Portofino's dining room. Both men looked glum and untrusting of their surroundings. Several tables were filled with other diners in various stages of their meal. Mickey Roach had already identified who the Russians had placed in the restaurant. Mickey never took his eyes from these tables and made sure Lucania and Rodio were aware of his surveillance. No words needed to be exchanged between Mickey and his Sicilians. His piercing eyes and furrowed brow told the story.

The two Russian mafia members walked slowly toward Gino and Ilir's table. Out of respect, the Italian and Albanian both stood but didn't offer a smile or their handshakes. Valbona stood a few feet behind Ilir as Mickey waited behind Gino. Nic Celaj was within a few feet of Ilir.

The four men seated themselves, and Mickey waved away the oncoming waiter, Rodio, who was prepared to take a drink order.

Unlike the Italians and Albanians there was no small talk, no "how is your family?" "How is business?" "How is the weather treating you?" "How about those Yankees?" The Russians made the first move.

"We have lost many of our people to you. I'm wondering if more will be lost after this cease fire," Petrov stated.

"There is no need for more loss. If we can come to terms, we leave here and go about our business," Gino promised.

"Our business seems to be no longer ours alone," Petrov said.

Gino gave a puzzled look. He knew what Petrov had in mind. The cat-and-mouse play was to begin. Each side would be moving pawns just as most chess matches begin.

"We are now told that our business is not acceptable to you. Our facility was destroyed, and valuable professionals were eliminated. So now you are dictating what we can and cannot do…in a free country," Petrov said.

"Nothing is free. There is a price that we all pay when business becomes dirty. In our minds, what you were doing is an abomination," Ilir said.

"So is selling drugs to children who commit crimes against the state to deal with their needs," Alexandrovich argued.

"Neither of our families is in the drug business," Gino pointed out.

"And I am not Russian. Please don't insult our intelligence. You are not talking to the district attorney," Petrov retorted.

"If you know anything about our history, you would know that the drug trade is not allowed and is punishable by death," Gino said.

"Perhaps many years ago, that was true. Today, your men are on the street, and the heroin flows like water. Your tribute is like ours: we don't ask where it comes from as long as it comes," Alexandrovich said.

"Our conditions have not changed. I will repeat myself; we are not in the heroin business. Perhaps in Sicily or Naples or Istanbul, there are some who are in this trade. Not in our family. Not here." Gino stated.

"And why are we discussing these matters? Our problems with you are strictly attached to the organ business, which we cannot abide," Ilir added.

"We have been doing business for years next door to you. Suddenly because of maybe our rapid success, you decide to put us under this edict. We have enough to worry about with the government. Now we answer to both of you as well?" Petrov demanded.

"You do not answer to us, Mr. Petrov. We know where this business is headed. It will bury us all," Gino said.

"We are very skilled at what we do. There is no reason for you to act as if the doors to your businesses will suddenly close. You do what you do, and we do what we do. Isn't that the American way?" Petrov asked.

"And when your business becomes a danger to us and the government cracks down on all of us, what are we to do? It wasn't as if we did not try to reason with you. We, both of our families, do not want this business on the streets that we share," Ilir explained.

"So now our business will suffer until the next thing you dislike comes along. Maybe it will be our insurance business next month, and, the month after, our..." Alexandrovich was interrupted by Gino.

"There is no other business that you are in that we are concerned about. Chopping up children and other vulnerable people is more than just criminal."

"You are now going to moralize to us. Unlike you, we do not believe in God. Our only god is money. So how will we compensated for the hole you have made in our affairs?" Petrov said.

"If that is your concern, then we should be discussing other ideas instead of religion," Ilir replied.

Mickey Roach noticed that one of the Russian plants stood and headed toward the men's room. He glanced at Lucania who slowly followed the Russian to the rest room.

Valbona fingered the pistol that she had concealed on her waist.

"What restitution do we get for the millions in losses that you have forced upon us? What about the funds we are losing on a daily basis? The numbers are adding up," Alexandrovich said.

"What are you proposing?" Gino asked.

"You let us rebuild and stop dictating to us. We will send you a bill for what we have lost so far," Alexandrovich said.

"That is not on the table, and it will never be. Ask for something else, and we will, as gentlemen, discuss what terms we can live with," Gino said.

Petrov put his hand on his brigadier's arm. He addressed Gino.

"We are looking for peace so that we can have our share of things. Your family has been here much longer than ours. You are entrenched in many things, but your power is not what it was. Your ranks have betrayed you; a blind man can see that. We are not in the unions, you have seen to that. Our territory is limited, you have seen to that as well. My *Bratva* should not be starved by your greed. Now come your friends, the Albanians, and, suddenly, we are the targets of your joint dislike of us. I am looking for a fair distribution of things that you have locked up since before we were all born."

"Your people have done great things with certain things of which we have no interest. Your expansion is limitless. You will have my word, our word, that neither of us will ever disturb your affairs," Gino promised.

"And when you are gone and the next one like you has amnesia, then where are we? Back at this table, asking for compensation like the immigrants you both want us to remain," Petrov conjectured.

"Those who come after us will have different problems. They will work out their differences as we will," Ilir said.

"Be reasonable, Mr. Petrov. What does your *Bratva* want from us? Let's not play "what if." What can be done now so that we can go forward?" Gino asked.

"Two hundred million dollars. And we will part friendly. Perhaps we can do business as we have in the past. The gasoline business was good for everyone. There may be another joint venture in the future."

"Good, at least we have a number to work with. You ask high, we say low, and we meet in the middle. Let's cut to the chase and settle on a more realistic amount," Gino said.

"What do you have in mind?" Petrov inquired.

The Russian returned from doing his business in the men's room. Lucania followed and resumed miming waiter duties.

"Our number is ten million a year for ten years paid from our activities," Gino offered.

"Five million now and fifteen million for ten years," Petrov countered.

"This is the best we can do: Five million now and seven for ten years. All in, seventy five million," Gino said.

Gino looked at Ilir. Ilir looked at his hands and cleared his throat.

"And never to return to the business that brought us here."

"Agreed," Petrov affirmed.

The Russians stood to leave. Petrov and Alexandrovich shook Gino's hand. They ignored Ilir Marku and left the restaurant. Two tables of Russians immediately left Portofino without paying a bill. Mickey Roach was proud of himself. He knew who the *Bratva* musclemen were all along. Valbona relaxed, never showing an emotion on her face.

"They behave differently, don't they?" Gino observed.

Gino felt that Ilir was snubbed, and it annoyed him.

"Animals. I am happy that they didn't shake my hand. My friend, you should wash your hands very well."

CHAPTER 59

"Mr. Rem, your client will face twenty years in a federal penitentiary. If history has shown these people anything, if they were even capable of learning from their mistakes, they would stop their criminal ways. I guess your client is just not smart enough. He should take the offered plea bargain. If not, the trial will drag out, make you rich, and Carmine Miceli, Jr., will still get the full sentence. Twenty years with the eighty-five-percent federal mandate is a very long time," Eamon Fitzpatrick III said.

Jim Rem, two of his assistants, Eamon Fitzpatrick III, Don Wilson, and several other white-shirted, stern-looking assistant attorneys met at neutral ground for a pre-trail conference. A conference room at the Princeton Club at Fifteen West Forty-Third Street in Manhattan was as good a place as any. Both Rem and Wilson were alumni of the venerable, ivy-league school. The idea of neutral ground was to get the bloviating Fitzpatrick away from his bully pulpit. The federal prosecutor was more likely to listen to reason at the Princeton Club or anywhere else for that matter, than to dig his heals in at his familiar Federal Plaza perch.

"Look, your case is flimsy at best. You really don't have much to go on, Mr. Prosecutor. We have listened to the wiretaps, and I can pick apart your assumptions. The grand jury will never indict my client, and you will not get a jail sentence at trial. Five years in prison? For what? To satisfy your obvious personal rancor for Italian-Americans? C'mon, will ya?" Rem argued.

"We don't need to make this personal, Rem. And I want to remind you, I put away one of the Gambino wise guys goombas with a wiretap a few years ago. He said 'where are my meatballs?' and that got him thirty plus," Fitzpatrick pointed out. He threw his shoulders back much like a peacock opens its feathers.

"I know that case. The context of the discussion made it obvious that Anthony Rella was looking for a piece of a drug-money deal. You won, they lost, and, at his age, he is doing a virtual life sentence. And, the truth be told, he likely deserved it anyway. My client is a stand-up citizen, and we will illustrate that to the court. You have shit on Miceli and you know it. Nothing that I have seen in discovery will stick. That's why you've made this flimsy offer, Mr. Fitzpatrick...with all due respect," Rem said.

"Suppose you are correct with your assumption and Miceli wins this case. Do you think for one minute that we will not pursue him for the next decade until we get something to stick?" Fitzpatrick asked.

"My client has just returned to his home from an extended family vacation to Puerto Rico. Carmine Miceli, Jr., is tanned, rested, and ready, willing, and able to fight these trumped-up charges of yours with all of his strength. I suggest that you reexamine your case so that we can discuss a different solution," Rem said to him.

"What do you have in mind, Jim?" Don Wilson asked.

At that moment, Rem knew that he had called their bluff. Fitzpatrick was more theatre than law. His booming voice, table pounding, hypnotic eye piercing, standing-like-a-red-gorilla-to-make-his-point histrionics would now take a second row to reality.

The feds had now shown weakness, and Jim Rem was all over it. Rem knew that he had to give Fitzpatrick and company a face saving escape route.

"Carmine Miceli will agree to plead to a lesser charge, let's say some anti-discrimination statute. One of his trucking companies hasn't hired enough minority drivers. He fires his general manager, pays a nice fat fine, hires some Puerto Ricans and blacks, and hangs his head in shame. You get something for all your effort, and my guy cleans up his unfair hiring policies. Case closed."

"Mr. Rem, I have no intention of playing this ridiculous game of chess with you," Fitzpatrick said.

"Sometimes, Mr. Prosecutor, a stalemate is as good as a win. Then we get a chance to play another game. I suggest this one is a draw," Rem said victoriously.

CHAPTER 60

The morning after the City Island summit meeting, Valbona was contemplating having a heart-to-heart talk with her *Babë*, Ilir Marku. She was torn between worlds and wanted to express herself, but her dilemma was complicated. She demanded to be a man and took a sworn oath. Would she approach Ilir as a man or as a woman?

Valbona's telephone rang. It was Shpresa Metalia.

"Val, how are you *zemer*?" Shpresa asked.

"I've been better. I tossed and turned all night. I don't know what the hell to do with my miserable life," Valbona professed.

"I have some news for you. Let's have coffee. Don't say French Roast again. How about the Bronx or Yonkers?"

"Okay, how about *La Parisienne Café* on Arthur Avenue, or is that neighborhood still off limits?" Shpresa asked.

"No, it's fine now. I can be there in a half-hour."

"I hope Dervish has some homemade *raki*. We are going to need some," Shpresa said.

Arthur Avenue was no longer in lockdown for fear of a Russian reprisal. Word had spread that the mob war was over and terms were met. The avenue was bustling again. The streets were as clean as ever, and every storekeeper was preparing for their day of commerce and hoping for the great weather to continue for the rest of the week. The aroma of fresh bread from Madonna Brothers and Addeo Bakery gave the street a homey, welcome feeling. A few diehards were eating a breakfast of raw clams in front of Cozensa's fish market. The indoor market sounded more like Naples than the Bronx with the fruit and vegetable men calling out in their dialect Italian. As the Dominican and Cuban cigar rollers at Paulie Cigar prepared to make their quota of smokes, the counter men at Mike's Deli did their normal stage performance for the early shoppers.

Across the street, Dervish opened for business at *La Parisienne Café,* setting out the tables and chairs on the sidewalk under the maroon awning. Parking-violation officers began their route, checking the parked cars for the appropriately timed tickets that drivers displayed on the dashboards. Everyone was hard at work. Life was good on Arthur Avenue for the first time in a long time.

Shpresa arrived and sat at one of the tables, catching the eyes of the NYFD men who were shopping in the neighborhood to stock their firehouse kitchen. Valbona arrived shortly after, dressed in a man's suit and tie, her short hair slicked back like any local gangster.

"Okay, so what's the big news? You know deep down I can't resist gossip," Valbona prodded.

"It's not gossip, *zemer,* just news that you may want to hear," Shpresa said.

"I'm all ears!"

Shpresa and Valbona ordered two *cappucini* with *raki* chasers.

"I'll get right to the point-Adem is coming home to see Ilir. He will be here from Tirana tonight," Shpresa informed her.

Valbona was speechless for a long moment.

"This is going to be very awkward. Is he planning to stay at his father's home?" Valbona asked.

"I suppose so. Why is that a problem?"

"Ah, duh, I live there in case you missed something."

"So come, and stay with Rick and me if it really bothers you."

"That will look tacky, Shpresa. After all, I was the one who ended the relationship."

"Are you interested?"

"My best friend, acting as the *shkuesi,* the lady matchmaker. This is too much to digest right now," Valbona said.

"You know he loves you like no other, and I know you have feelings for him whether or not you want to admit it."

"I don't know what I feel anymore."

"It's a good time for you to start deciding if you want to be the *burrnesha,* the *virgjinesha,* or whatever you want to call it or if you want to start a normal relationship with a great guy who wants a traditional family," Shpresa said.

"Like he will accept a woman who became a..."

"Stop right there. I don't want to hear what you've done. Adem doesn't have to know either. What's done is done, and now it may be time to reinvent yourself again."

Valbona took the shot of *raki* in one gulp and waived her glass to the waiter for a refill.

"What do I say to him? 'Sorry, I had to go find myself in the mob, and now I want you back?'" Valbona asked.

"Ah...yeah. Or something like that. The words will come, Valbona."

"And I show up dressed like this with my short hair greased back and my fingernails like a farmer. My eyebrows look like two caterpillars on my forehead. What the fuck?" Valbona exclaimed. She downed the second raki and waived for a third.

"We have the entire day to fix all that. You are still the same person he remembers just with short hair."

"And if he says no? If he demands that I leave the business? What do I do then?"

"You decide what you want in life. Decide what is most important to you, being a gangster or a mom. I'm sure he will take you back."

"And I live like a good *nuse* in Albania. My God, Shpresa, I'm not sure if I can move to Europe and put this country behind me."

"Adem would live with you on the North Pole. That whole *nuse* thing is ancient history. The dutiful wife is a thing of the past. You can work through that, *zemer*."

"First things first. I need to speak with Ilir. I need his blessing."

CHAPTER 61

After a few more shots of homemade *raki*, Valbona headed home to the Marku estate in Scarsdale. Luckily, she was not stopped on the Bronx River Parkway by any of the ball-breaking, Highway One units, who without a doubt would have given her a field sobriety test, partly since she was swerving on the parkway but largely because the cop would have had a field day back at the precinct. A woman, a hot woman at that, dressed as a man would have been the talk of the stationhouse.

Ilir was meeting with his real estate and financial people, deciding how to liquidate his considerable portfolio. The meeting was taking place in Ilir's study as all very important meetings did at the Marku estate. Reams of financial statements and piles of property books and building photographs made for no flat surfaces on Ilir's desk and conference table. Breaking down a vast, real-estate empire was not going to be an easy task. Ilir wanted to cash in, take his chips off the table, and move on with his life. His home in Albania was being renovated and prepared for his arrival in the not-too-distant future.

Valbona walked into the meeting, not noticing the abundance of cars behind the gated home. After all, she was distracted by what was on her mind and the abundant *raki* that she had downed.

"*Babë*, I'm so sorry. I didn't know you were so busy," Valbona said apologetically. Ilir noticed her state immediately.

"You are never a bother, Val. I will leave these good people to their charts and numbers. I will meet you in the living room," Ilir said.

Valbona went down the hallway and into the large living room, pacing the floor and practicing her opening lines. In a few minutes, Ilir arrived looking concerned, but calm.

"Babë, I need to speak with you. Something important." Valbona's tongue was thick from the shots.

"Val, I have never seen you in such a state. I'm quite surprised at you. A man must be able to hold his liquor."

"I'm sorry, I know that I should have waited for a while, but I have much to do before tonight."

"Tonight? What is so pressing that you had to fortify yourself with alcohol and interrupt my meeting?"

"I understand that Adem will be here, that he is coming for a visit with you."

"Yes, he is. I asked to see him, and, as a good son, he is on his way from Tirana. He will stay for a few weeks, maybe a bit longer. What does that have to do with you?" Ilir asked.

"Babë, I am torn between two worlds. Part of me wants to be what I am as you see me now, and the other part wants to stay as a woman, to be married and have children, and raise them in the traditional Albanian manner. I am so confused. You must think I am crazy."

Ilir directed Valbona to sit on the sofa. He sat across from her in a cushy, upholstered club chair.

"So this life is not for you after all. Have you gotten it out of your system?" Ilir asked.

"That's my problem. I like the life very much, the power, the complicated decisions that need to be made, the difficult action that must be taken, all of it. I regret nothing. I would do it all over again. *Babë*, I feel a calling in my soul."

"And you expect Adem to welcome you back with his arms opened, to forgive you and the way you sent him away. I'm not certain this will happen for you. Regardless, you will always be part of the Marku family. In the old tradition, you still belong to us," Ilir said.

"I am eternally grateful for that. Being part of your family is what kept me alive."

"Valbona, in life, one must find what is right, what is his or her destiny. If you desire to break your vow of *berrnesha*, it is something that is easily done, but do not think you can flip back and forth like turning on a light switch. You must make your decision and live with it."

"*Babë*, you just called me Valbona."

"You have no idea how difficult it was for me to refer to you any other way. I went along with your wishes out of respect for you and respect to the *Kanun,* our code."

"I knew that all along. I knew you would have laid your life on the line for me if it became necessary as I would have for you."

"Do you love Adem, or are you using him as a means to get what you want?" Ilir asked. Ilir's tone changed, but his eyes betrayed nothing of his feelings.

"I don't know. Adem came into my life at my darkest moment. He is a man whom I would certainly have spent the rest of my life with if that's what you're asking," Valbona replied. Her eyes welled with tears.

Ilir stood from his chair and slowly went to his daughter-in-law. He took both of her hands into his.

"In our culture, there are arranged marriages as you know. Your parents, myself and my wife, and all of our relatives had these marriages. Naturally, there was never love between a man and woman when they were selected for one another. As the old timers always said, 'in time, love will come.' Go and prepare yourself for my only son."

CHAPTER 62

Marty Craig always did things on the up-and-up. From the time he was a young man, his ethics in business were unquestionable. He and his partners and their employees and vendors all did well, and they respected him to the utmost. Everything he touched turned to gold. He had the Midas touch, everyone would say, but his King Midas legacy was beginning to fail him.

"Marty, do you think it's *Karma*? How could things start to unravel and on every front?" Ericka asked.

"Would you stop already? Business runs in cycles, and we find ourselves on a downward turn, that's all. We have plenty of money," Marty snapped.

"It seems that, ever since that bonehead move of yours with Lloyd's kidney, we are sinking pretty fast."

"Bonehead move? I would do it again tomorrow to make my son have a second chance at life. If I had to live in a one-bedroom apartment above a bakery in Brooklyn like my parents did, I would sell everything I own. You still don't get it, do you?"

"There was a time when I would have been happy to live above that bakery with you. Not so much anymore," Ericka said. There was a spray of sorrow in her voice.

"So I guess you just got used to the fucking good life, Ericka. The jewelry, this house, sports cars, designer clothing, and big-time vacations. I can go on and on. Now you start singing a different tune. I never would have expected this from you."

"And I never would have expected you to be part of a young girl's murder. It was that evil that turned me off. You could have been richer or poorer for all I care. Yeah, richer is better with all the trappings, but you were nothing when we met. I didn't marry you for money."

"It sure seems like that now, doesn't it?"

"Lloyd is getting better, and stronger every day. Gianna is doing great. There is enough set aside for their educations. They will be just fine. But us, that's another story altogether.

"Jesus Christ Almighty, Ericka. I thought we were past all that. Now, after some bumps in the road, you are willing to throw in the towel. It's only money. It comes, and it goes, and I will make up the losses. So maybe I have to get back out there and hustle a little again. It's not like I haven't provided for us and then some for all these years."

"Providing things was one thing. Stepping over that moral line was another. You are being punished, Martin Craig, punished for losing your way, for letting the devil control you. The devil was your money."

"You sound like one of those ministers on television that we always laughed about," Marty rolled his eyes in disbelief.

"Are you so far above it all not to see what you have done to us?"

"Done to us? Our son is well. He can lead a normal life because of what I did. Fuck that moralizing crap. If you can't deal with it, then do what you have to do, Ericka."

"I already have, Marty. I went to see a lawyer. I'm filing for divorce. I just can't be with you anymore."

"You're kidding, right?"

"I wish I were kidding. Don't worry, I will not take you to the cleaners as they say. God above will take care of that."

CHAPTER 63

Half way through the almost fourteen hour trip, Adem started regretting not taking his father's invitation to fly business class on Turkish Airlines. The decision to take a coach flight was purely economics for the young singer. Three thousand versus nine hundred eighty euros was just too much for Adem to swallow, even if it wasn't his own money.

The flight from Tirana's *Nene Tereza* Airport to Istanbul then a layover and on to JFK was exhausting, even at his age. The flight arrived in New York at almost five in the afternoon. After a long wait at customs, a full search of his luggage, and navigating to the waiting car, he arrived at the Marku Estate at nearly seven in the evening. Ilir sent his trusted bodyguard and two of his men to greet his only son.

The embrace between Ilir and Adem was worth every second of the trip to the aspiring entertainer. He saw a tear in his father's eye that choked him up a bit, but he held his composure.

"My son, you look a bit thin to me. Handsome as ever, but my cook will fatten you up a bit," Ilir said.

"*Babë*, the camera adds fifteen pounds. Even in Tirana, thin is in, but I will not pass up one forkful of your food. I remember it too well."

"And how is your mother? Well, I hope."

"You know, the normal aches and pains of age, but *Nane* is fine and sends her best wishes to you."

"I am happy to hear that. And how is your life going back home?"

The staff rushed to serve a plate of appetizers and coffee.

"I'm doing well. There are a few very good offers on the table. I will be releasing a new album very soon, and I have a feeling that you had some influence."

"Congratulations, but your talent speaks for itself. Maybe a phone call or two helped, but what do we have friends for?" Ilir smiled broadly at his son's success.

"Thank you, *Babë*. It's not easy in this business, even in Tirana."

"Are you seeing anyone special?" Ilir asked.

"No, it's been too soon for me. It may take some time for me to get over Valbona. Is she here? Or should I ask if he is here? Word travels quickly, you know."

"Yes, she will be here shortly. Come, have some food; you must be hungry from your trip. Your room is upstairs next to mine."

Ilir's wife came into the room and greeted Adem warmly. His presence was not a problem for her. She came to accept Adem after her son was killed. She had a warm spot in her heart for her husband's son.

Shpresa dropped Valbona inside the gate of the Marku Estate.

"Wish me good luck, *zemer*. I'm trembling inside and out," Valbona said.

"Be yourself; that's what Adem fell in love with. Call me later without fail," Shpresa urged.

Valbona walked to the door and was let in by Nic Celaj. She walked slowly into the living room.

Adem was sitting next to Ilir on the long sofa, sipping coffee and chatting, when Valbona entered the room with demure hesitation. Valbona smiled at Adem and walked toward him, her eyes glistening with tears.

Valbona, my goodness, you look beautiful," Adem exclaimed. The two embraced for a long, almost uncomfortable moment.

"I have things to attend to. Dinner will be in an hour. My wife will call for you," Ilir said and made a quick exit from the room.

Valbona took Ilir's spot on the sofa, and Adem sat near but not close to her.

"You look great, Adem," Valbona said.

"*Babë* thinks I'm too thin, but enough about me. I want to look at you for a moment."

Shpresa's day of beauty turned Valbona from a man into a virtual Vogue cover. Valbona's men's haircut was slightly blown out and mildly gelled and partially spiked on top. Her long neck was accented by large, gold, loopy earrings, which matched a fabulous, glimmering, gold and platinum necklace that ran down to her bust line. Her shoulders were exposed as well as a slight hint of cleavage in a floor-length, emerald green dress, which hinted at her magnificent, curvy figure. Her shoes, strapped espadrilles, with her red, pedicured nails, matched the color of her freshly done French manicure. The caterpillars were gone from above her now-threaded eyebrows. Valbona was all woman!

"I was expecting to see the *burrnesha* that we have seen in old photographs. You know, with big trousers, a too large jacket, holding a rifle-not this," Adem remarked.

"But my hair is still short. It will grow," Valbona said.

"It is very becoming on you, Valbona. So tell me about that experience. Needless to say, I was shocked that you made the transformation."

"Adem, that is all behind me now. I guess in my continued grief, I had to find who I was. I can say now that I am what you see before you, and there is no going back," Valbona promised.

"And your grief?" Adem asked.

"I will always grieve for what could have been. My beautiful husband and son will always be in my heart and soul. If I learned one thing, it is that life must go on. I am willing to try again, Adem."

"I'm afraid to be thrown away like yesterday's trash again, Valbona. Maybe you need to go out a bit, date some men, and see the world before you make the next move in your life," Adem suggested.

"Adem, I am willing to try again with you. You were my salvation, you kept me alive with your voice, your strength, your compassion."

"I'm not so sure I can endure another disappointment. I'm still not right about how things ended, Valbona."

"You said you loved me many times. Is that still the case, Adem?" Valbona asked. She dropped her eyes as if waiting for bad news.

"Do you think love is like a faucet to be turned on and off on a whim? I will love you until the day I close my eyes for good."

"Then Adem, I am breaking all the rules right now. I've broken the rules of God, now I will break the rules of our forefathers. I will now make my last act as a man.

"Adem, will you marry me?"

"Hold on just a minute. You are in no condition to ask me or anyone else to marry you. Valbona, I am not going to be your savior, nor do I want to be your security blanket. Perhaps before when we were dating, the thought of marrying you was on my mind, yes. Now, after you have sworn an oath without too much thought I may add, to become a sworn virgin, I see that you are acting very impulsively. There is no way that you are ready for marriage at this point in time," Adem said firmly.

"So you no longer find me attractive, is that it?" Valbona asked.

"You're missing the point. I have a career to think about. I'm no doctor, but I know a bit about post-traumatic stress disorder. When you were in the nearly comatose state you were in after what happened to you, I did quite a bit of reading on that subject. I'm not convinced that you are thinking clearly right now. I think you need to talk to someone who can walk you through things."

"So, suddenly, I'm crazy to you?" Valbona snapped.

"I never said such a thing. You are doing compulsive things. That's not crazy at all, but you need to find out why your behavior is so erratic. You need to search yourself, your true feelings. Sure, I'm attracted to you. Any man in his right mind would be, but that's not the only reason to be married."

"So what are some other reasons, Adem? Enlighten me please." Her voice and manner were terse. Valbona sat back on the sofa and crossed her arms over her breasts.

"To be with a person for the rest of your life, to start a family and raise children, just to name two that come to mind."

"I want children. Is that compulsive?"

"Maybe, at this time, the answer is… yes, it is. So what happens if the children are not exactly as you thought they would be? Will you change your mind and move on? I'm not so sure that you will be able to deal with all the stresses that comes with that life," Adem protested.

"Now you are saying I may abandon my own children? That's ridiculous!"

"And so is becoming a man and doing what you thought you needed to do to get even with society, to satisfy some vengeance that remains in your soul. You worked your way into my father's world, which is something I, myself, rejected immediately. He is a great man, but his life is immoral and unjust. I could never for one minute guess you would be attracted to that life. So what am I to think now? Is this just another phase of Valbona Marku or Val Marku, as you wanted to be called? Am I just an easy mark for that phase? There are a whole lot of questions you need to be asking yourself."

"I want to have children to teach them the right way to live, to show the entire world that I would have been a great mother, the best who ever was, to nurture and to love my kids. Is that such a bad thing?" Valbona asked. Her voice trembled.

"And you want me to sire those children. Am I just a breading horse? Then where am I if you suddenly decide that you have what you want and I'm out again?"

"I guess your precious career is what the real issue is, Adem," Valbona challenged.

"Are you kidding me? Of course, I would want a family one day. Tell me what changed your mind, Valbona, to want all of the sudden to be married and have babies. Be honest with me please," Adem pleaded.

"Having the power to give life, to make a real mark in this horrible world we live in. Something happened, I don't wish to go into the details, which made me stop and think about what I was doing. I saved a young girl's life, and it made me think of my baby. Is that so wrong? Am I that fucked up that I can't tell reality from fantasy?"

"What you did, whatever it was, I am sure it was noble. You have a great heart and a capacity to love deeply. That is more attractive to me than this beautiful package I see in front of me, sitting on this couch. You need to be certain without a shadow of a doubt that this is your calling in life, to be a mother and a wife. All I'm saying is that you need a lot more time to search your soul, to make absolutely sure that the next stop for you will be the last," Adem stood from the sofa and walked around the room. His hands were trembling.

"So now what? What am I? A failed woman, a failed man, a failed human being?"

"These are questions that only you can answer. I am willing to see you through the maze that you have been in since Lekë was killed, but only under certain circumstances will I remain in your life, Valbona."

333

"Such as?"

"For starters, you must find someone who can help you to heal emotionally and mentally, a professional, who has lots of experience with grief counseling and PTSD. Then you leave my father's life completely and totally. He is preparing himself for retirement. You cannot think for one moment that you will be involved with his organization. If that's what you want, all I can say is goodbye forever," Adem stated. He sat back on the sofa and took Valbona's hands in his.

"Maybe then I can get to know the real Valbona as my half-brother did," Adem said.

"I need time, time to think these things over," Valbona muttered.

Adem stood again and hovered over Valbona.

"Yes, I know you do, as do I. I came here to visit my father. Now I'm beginning to think that he wanted us to see each other again, to rekindle our romance so that he could see his legacy go forward. If God has that in his plan for *Babë,* he will live to see that day. If not, then so be it. I will not allow myself to be trapped into that world or allow my sons or daughters to follow that road to perdition."

CHAPTER 64

Two weeks passed after the City Island meeting of the three mob factions took place. There was no hint of recrimination by the Russians, and business was back to normal. Ilir gave strict instructions to his people as did Gino. There were to be no petty skirmishes, no territory conflicts, nothing that would start problems with the Brighton Beach mafia. Anything unusual that was noticed on the streets was to be reported back without delay.

Ilir went for the additional tests that Dr. Mark Kaplan had ordered. Ilir's stomach pains had worsened. Ilir had noticed that, along with the gnawing stomach pain, the palms of his hands and his feet were itching as of late. He was feeling poorly in general, but he did not allow anyone to see his discomfort. Ilir spent every moment possible with Adem.

Ilir and Adem were sitting by the outdoor pool at the estate, at a round table under an umbrella, sipping cognac and smoking Cuban cigars.

"*Djale,* I don't want to intrude into your life. Please forgive an old man his curiosity," Ilir began.

"*Babë*, you are not old first of all, and you may ask me any question your heart desires," Adem said.

"My thoughts are of you and Valbona. I notice that you are both cordial to one another, but I don't see that spark that I was expecting."

"She needs to take her time with deciding what she really wants in life. Believe me, *Babë*, I am still deeply in love with this woman. If she takes a few steps that I have asked for, in time, we will see if we are meant to be together."

"I was prepared to visit her father with you and ask for her to be your *nuse.*"

"Way too soon. There is no rush. I plan to return to Albania in a few weeks and to see which way the wind blows. I have work to do as you know. I promise you one thing though. You will be the first to know if there is anything that hastens my return," Adem vowed.

"She has decided to leave my organization. Is that one of your conditions?" Ilir asked.

Adem took a long, slow sip from his glass then a long pull on his cigar.

"Honestly, yes, I asked her to decide what she wants to do. Frankly, I find it hard to consider a wife who is involved in the kind of business you are in. I say this with all due respect."

"No offense taken, *djale*. I would have thought that you would have demanded that. I am very relieved that Valbona is no longer with me."

"Demanded is too strong a word, *Babë*. I think it was more of a request. I also asked that she seek professional help, you know, a psychiatrist, someone she could talk to about the tragedy, to help put her past behind her."

"I must laugh at this, Adem. Where I am from, there was not even a doctor available never mind a psychiatrist. I guess this world had passed me by," Ilir said.

Ilir moved forward in his chair, which seemed to relive his discomfort.

"*Babë*, are you all right? You seem to be not yourself lately."

"I am fine, I just have some stomach issues. Perhaps a more bland diet is what I need. Now you know I am retiring to come and live in Albania and that my plans are to pass on my chair to someone. You've made it quite clear that you would not be interested in my business. A father always wants to pass on his legacy to his son. Lekë was to fulfill that dream, but his future of my family was taken from us. You can manage my legitimate business affairs and be a very wealthy man here. I will put everything on hold if you just say the word," Ilir offered.

"I am grateful that you would even consider me. My life is my art. I don't see myself running your ..."

Ilir interrupted Adem.

"My business is totally legitimate. I have kept the two worlds separate, which was not an easy task. I will find others to take over the side of my affairs that you want to stay away from. Lekë is dead because of the things that we do and I will never forgive myself for that," Ilir said.

"Please, *Babë,* you should not blame yourself for Lekë. This is the business that he wanted, that he felt comfortable with. It was fate that intervened."

"Well, in any case, you will be a rich man in Albania after I'm gone, but I'm offering you a choice," Ilir said.

Bekim Selca came to the table and whispered in Ilir's ear.

"Adem, I have a visitor. Enjoy the drink and the cigar. I will be back with you as soon as I can. Every moment I spend with you is like being in heaven. I wish things were different in life, my son. We lost many years not being together, so now we will make up for lost time."

The visitor was Dr. Kaplan. He waited in the study for Ilir.

"You're visit to me is always welcome, Mark. How is your family?"

"Ilir, I have some unpleasant news to discuss. I wish the visit were social," Kaplan said carefully.

The lady from Ilir's kitchen staff brought Turkish coffee and homemade *sheqerpare*, Albanian sugar coins. Kaplan ignored the woman, and the treats.

"You look serious, Mark."

"Ilir, the tests that you took show that you have an endocrine tumor of the pancreas. The tumor is cancerous. I notice that you are a bit jaundiced and your eyes are a bit yellow. I also notice that you are scratching your palms. These are all symptoms along with your stomach pain."

"So what needs to be done?" Ilir asked.

"Surgery. I know the best surgeon in the country for this disease. He works at Presbyterian Hospital in Manhattan. I will set up a consultation for tomorrow if possible so we can determine what course of action to take," Kaplan explained.

"How long do I have, Mark?" Ilir asked pointedly.

"Now that is a question that is very premature. Let's first get inside and see what's going on with you. Then we will know more."

"I had a cousin with this. He died within three months," Ilir said.

"Every case is different. I've seen patients last for years, and they had good years. There have been some cases that were actually cured, but I will not lie to you. Cancer of the pancreas is no picnic, and a cure is not very realistic," Kaplan said.

"I am in your capable hands, my friend. I imagine my plans to retire to Albania are unlikely."

"Let's wait and see. Maybe a visit after your surgery, but I want you around here for treatments. Your home country has very little to offer in terms of sound medical management."

"I understand. Please, take your coffee."

"Ilir, I am so sorry to tell you this news. You are much more than a patient to me. You are my dear friend. I will do everything I can for you," Kaplan promised.

"Mix a love potion for me, Mark. I have use for that at the moment."

Shpresa and Valbona talked for over an hour on the telephone as they did when they were teenagers. Since the day Adem returned from Tirana, they talked daily, going around and around about Valbona's future.

"So now what are you going to do with yourself, *zemer*?"

"Hang out with you a lot, grow my hair long again, and see the shrink weekly. Other than that, I'm just going to chill out and relax. Can you imagine if I needed a real job?"

"You can always work with me and Rick, just for something to keep your mind occupied.

"That is such a nice thing to say. Maybe, let's see how things go. Can you and Rick come over tonight? Adem will be singing his latest songs for his *Babë* and the rest of us.

Shpresa almost shrieked with joy.

"We wouldn't miss that for the world."

CHAPTER 65

Carmine Miceli, Jr., was relaxed at home in his Manhattan townhouse. Gino was on his way to discuss the resolution to the Russian issue. There was other business that needed to be brought to Carmine, Jr.'s, attention, but the overriding topic was to be the Brighton Beach mafia and how they would be paid the large sum of money that Gino and Ilir promised.

Carmine, Jr., had a different agenda.

Gino left Joey Clams and C.C. in front of the townhouse. The two-friends-turned-mob-guys would hang around Madison Avenue and wait for Gino's call to collect him and go back to the safe house. Mickey Roach thought it best that Gino stay in the place that they rented from Rick Metalia's client until the coast was clear. To Mickey, the coast would never be clear, but, at the price the family was paying for the safe house, Gino agreed to stay just a few more days.

Joey Clams and C.C. would mull around the fancy designer stores and rate the women as they passed. The scale was one to ten, but C.C. occasionally would rate the hottest looking girls as much as a twelve. The game passed the time for them. Joey Clams would never say a word, but C.C. offered a "hello, beautiful," or "good afternoon, gorgeous," hoping for a response. A smile was the most he would get.

"Gino, you look great. I guess I should congratulate you in person. You did a yeoman's job against those Russian bastards," Carmine, Jr., said.

"I had a lot of help, Carmine."

"Your game of chess ended in victory for us. Why not bask in the glory? You beat them at their own game."

"There is no glory in a stalemate, Carmine. I guess winning would have been a lot more bloody. Besides, when I tell you what it cost us, you may freak out on me."

"That's what I wanted to talk with you about. I don't care what it cost. Let me explain what I mean.

"Jim Rem did an absolutely amazing job with the feds. Talk about playing chess with the masters of the game. Rem got them to drop the big charges for a bullshit plea. I'll pay a fine, not do any time, and not have a big media circus trial. It's just like a smack on the hands. I'm in the clear. But I need to explain what I mean when say I don't care," Carmine, Jr., went on.

"I get it; it's only money, and we can make it up," Gino said.

"Not really. I don't have what it takes any more. Maybe I never really did. My fastball is gone. I don't want to play in this game anymore. I want out. My father is rolling in his grave right now but I made a decision for my family and me. I'm retiring. I have enough money for the rest of my life and probably for my great grandchildren's lives. This thing with the feds scared me shitless. The idea of doing a long stretch in prison, not seeing my kids grow up, leaving my wife alone was all just too much for me to handle. I guess I'm not like the Mustache Petes from Sicily who thought of prison as part of the deal. I'm done, Gino."

Gino paused, his brain almost unable to compute what he just heard.

"Look, Gino, it's all yours, all of it, and I can't think of a better don than you."

"Carmine, I never wanted this in the first place. I backed into the life, then I filled in for you temporarily. Unlike you, I wasn't born and raised into the life. I'm not your guy," Gino insisted.

"Then who is? You were the only one my father really ever trusted. Our families were attached at the hips, back in Sicily and all the way to New York. You have this life in your blood… your soul."

"I made my living in the real-estate business, Carmine. I raised my family, and I can live nicely on my investments and my pension. I had my ups and downs, but it was totally legitimate. You are asking me to run one of the biggest syndicates in the country. Talk about rolling in his grave? My mother is doing fucking cartwheels right about now," Gino protested.

"Don't tell me, sitting here right now just me and you, that you didn't get a rush going up against the Russians. They want to take over our whole world, and they don't have one scintilla of decency. Is that what you want? For them to go back to chopping up kids and God only knows what else they are capable of?"

"Is that what *you* want? You are willing to walk away and dump the whole thing in my lap. Do you think I want to spend whatever time I have left behind bars in some federal lockup? Or be shot dead in a barber's chair like Anastasia? As it is, I can't make a move without Clams and C.C. I dragged these poor bastards into the life, too."

Gino felt his ears getting hot.

"Gino, what choice do I have? I just can't do it anymore. You take over for a while, then you can pass things on to people that you trust. It's all about the people you place around you, who protect you just like the chess game you always talk about. Look, I had you, and you watched my back. You saved our family from these Brighton Beach maniacs. Nobody we have could have done the job you did…nobody. And you can always ask for my opinion on things, always."

"And how am I supposed to handle the problem with the Gambinos?" Gino asked

"What problem?

"The problem with that lowlife Jimmy Nardone."

"Nardone is a piece of shit, always was," Carmine said dismissively.

"I'm pretty sure he is in bed with the Russians with that organ transplant business. He's going to be a real problem."

"You need to be absolutely sure, Gino. My father used to say, 'Cui scerri cerca, scerri trova.' Know what I mean?"

"Yes I do, 'who looks for a quarrel finds a quarrel.' I will find out for sure, Carmine. You know there are no secrets in our world. Sooner or later, the shit comes out. This Nardone prick is bad news. How can I trust our own kind when they are partners with our enemy? This guy can make this whole agreement we made with the Russians collapse. This is the garbage I need to deal with. It's not just the feds I have to watch for. I need eyes behind my head with this guy," Gino complained.

"If you find out he is dirty, you go and sit down with his boss. Be guided by how they react. On the other hand, give it to Mickey Roach. He can make that problem disappear," Carmine said.

"Now I'll tell you what *my* mother used to say to me all the time: '*E cchiu facili a fari beni chi mali.*' And she was one hundred percent correct," Gino said.

Carmine, Jr., looked into Gino's eyes and understood exactly what his mother meant.

"Yes, she was right, Gino. It is easier to do good than evil."

CHAPTER 66

Another two weeks passed, and the Russians received their initial payment from the Marku and Miceli families as promised. The Petrov *Bratva* was now five million dollars in cold cash for the better, and the Beluga caviar and Dom Perignon flowed enthusiastically in Brighton Beach.

Ilir Marku had his surgery at Presbyterian Hospital, Weil Cornell Medical Center. His surgeon and his personal physician were in agreement that he would stay at the hospital for at least five days to ensure that the surgery went well and to await further test results on his condition.

Nic Celaj spent twelve hours each day outside Ilir's door with two other Marku soldiers. Three loyal, hulking, Albanian bodyguards manned the other twelve hours just in case anyone had any ideas to take recriminations against their ailing boss.

Gino paid a surprise visit to his friend at Presbyterian, guarded by Joey Clams and C.C. The three men waited for the elevator to take them to the private room where Ilir was convalescing.

"Well, hello, beautiful." C.C. couldn't help himself from his usual flirtation when a gorgeous blonde appeared, waiting for the same elevator. She was with a teenage boy, and the young woman ignored the overt knuckleheaded line. The teenager didn't hear anything as he was listening to music on his cellphone's ear buds.

Gino flashed a disapproving eye at C.C. while Joey Clams restrained himself from smacking his friend on the back of his head.

"Ma'am, I apologize for my associate's inappropriate behavior. Sometimes, men cannot control their ignorance," Gino said sincerely.

"Thank you, sir. I would expect that kind of line in a bar but certainly not in a hospital," the woman said.

"We've come to visit a sick friend, and I guess he just wanted to break the tension. Again, my sincere apologies," Gino said.

"No harm, no foul. It took a gentleman like yourself to call your friend on his *faux pas*."

Just then, the elevator door opened, and there stood Dr. Pretesh Gupta. The doctor greeted the young woman and the teen.

"Well, there you are Ericka. I just came down to meet you. I wanted to make sure you knew that we were meeting on the nineteenth floor. Hello, Lloyd, you are looking very fit," Dr. Gupta commented. He kissed Ericka on the cheek and vigorously shook Lloyd's hand

The elevator filled quickly with the doctor, Ericka and Lloyd Craig, Gino, and his bodyguards. C.C.'s face was red with embarrassment.

Gupta pressed nineteen, and Joey Clams pressed twenty-six.

"It certainly is a great day today, Ericka. Lloyd gets his final 'okay' to return to Boston. We have another kidney transplant patient who is exactly your age, Lloyd. Perhaps, you can stop by and give him a few tips on his recovery," Gupta suggested.

The elevator stopped at their floor, and the doctor and the Craigs exited. Ericka stopped, held the door open for a few seconds, and looked at Gino.

"Thank you again. You certainly bring back the word 'chivalrous' to my vocabulary," Ericka said.

Gino smiled as the elevator door closed.

"C.C., what the fuck? Save that shit for the strip joints," Gino reprimanded.

"Sorry, boss, but did you take a look at her? A twelve, maybe a thirteen," C.C. said.

"Quit while you're ahead, you moron," Joey Clams said to C.C. Joey cuffed his beefy hand on the back of C.C.'s large, balding head.

When Gino approached Ilir's room, Nic Celaj greeted him with a two-handed shake and opened the door to room twenty-six fifteen. Joey and C.C. stood like centurions outside the room.

Inside the room, Ilir was sitting comfortably on a Stratolounger, and Adem and Valbona were sitting on folding chairs on either side of Ilir.

"Look who came to visit me? I am honored, but you did not need to come out of your way, Gino."

Gino walked over to Ilir, bent down, shook his friend's hand, and kissed him on both cheeks.

"Gino, how is your family?" Ilir asked.

"Everyone is fine, my friend. How are you making out?" Gino asked.

"I feel like I can run in Central Park. Have you met my son, Adem?"

"Yes, we have met. How are you, Adem?" Gino asked. Adem, already standing, greeted Gino warmly.

Gino kissed Valbona on both cheeks.

"Valbona, please call the nurse. We must offer coffee to my friend," Ilir implored.

"No, no, please. I just came to see how you are doing and if you needed anything."

"Gino, right now, this is my home. In Albanian culture, we must see to the comfort of our guests."

Dutifully, Valbona left the room in search of coffee.

"So tell me, Gino, how is Carmine doing since he is back home? Are he and his family well?" Ilir asked.

"Very well. He sends his best wishes, and he hopes you have a speedy recovery."

"Look at that bouquet of flowers in the corner. From Mr. and Mrs. Miceli…get well soon. It took two men to carry that monster in here. He is much too gracious," Ilir said.

"You deserve an entire room full of flowers, my friend."

"Gino, can you believe this? My son has a new album that he is releasing in Albania, and he put off going back until I am up and around. I may complain about pain just to keep him here with me," Ilir teased.

"*Babë*, I have something to tell you. I can have a release for the album right here from New York. The producers said it will look more international, and we can capture the Albanian-American audience at the same time. I'm planning on staying here for a while," Adem assured him.

"That is wonderful news, *djale*. We will make a big party for you here. Gino, you brought me this good luck," Ilir said.

Valbona returned with four black coffees in Styrofoam cups and four, small, Drake's coffee cakes.

"This is the best I could do on short notice. Sorry for the cups, Gino."

"Are you kidding? This is the best coffee break I could imagine."

CHAPTER 67

It didn't take Gino very long to discover that what he had suspected about Jimmy Nardone was true. The Gambino *capo* was indeed involved with the organ piracy scam along with the Brighton Beach Russian mafia. The only thing that Gino could not determine through his contacts in Brooklyn was whether or not Nardone was kicking up his piece of the profits to the Gambino family.

Gino decided it wasn't worth the risk of confronting the boss of the Gambino family. He wanted to solve the problem the old-fashioned way.

He gave the job of Jimmy Nardone's disposition to the man whom he trusted above all men...Mickey Roach.

A week after Gino met with Mickey Roach, the old-time Sicilian, as usual, had his plan in place.

Nardone and his driver made their routine rounds, hitting the strip joints and gentlemen's clubs in Brooklyn and Queens. Their piece of the action consisted of partnerships that the mob had with some of the owners and protection money with some of the others.

One of their stops, Sugarbabies, near the Ed Koch Bridge in Long Island City, was a regular, twice-a-week envelope pick up for Nardone.

On this particular Thursday evening just before midnight, Nardone and his driver arrived like clockwork. They found a cherry parking spot right out front of the club.

Nardone's driver fancied one of the strippers, who took the young Gambino soldier by the hand up a spiral staircase to one of the six "executive lounges," where the girl always plied her special talents. Nardone went to the bar to enjoy the floor show and have a few drinks.

Nardone spotted a familiar face getting a lap dance. It was none other than Mickey Roach of the Miceli family. Nardone sauntered over to the booth where the older gangster was burying his face in the young woman's breasts. The girl was gyrating her body to an old, Donna Summer tune while straddling Mickey.

"Ohhhh, so look who finally got a date. Mickey, what the fuck you doin' here? I thought you only trawled up in the Bronx," Nardone demanded.

"Jesus Christ, Jimmy! I figured I would just stop in for a drink, and this doll's got me in for a C-note already," Mickey said.

"You do know this joint is with me, right?" Nardone said.

"I had no idea. Trust me, I ain't doin' no business here tonight. Only monkey business."

Mickey moved the girl off of his thighs, gave her a twenty, and told her he would see her later.

"Lemmie buy you a drink, Jimmy. Last time we was together, we had a little bit of tension goin' on. I was meanin' to make a visit to Brooklyn and tell you that I felt shitty about that," Mickey explained.

"Sure, but this is my turf, and your money's no good. I got the drinks," Nardone offered.

The two wiseguys had three drinks apiece. They talked about who was away at college-mobspeak for prison-and who was sick, dead, or in hiding from the life.

"Ya know, Mickey, you ain't such a bad guy after all. I remember you from when you was with old man Miceli. You was always serious but never a scumbag like you was to me with that Gino prick," Nardone said.

"What can I tell you, Jimmy? These new people ain't like we was in the old days. I'm goin' back to the old country, where I can earn a livin' and not be pushed around. By the way, you ain't such a bad guy yourself," Mickey added.

"Minkia, look at the time, Mickey. It's almost one. Where the fuck is my guy? Maybe he fell into that *putana's* hole. Lemmie go up and see what's goin' on."

Nardone went up the spiral staircase and was stopped by a Lou Ferrigno-look-alike bouncer, who refused to let him into the rooms.

"You know who I am, asshole? Step aside before you wind up with a problem."

"Sir, I have my orders. Nobody passes without one of the girls. Anyway, there's nobody in any of the rooms," the bouncer replied.

"My guy came up here a while ago with that short, black chick. He's here all the time with her."

"Yeah, they left together about twenty minutes ago, sir, out the back stairway."

The Ferrigno clone was now on the Miceli payroll. The short black chick and the driver did indeed go out the back stairwell-in matching duffel bags.

Jimmie's horny and unsuspecting driver and his sugarbaby went into the darkened executive lounge, meeting up with a couple of friends of Mickey Roach. Cristofo Rodio garroted the unsuspecting and horny driver while Lucania took care of the girl in the same manner.

Not finding his driver, Nardone flew down the staircase in a near rage. Mickey was waiting for him at the bottom of the steps.

"Jimmy, what's the matter?" Mickey asked.

"Can you fucking believe this kid? He leaves me here to go with that *tutzoon* bitch. Lemmie go see if he's out by the car. I'm gonna kick his balls into his throat, that little bastard. I'll see you around, Mickey," Nardone said.

Mickey followed Nardone out onto the sidewalk.

"Gone! The friggen' car is gone. He's done. That asshole is as good as dead. Now how the hell do I get back to Brooklyn?" Nardone fumed.

"Relax, Jimmy. I'll take you back. I can say hello to the old crew in Bensonhurst. I haven't seen them in so long."

"You are such a good guy, Mickey. Maybe you can jump ship and work with us in Brooklyn," Nardone mused.

Jimmy's car was brought to a junkyard owned by one of the Miceli cousins at the end of Boston Road in the Bronx. The car was stripped then crushed into a nice, flat package. Then it was put on a flatbed truck to its ultimate destination, a steel mill in Newark, New Jersey.

Lucania and Rodio returned the next day from JFK Airport to Palermo, Sicily.

Jimmy Nardone, his driver, and the stripper are now buried under vertical piles of the new Tappan Zee Bridge.

CHAPTER 68

What started out as an intimate party at the Marku Estate soon grew to over two hundred guests.

Ilir planned the house party for Adem to sing a few of his songs to a select few family and friends. Instead, word got around the community, and Ilir did not want to offend his extended circle.

The best Albanian singers in the United States would warm up the crowd for Adem. This would be the prelude to the much larger event when Adem and his producers did the official album release.

Gino Ranno and his inner circle were invited as was Dr. Mark Kaplan and his family. A state senator, a United States congressman, and a judge were the only non-Albanian guests at the event. Only the doctor and Ilir knew of his prognosis as Ilir wished.

Remi Jakupi, the famous singer and songwriter, Gezim Nika, maybe the best Albanian, male singer on the planet, and the gorgeous Arberie Hadergjonaj would perform at the party.

Gino was one of the first to arrive with Joey Clams, C.C., and Mickey Roach in tow. Gino went to see Ilir, who was sitting in an upholstered wing chair under a massive tent set up by the Olympic-sized pool. Marku bodyguards encircled the property and checked in each guest from a list that Ilir himself prepared.

"Ilir, my friend, you look amazing. I am so honored to be invited to your home."

"Gino, how is the family?" Ilir asked.

"Good, thank God. I hope yours is as well."

"Yes, *Mash'Allah*. I have just one bit of business to discuss with you. Please pardon my rude behavior," Ilir implored.

"By all means. Before the crowd arrives, we can have a few minutes together," Gino said agreeably.

"The disappearance of that man, the Gambino capo, has his people asking around as to his fate."

"Yes, I know. Jimmy Nardone. I heard about this. Very strange thing indeed. It looks as if the Russians may have had their hand in the matter. This is what they do when they are unhappy with one of their partners," Gino winked at Ilir, who had already figured out the situation.

"They are a strange group of people, my friend. I know you don't need my counsel on them, but I must tell you what you already know. They are not to be trusted. Their word means nothing," Ilir warned.

"I agree. So far, they have lived to our agreement. Only time will tell."

"Ah, here comes Valbona and some others. Enjoy yourself, Gino. My home is yours," Ilir said graciously.

The crowd arrived between seven and seven thirty, and it was an amazing feat for Albanians to be on time. Who would dare come to Ilir's home late?

Rick and Shpresa Metalia paid their respects to Ilir and made a beeline to Gino.

"Shpresa, Rick, how wonderful to see you both. How are you?" Gino asked.

"We are good, Gino. This will be a party to remember. Did you see the food that Ilir's staff put out? It looks like a feast. Seven roasted lambs and enough food to feed a small army. You do know you will be expected to eat a lamb's head as an honored guest," Rick said.

"Of course. I grew up eating *cappuzella*. The Sicilians and Albanians I swear are one people," Gino observed.

"Yes, but our music is much louder. I hope you brought ear plugs, Gino," Shpresa cautioned.

"So tell me, Shpresa, before she arrives, how is Valbona doing?" Gino asked.

"She is doing what she needs to do. Only time will tell," Shpresa replied.

"I just said that very thing to Ilir about another subject. We have a saying in Sicilian, '*Lu tempo e priziusu*.' Time is precious," Gino said.

"No truer words were ever spoken," Rick concurred.

At nine o'clock after every guest had been served amazing food by a battalion of waiters, the musical extravaganza began.

The band went from the soft music of a cifteli, a traditional Albanian, guitar-like instrument, to all-out, maddeningly, loud, Albanian music.

Alberie Hadergjonaj was first to perform. The crowd went wild when she appeared on the stage. She was dressed in an evening gown that made her movie-star looks pop out under the stage lights. Alberie sang for thirty minutes to the traditional throwing of money in packs of fives, tens, and twenties. No singles for this crowd.

Alberie made an announcement that all money was to be donated to the Kosovo orphans and that their host would match the funds collected. The crowd went wild, and the money rained down on Alberie and the stage.

Remi Jakupi took the stage next. His rendition of classic Albanian songs had the crowd singing along and dancing in circles around the stage. Shots of homemade *raki* and fine *cognac* were served on silver platters by the wait staff.

The band seemed to turn it up a notch, welcoming the great singer Gezim Nikaj. Gezim, cupping the microphone in is hand, sang his heart out. His beautiful wife, Angelina, was beaming, watching her talented husband as if it were her first time seeing him.

After his third song, Gezim waved Alberie and Remi to the stage. The band didn't miss a beat, and the pounding music of the Balkans filled the evening air.

"Madonna mia. These people know how to party!" Mickey Roach exclaimed.

"What? What did you say?" Gino pointed to his ears, feigning deafness.

"These women are all gorgeous," C.C. said.

"Keep your eyes in your head, Charlie, before I throw you in the damn pool," Joey Clams mockingly threatened.

The three singers ended with a flourish. The crowd went crazy at their finale.

Ilir Marku took the stage. The crowd went silent, another first for Albanians.

Ilir spoke in English for the benefit of his non-Albanian-speaking guests.

"Thank you all for joining me at my home tonight. It is with great pleasure that I introduce my *djale,* my son, Adem Marku.

Adem jumped onto the stage to a raucous ovation from the crowd.

Adem, dressed in a black suit and shirt, asked the crowd for quiet. That took a few minutes. The band remained silent.

"Good evening, ladies and gentleman. I am honored by your presence. I am grateful to my father for his hospitality tonight and for all of you for your generosity to the children of Kosovo. I must say, after hearing these wonderful performers, I hope I can live up to your expectations. They are a tough act to follow."

Another wild ovation erupted as the band began playing the first song, a love ballad.

"This song is the lead of my newest album. It was written by the talented musical genius Remi Jakupi.

Adem started the song with his eyes closed. After the first few lines, Adem opened his eyes and sought out Valbona from the stage. Valbona was standing next to Rick and Shpresa. It was as if he were singing it to her and her alone.

Dy kandila
Dy kandila… në gjithësi,
Pranë njëri-tjetrit si unë dhe ti,

U zgjuan epshet e dashurisë,
Një kujtim
Two candles....in space
Near each other like you and I
Awakening lust
One memory
Në errësirë, unë dhe ti,
Sytë e tu, në sytë e mi,
Dora jote, në gjoksin tim,
Ouooooo...
In darkness, you and I
Your eyes, in my eyes
Your hand on my chest
Ouoooooo
Dy kandila në gjithësi,
Pranë njëri-tjetrit si unë dhe ti,
U zgjuan epshet e dashurisë,
Një kujtim...
See above
Në rrugët e qytetit, një kandil,
Ende po shndrrit...
Malli po djeg, e loti loton,
Ty duke prit,
Ouoooo....
In the streets of the city, one candle
Still flickers
Yearning is burning, and tears are tearing
Awaiting you,
Ouoooooo
Në errësirë, unë dhe ti,
Sytë e tu, në sytë e mi,
Dora jote, në gjoksin tim,
Ouooo.....
Dy kandila në gjithësi,

Pranë njëri-tjetrit si unë dhe ti,
U zgjuan epshet e dashyurisë,
Një kujtim….
Në rrugët e qytetit, një kandil,
Ende po shndrrit,
Malli po djeg e loti loton,
Ty duke prit,
Ouoooo…

Valbona was in tears. In fact, there wasn't a dry eye in the house.

CHAPTER 69

It's true that old habits die hard. The same night that Adem had his album launch party at his father's home, Boris Petrov, Andrey Aleksandrovich, and two twenty-four-year-old Russian beauties had dinner at Tatiana's Nightclub at Brighton Sixth Street on the boardwalk in Brighton Beach.

It wasn't too long before this evening's dinner that Anton Tropanov was executed right under the boardwalk. His murder did not even enter the two Petrov *Bratva's* minds. Tropanov failed, and he was summarily eliminated-it was a simple fact of life in the brutal world of the Russian mafia. He was yesterday's news, and dead was dead to Boris Petrov.

The two stunning young women were the new sidepieces to the *pakan* and his brigadier. The girls were yet another set of eye candy for the rest of the Russian community to fantasize over, and they added to the mystique of the *Voy v zakone*, the so-called thieves-in-law.

Boris Petrov did not feel any imminent danger from the Albanians and Italians on this particular night. His agreement with the rival mobs seemed to be going along smoothly, and the five-million-dollar deposit on the ten-year, restitution deal had filled the Bratva's coffers nicely.

Only three of Petrov's *byki* were in Tatiana's to assure the boss' security. Life was good, so there was no need for the type of protection needed during the recent mob war.

Tatiana's was filled with the usual crowd, who were on hand to enjoy the fabulous Russian food and floorshow at the glitzy nightclub.

"Word has come to me that Gino Ranno is now the official head of the Miceli family. It seems that Carmine Miceli, Jr., has lost his appetite for his father's business. This is the problem when there is no hunger in the belly, Andrey," Petrov said.

"And I have further intelligence that Ilir Marku is gravely ill. I am trying to confirm some new information that just came to me. If he is indeed on his way out, those Albanian dogs have no one on the horizon to take over. That weakness will mean growth for us in many areas," Aleksandrovich added.

Petrov was sipping on imported Russian vodka with lime juice. He waived to the nearby waiter for service.

"Bring us a seafood tower for four. We will order more after the show ends," Petrov requested.

"Bring some *hachapuri* with that," Aleksandrovich continued. The Georgian-style cheese pie was a favorite of both he and Petrov.

"Good idea. I feel hungry tonight," Petrov said slyly. The *pakan* placed his hand high up on the thigh of his female companion. He winked at the girl, who smiled coyly behind her champagne flute.

The lights dimmed in the restaurant as the show was about to begin.

The dutiful waiter and his assistant busied themselves at Petrov's table, setting up the metal frame and shaved ice for the soon-to-come abundant shellfish, lobster, and shrimp for the famous seafood tower.

A second waiter delivered the warm cheese pie, serving each of the four in Petrov's party from a large, family-style platter.

Eight dancers, four very fit, young men dressed in traditional Russian shirts and baggy pants swung themselves across the stage to the band playing a well-known Russian standard. Four shapely, young women outfitted in brocade *sarafan*, the traditional peasant dress, danced in a small circle on the stage.

Boris Petrov grabbed a piece of *hachapuri* from his plate and wolfed it down. He followed the cheese pie with a large gulp of vodka.

Within thirty seconds, Boris Petrov began to twitch, his face frozen in a bizarre grin, his face taking on cherry-red hue.

"Are you okay?" his young female companion asked.

"My heart, it's beating too fast," Petrov answered through a pained grimace.

Petrov began to convulse, and chalky-white foam formed on his lips. He collapsed onto the table.

Both girls at the Petrov table screeched. Aleksandrovich stood and waived the bodyguards over to the table. Two men drew their pistols. The third, seeing that no attack was being made on Petrov, dialed 911 for an ambulance.

An hour later, Boris Petrov was pronounced dead at Coney Island Hospital.

Just as Boris Petrov had poisoned his predecessor, Grigor "The Czar" Grigorovich, the Petrov *Bratva's* brigadier, Andrey Aleksandrovich slipped a cyanide capsule into his boss's Georgian cheese pie.

The Russian mafia power brokers in Moscow sanctioned the killing of Boris Petrov. The big boys felt it fitting that Petrov should meet the same assassination end that he perpetrated on Grigorovich. The new *pakan* of the Brighton Beach mob was Andrey Aleksandrovich, and the *Bratva* now had his surname.

His first order of business was to send a message to Gino Ranno through an intermediary and former gasoline-scam partner with the Gambino crime family.

The message was clear and succinct.

The deal between us is no longer valid. Your deal was with a dead man. The money you paid was for losses we received due to your actions. You will not intimidate us any longer. You and your partner are no longer a threat to us. We intend to rebuild our facility, only, this time, it will be bigger and better.

The new chess game had begun.

Aleksandrovich sent a final, one-word message to Gino Ranno, written on the inside of a pack of Tatiana matches.

CHECKMATE!

About the Author

Louis Romano was born in The Bronx, New York in 1950. He began writing urban poetry at the age of 18 and, in addition, started writing fiction in 2010.

To connect with the author:

https://www.facebook.com/LouisRomanoAuthor

https://twitter.com/LRomanoSrAuthor

http://instagram.com/louis_romano_author/

https://www.pinterest.com/louisromano/

His debut mob novel FISH FARM, a favorite of his fans, introduces Gino Ranno and his buddies, who are also seen in Mr. Romano's 2nd mob book, the 5-time award-winning BESA. GAME OF PAWNS is the third in this series.

BESA is currently under film production. Follow the making of the BESA movie at:

https://www.facebook.com/pages/BESA/1527054917580749

About the Author, cont.

Romano's first book in his Detective Vic Gonnella series, the smash hit INTERCESSION, is a semi-fictional novel set in 2012 involving the revenge of a psychologically damaged man who was abused by his priest as a young boy. The screenplay for this novel has also won numerous awards.

Been abused? Please contact Road-to-Recovery, a non-profit on which Louis Romano is a board member:

https://www.facebook.com/roadtorecovery.info?ref=br_tf

CPSIA information can be obtained at www.ICGtesting.com
Printed in the USA
BVOW06s1935220316

441349BV00019B/117/P